BLACK WIDOW
WHITE LIES

Margaret Tessler

BLACK WIDOW
WHITE LIES

Characters

Salazar Family

Sharon & Ryan Salazar, whose plans for a "perfect" vacation
    go terribly awry
Alana & Beto Meléndez—Ryan's sister & her husband
Carlos Meléndez—Alana & Beto's 10-year-old son
Omar Meléndez—Carlos's 10-year-old cousin
Ysela & Ricardo Salazar (Amá & Apá)—
    Ryan & Alana's parents
Tía Eppie (Tía Dippy)—Amá's flamboyant sister
Tía Marta—Amá's straight-laced sister
Uncle Javier and Aunt Maribel—Apá's brother & his wife

Wendy & Bonsall Johnson—owners of the Parlor Car
    Bed and Breakfast in Chama

Joaquín Álvarez—89-year-old widower who seeks romance
    through matchmaker ads
Alicia Mondragón—Joaquín's daughter
Vanessa Mondragón—Joaquín's granddaughter

Jimmy Romero—private investigator who helps Sharon
Andy Estrada—lawyer who helps Sharon
Luis Tovar—sheriff's deputy
Kent Vigil—Méndez family friend

Méndez Family Tree
Children & Grandchildren of
Ernesto & Juana Méndez

1. Perlita (Méndez) & Hector Peralta (ages 68)—parents of
      Bernice Peralta—Salazar family's old nemesis
2. (Ernesto (Neto) Méndez, Jr., age 67)
3. Connie (Méndez) & Sergio Bustamante (ages 66)—
      parents of
         Sylvia Bustamante (Bernice's cousin)
         Family moved to Coyote, New Mexico,
         after a mysterious "accident"
         caused by Bernice
4. Kiko Méndez, age 63, lives in Tres Piedras, New Mexico
5. (José Méndez, age 60)
6. Flavio Méndez, age 57—address unknown
      (in and out of prison)
7. Rafael Méndez, age 54, lives in Dallas;
      temporarily visiting in Gallina, New Mexico
8. Rita Méndez, age 39—Perlita's youngest sister;
      Bernice's aunt and look-alike

In memory of Vivette, who still inspires me

COLORADO

DULCE ◆   ◆ CHAMA

EL VADO LAKE ◆   ◆ T.A.   ◆ TRES PIEDRAS

GALLINA ◆   COYOTE ◆   ◆ ABIQUIÚ

◆ ESPAÑOLA

◆ SANTA FE

◆ ALBUQUERQUE

NEW MEXICO USA

◆ ROSWELL

CARLSBAD ◆

T.A. = TIERRA AMARILLA

SCALE NOT EXACT

Acknowledgments

The incidents in this story are entirely fictional. However, many of the people and places named herein are real. I would especially like to thank Wendy and Bonsall Johnson for allowing my imaginary family to spend their imaginary vacation at the Johnsons' very real Parlor Car Bed and Breakfast. A grateful thanks also to Deb Williams, Jill and Jim Lane, Wiley Jim Pfeiffer, Charlotte and Marvin Wilke, and Ted Rembetsy for appearing as themselves, however briefly.

This story could not have been written without the kindness, patience, enthusiasm, and expertise of everyone who answered my countless questions and encouraged me along the way. A heartfelt thanks to Don Bullis, Margaret Coel, Damon Fay, Maureen Gonzales, Adán Gutiérrez, Dr. D.P. Lyle, Angie Manzanares, Jeffrey Marks, Margaret Martínez, Margaret Palmer, Marji Patterson, Lucinda Schroeder, Margaret Williams, and my daughter Mary Behm.

Additional gratitude goes to Gayle Trent for her editorial insight and to everyone who proofread my first drafts and offered valuable feedback—Jerry Aguirre; Paula High; Luis Tovar; my comadre Merlinda Sedillo; my sister Louise Gibson; my daughter Valerie Coffee; my husband, Howard; and members of my writing workshops: Dave Bachelor, Maxine Conant, Edie Flaherty, Jeanne Knight, Betsy Lackmann, Marcia Landau, Jan McConaghy, Helen Pilz, Ronda Sofia, Pat Wood, and Mary Zerbe.

Any mistakes are mine, not theirs.

Author's Note

As in other towns, businesses in Chama may come and go. Although some of the places mentioned in this story might not be around in years to come, I hope seeing their names will bring happy memories to those who "remember when."

Black Widow
seeks to exploit, annihilate
rich elderly widower(s)

Of course it didn't read this way. Instead, the small item on the matchmaker page of *The Santa Fe Journal* advertised

Beautiful Lady
Fun-loving redhead, 35,
seeks mature gentleman
for companionship, possibly more.

She was none of these things. Shaving a few years off her age could probably be overlooked. Calling herself either beautiful or a lady was imaginative. "Redhead" was a stretch too—the last time I'd seen her, her hair could only be described as a ghastly shade of orange.

But it was remembering her idea of "fun" that made my blood run cold.

Chapter 1
Spring 2003

What began as a romantic holiday for two somehow evolved into a family vacation for twelve adults, seven kids, one golden retriever, two schnauzers, one tiger-striped cat, and one hamster. By Salazar standards, this was actually a small group, but since it wasn't an "official" family reunion, we managed to keep the numbers down.

My name is Sharon Salazar. My husband, Ryan, and I live in San Antonio, Texas. Nearly all hundred-fifty or so members of the Salazar clan live in Zapata, a small town two-hundred miles farther south. All three members of my immediate family live over a thousand miles away.

Ever since Ryan and I had spent a few days cross-country skiing in Chama, New Mexico, we'd talked about going back the following summer to ride the Cumbres-Toltec narrow-gauge train. We'd fallen in love with the town and were giving Ryan's sister and her husband—Alana and Beto Meléndez—a glowing report one evening while playing cards at their home.

"Where is Chama?" Beto asked.

"It's kind of a remote little village in northern New Mexico, just a few miles south of the Colorado border," Ryan said.

Alana raised an eyebrow. "Remote? As in dirt roads and no electricity?"

I laughed. "Hardly. It's quaint in some ways, but has all the modern amenities. Better than that, it's almost completely surrounded by mountains—the scenery's gorgeous."

"A mountain hideaway," Alana said, a wistful look in her deep brown eyes. "Imagine. Cool summer breezes."

Since summer temps were frequently in the 100s in Zapata, the cooler weather must have sounded especially appealing. Ryan and I exchanged glances. He winked as if we'd read each other's minds.

"Why don't you come with us?" I asked.

There was no one else I'd rather invite. Alana—good-hearted, spirited, and beautiful—was truly a sister to me. Beto reminded me of a lovable teddy bear. He called himself a computer nerd, downplaying his technical skills.

Alana frowned. "Oh, Sharon, I don't know...."

"Got a better offer?" Ryan teased.

"Ay, Corazón." Beto's gray eyes twinkled behind his rimless glasses. "How long since we took a vacation?"

"Even longer for Amá and Apá," Alana replied.

"Well, let's ask them too!" I blurted out without stopping to check Ryan's radar before including his parents.

Ryan raised his arms over his head and clasped his fingers together, cracking his knuckles. "Whose deal?"

"Or maybe next time," I murmured as I dealt the cards for our next round of rummy.

"No, you're right," Ryan said, grinning at me as he picked up his cards. "They deserve a getaway, and I'd like a chance to do something for them. Problem is...."

Alana rolled her eyes. "Tía Dippy."

Epifiana Jiménez, "Tía Eppie" when we were being respectful, was one of Amá's older sisters. The oldest of the trio was Tía Marta, who had never married and was as set in her ways as Tía Eppie was unconventional.

Tía Eppie, a.k.a. Tía Dippy, not only had a bizarre sense of style, but a wide range of opinions that she delighted in sharing with everyone. Actually, all three sisters, all in their late sixties, were highly opinionated and bickered with each other constantly. Yet they were practically inseparable since Tía Dippy, newly widowed and lacking someone to argue with, had recently moved back to Zapata.

Amá wouldn't want to leave Tía Dippy alone. "*Pobrecita*," I could hear Amá saying. "Poor thing. She can't help herself. She's still grieving."

If tales were true, Tía Dippy was glad to be free of her hard-to-please husband, and after a month or so of self-imposed mourning, seemed to be coping nicely. She'd traded her widow's weeds for shimmery blouses made of colorful scarves, miniskirts that revealed scrawny black-stockinged legs, and a dozen jangly bracelets.

"Look," I said, "your folks can come along in that brand-new motorhome that sits in their carport. If they decide to invite Tía Dippy...." I shrugged.

Alana brightened. "That's true. That Winnebago fits any number of people. And Apá's been looking for a chance to take it a little farther than Port Isabel."

We gave up focusing on our cards and began figuring the logistics of our proposed trip. The more we talked, the more enthusiastic we became.

"It's going to be so much fun," Alana said. "Nothing can spoil it—no matter who shows up."

Nothing. Nothing but a convoluted chain of events that threatened to turn our holiday upside-down. And the person who "showed up" unexpectedly was at the root of the trouble.

* * *

5

After many phone calls, a few meetings, and much discussion, our ideas blossomed into concrete plans. When I called Wendy Johnson several weeks later to make reservations at their B&B in Chama, she sounded distracted.

"Is everything okay?" I asked. It was easy to picture her clear green eyes and her light brown hair that framed a heart-shaped face. But I had a hard time matching the strain in her voice with her friendly disposition.

"Mm. Yes." She hesitated. "Everything's fine."

"Would another time be better?"

"Oh, no," she answered quickly. "We'd love to see you. Bonsall and I are still talking about how much we enjoyed your last visit."

I smiled. "So are we."

"How many did you say?"

"Too many altogether. But only four of us will be staying with you. The others will be staying at a hotel or at the RV park up the road. The kids want to camp near the train."

"That'll be fun. And that's a nice campground too—right by the river."

After ending our call, I still felt vaguely uneasy. I hoped whatever was bothering Wendy would resolve itself by the time we got there. If not, maybe it was something she'd feel more comfortable discussing in person.

Chapter 2
Summer 2003

Four months later, on a sultry morning in mid-July, Ryan and I headed northwest from San Antonio on I-10. I cranked up the A/C a notch. Despite its color, our little white Accord was no match for the sun.

And despite the muggy beginning, I was excited about our trip. Everyone else lived in Zapata and had left from there a day or two earlier. We'd all arranged to meet in Carlsbad to visit the caverns before traveling farther.

"When you agreed to marry me," Ryan asked as we hummed down the highway, "did you stop to think you'd be marrying a whole family? My whole crazy family?"

I looked up from the roadmap I'd been trying to refold and laughed. "Well, since we were in second grade the first time you asked me, I probably took it for granted."

Ryan chuckled. "Good thing you had all that time to think it over."

Although we'd grown up together, I had moved away when we were teen-agers, and we'd lost touch with each other till a few years ago when we were both in our mid-thirties. The connection we'd felt as children was quickly rekindled, and we were married shortly afterwards.

Ryan didn't mention that marrying into *my* "whole family" was relatively easy. I was an only child whose mother was as detached as Ryan's was nosy. I liked my stepfather, but since he and my mother lived in Minnesota, visits were infrequent. My biological father had recently moved to

Florida, making it hard for him to interfere in our lives, even if he'd been the type.

I gave up on the map and stuck it crookedly in the side pocket. "I suppose it helped that I practically grew up in my best friend's big noisy family.... And yours too," I added.

"Is that the real reason you married me?" Ryan glanced over at me, his brown eyes warm and teasing. "The nutty in-laws?"

"Yeah. You had nothing to do with it," I teased back.

He tried to scowl, but his grin got in the way. "I'll ditch this trip then, and leave you to 'em."

I reached over and patted his arm. "You can't do that. Think how disappointed Tía Dippy would be."

"Okay, I'll tag along. But only for Tía Dippy."

I laughed and blew him a kiss. "Touché."

* * *

Alana and Beto's two oldest sons had stayed home to manage Beto's computer business. So Carlos, the youngest son, was allowed to invite his cousin Omar Meléndez to come with them. The boys, both ten years old, had also brought along their respective pets—Carlos's cat, Spot, and Omar's golden retriever, Digger—thanks to Amá and Apá, who had brushed aside Alana's objections and offered to let the pets stay in their RV once we all arrived in Chama.

The largest of the families in our group—another cousin, her husband, and their five children—were also the most adaptable. They were traveling in a fifth-wheel trailer ingeniously designed to convert dining and living areas into bedrooms when needed.

They'd been through Carlsbad Caverns before, so agreed to look after Spot and Digger while the rest of us took the tour. They had their own pets, two schnauzers named Yippy and Yappy, and a hamster named Derek. While Spot accepted Digger and might have been curious about Derek, he took an instant dislike to the schnauzers. Spot hissed, bopped Yippy on the nose, and promptly disappeared under a recliner, where he stayed till we returned.

The next morning, we drove the short distance to Roswell. Carlos and Omar had begged the grownups to let them explore the UFO museum. I guess it was worth the trouble, since they both claimed an uncanny ability to spot alien lifeforms all the way to Albuquerque, the next stop on our itinerary.

Our entire group (not counting the menagerie, of course) converged for dinner at Papa Nacho's, a homey family restaurant Ryan and I had discovered on our last vacation. Over chips and salsa, we revised our travel plans. Ryan and Alana's parents had generously invited both Amá's sisters to travel with them in the motorhome. But Tía Marta and Tía Dippy wanted to visit several art galleries in Santa Fe, and—in a rare moment of solidarity—decided to rent a car in Albuquerque the next morning and re-join us in a day or two.

"I hate to be a killjoy, but there's no place to return rental cars in Chama—and no bus service either," I said.

"You could take our tow car," Apá said, referring to the 1976 yellow Volkswagen they pulled behind their motorhome.

Amá's eyes glazed over, maybe at the thought of Tía Dippy behind the wheel of their vintage car. She quickly recovered and agreed to the plan. "We won't need it till we get to Chama."

"And Marta is a good driver," Apá added smoothly, "so I know it will be in good hands."

After dinner, with modified plans in place, we all headed for our respective hotels and RV parks, where we would spend the night before continuing on toward Chama. Before going our separate ways, Ryan and I caught up with Alana and Beto outside the restaurant. The kids, who'd been taking turns checking on Digger and Spot, ran ahead to the van.

"I'm glad our tías found something they could agree on," Ryan remarked.

Alana nodded. "Breaking up their trip should give the folks a sanity break. I don't know how Apá holds up with all their clucking and cackling."

Beto put his arm around Alana. "Now remember, Corazón. You promised not to worry about those things. Apá can hold his own."

"Good advice," Ryan said.

"Definitely," I added. "Worrying is against the rules."

A voice inside my head, shrieking like a broken car alarm, tried to make itself heard—something about "best laid plans." I told it to be quiet, and it faded away to a dull whine.

Chapter 3

As we drove north from Albuquerque, I was once again mesmerized by the scenery. There was something almost surreal about the large cottony clouds bursting out of the royal-blue sky, and the round green clumps of piñon and juniper dotting the sandy mesas. In the background loomed the Jémez Mountains to the northwest and the Sangre de Cristos, northeast.

"I feel like I'm in the middle of a Peter Hurd painting."

Ryan nodded. "I'm glad we're coming back this way." He reached over and squeezed my hand. "And I'm glad my folks came along too. Apá's really looking forward to taking the boys fishing."

"They'll have fun. Apá got them each new fly rods. That's all they've talked about for days."

Near Abiquiú, the highway became a series of curves. Sandstone cliffs rose to our right—cliffs that nature had painted a deep red. Farther north, the colors changed, became muted. The steep bluffs—now layered in pale shades of gray, mauve, lemon, coral, and ivory—still looked rugged and imposing. In marked contrast, we drove along a brief stretch of road where a drop-off on the opposite side led to a grassy meadow. Here we could look down at the Chama River, a ribbon of silver banked by cottonwood trees, meandering through a peaceful green valley.

Ryan swung onto a wide pullout and shut off the engine. We got out and stood hand in hand, listening to the silence that was broken only by the soft rush of wind and the occasional scolding of a magpie.

For a few moments I closed my eyes and held out my other hand, as if to touch the ghosts of the Ancient Ones whose presence I felt so strongly here.

I opened my eyes and found Ryan regarding me curiously.

"Don't you feel it?" I whispered.

"Like we've stepped back in time?"

"Very far back."

He put his arm around me and I leaned into his solid warmth. We continued gazing at the beauty around us, in no hurry to leave, until the spell was broken by the squealing tires of a gold Porsche as it rounded the curve too fast. The car straightened, then careened around the next curve.

"Idiot," Ryan muttered.

I shivered. "The way that Porsche was speeding—even though it was the wrong color—for a minute I had a bad case of déjà vu. Like Bernice was going to barge in on us and demand to know why we're here."

"Well, you don't need to worry about that. She's long gone. Probably in South America by now."

We got back in the car and buckled up. Ryan pulled onto the highway and headed north again.

"That's very optimistic of you, thinking we've seen the last of Bernice," I said when we were a few miles down the road.

"What makes you think we haven't?"

"I don't know. But what makes you think she won't come back? I don't mean to Zapata—but back to the U.S. She could get lost in this country as easily as Mexico. Besides, she has relatives who live in New Mexico."

"Sharon." Ryan sounded exasperated. "Don't borrow trouble."

"I'm sorry. I don't mean to argue, but...."

"But—but you can't help it. You're a lawyer." He smiled. "A blonde one at that."

I made a face at him. "Actually, I'm hoping you'll *win* this argument. Convince me beyond a doubt that Bernice has gone so far south she's reached Antarctica."

"Honey, wherever she is, I don't want to waste any time thinking about her. Trust me. She's at the South Pole even as we speak."

I didn't want to think about her either.

Bernice: *La Fea*, "the ugly one."

A few years ago, her vindictiveness had brought heartache to Ryan's family. But before she could be hauled off to court and charged with anything, she managed to escape to Mexico. Since she was driving a bright red Porsche at the time, she was hardly inconspicuous, so we assumed she'd parted with it. She loved that car, so my uncharitable hope was that she got stuck with some beat-up rattletrap afterwards. One that got her as far as the South Pole before breaking down, I amended silently.

* * *

Ryan and I arrived in Chama about noon and stopped at J.V.'s Place for lunch. This was a family-run café that served the best green-chile cheeseburgers we'd ever found. J.V.'s was small, with no more than ten or eleven tables, but cheerful and friendly. There were a couple of tables outside as well, so we decided to eat at one of those.

"Pretty hot out here, ain't it?" another customer remarked on his way inside. "Over eighty already."

Ryan and I looked at each other and laughed. The weather felt very mild compared to what we were used to.

"I think I can learn to like this," Ryan said.

After lunch, we went to the Parlor Car B&B and unloaded our suitcases. The Parlor Car was a lovely Tudor-style home on the main street across from the train station. Lace curtains graced the bay window downstairs as well as the upstairs windows. The grounds were green and spacious, with a variety of flowers and trees, including several blue spruce and white fir that towered above the rooftop.

Wendy gave us a warm welcome, but she looked drawn. I wondered once again if something was bothering her.

"Your sister and her family are already here," she told us. "She and her husband went down to the campground to help your parents set up."

"Yes," I said. "The boys are going to camp beside their grandparents' RV."

Wendy laughed, and it was good to see her face lighten. "Well, right now they're in the back with Bonsall. I think your nephew was concerned about leaving his cat here, so Bonsall suggested they stay and check out his clinic."

Wendy's husband not only helped run the B&B, but also had a veterinary practice set up in a mobile unit behind the house. We had arranged to board the pets with him on the day we rode the train.

"Knowing Carlos," Ryan said, "he's probably talking Bonsall's ear off."

"I'm sure Bonsall doesn't mind. They're both nice boys. And you're right, Carlos did tell us how he saved Spot from the coyotes. Come on, I'll take you back there."

We found them outside, Spot curled up in Bonsall's arms, and Digger standing next to them. Bonsall was tall and slim, with brown hair and eyes. Wearing a Western shirt, jeans,

and boots, he looked more like a rancher than a doctor.
That in itself must have put the boys' minds at ease.

Carlos greeted us with a big smile. "Spot's really going to
like it here. He started purring the minute Dr. Johnson
picked him up!"

I hugged both kids. "What did I tell you?"

Ryan tousled Omar's hair. "What about Digger? You think
he'll be happy too?"

Omar grinned. "Yeah. Look at his tail waggin'."

* * *

Ryan and I walked with the boys and their pets over to
Rio Chama RV Park. On the road beside us bloomed Queen
Anne's lace and fragrant sweet yellow clover. Ahead of us
we could see mountains, evergreens, and aspens—an
artist's delight.

"We should come back in the fall to see the leaves change
color," I said.

Carlos's face brightened. "Maybe I can get out of school."

"Me too," said Ryan.

Carlos looked surprised. "I thought teachers could get out
of school any time they wanted to."

"Good idea—I'll suggest that to my principal at St.
Mary's."

Amá and Apá were parked under a large cottonwood tree,
and Beto had laid out the gear the boys needed on a picnic
table in the tent area.

"You need to pitch your own tent," Apá told them. "But
it's sure not like when I was a kid. Back then you had to
square it up before pounding stakes in the ground and make
sure the poles were even, and I don't remember what else.
But nowadays—" He waved one hand as if brandishing a

magic wand, then snapped his fingers. "Flip, zip! It goes up with the touch of a button."

"They'll still need to secure it and arrange their sleeping bags and stuff. Don't worry, Apá," Alana said, hugging him. "They still have a little work to do."

"And a few rules to follow. We want to be good neighbors."

He took the boys aside to explain what was expected of them, while Alana and I checked on Amá, who was happily puttering around inside her little home on wheels, adding decorative touches here and there.

"Come in, *mijitas*!" she said with a smile, as she drew us inside and encircled us both in her arms. The endearment always warmed me like a soft blanket.

We chatted while the kids and animals got situated; then Alana, Beto, Ryan, and I walked back to the Parlor Car, where we sat on gliders in the garden.

"It's so peaceful here," Alana said dreamily. "I could stay here forever."

I hoped her mood would rub off on me. Try as I would, I couldn't shake either the nagging memory of *La Fea* or my worry over the anxiety I sensed in Wendy.

Ryan's right. Don't borrow trouble, I chided myself. While you're at it, mind your own business. Don't let your imagination run away with you and spoil this holiday.

Still, the feeling persisted that somehow Bernice was nearby. After all, if vampires could slither out of coffins, I was sure mere continental boundaries couldn't contain *La Fea*.

Chapter 4

Apá's brother and his wife—Uncle Javier and Aunt
Maribel—had checked into a hotel near the Parlor Car earlier
that morning. The cousins with the large family arrived at
the RV park later that afternoon and pulled in near the
Salazars. They also set up a double-size tent to house their
offspring, plus Yippy, Yappy, and Derek.

The next morning, the men, kids, and dogs went fishing
on the Chama River. Derek, having exhausted himself
traveling many miles during the night on his exercise wheel,
snoozed in his nest of cedar shavings. Spot stretched out on
the dashboard of the Winnebago, where he could enjoy the
sun and watch for chipmunks. The rest of us were left to our
own devices—reading, hiking, exploring the town—whatever
sounded appealing.

It was the first chance I'd had to visit with Wendy alone.
We sat out on the back patio by the tall pink hollyhocks,
drinking lemonade and relaxing. I lost the argument with
myself about minding my own business and finally gathered
the courage to ask her if something was wrong. She looked
almost relieved that I'd opened the subject.

"Well, it's no secret. In a small town like this, everyone
knows everything. For some people, it's just idle gossip. But
for those of us who care about Joaquín Álvarez, it's rather
disturbing."

"Who is he?"

"He's one of the old-timers who's lived in Chama forever.
His wife died about...let's see...well, less than a year ago.

His daughter and granddaughter wanted him to move in with them, but he said he wanted to stay in his own home. Since they live nearby, they figured it wouldn't be a problem."

Wendy traced slow circles on the frost that had collected on her lemonade glass. "He's such a sweet man—or used to be."

"His personality is changing?" It sounded as if he might have developed dementia, but I hated using that word since I know how harsh it sounds, especially if the family hasn't acknowledged it.

She hesitated, then continued in her gentle way. "That's one way of putting it. Not long after his wife's death, he signed up with a dating service."

I could imagine the family's dismay, but I could also imagine Mr. Álvarez's loneliness—a loneliness that even a devoted daughter and a small grandchild couldn't fill. "I know a number of people who've met through dating services—and even online. Not sure I'd recommend it, but it's worked out for my friends."

"Are any of them eighty-nine years old?"

I nearly choked on my ice-cubes.

Wendy reached over and patted me on the back. "I'm sorry, but now you understand how shocked everyone was."

I recovered and slipped into my "devil's advocate" mode. "Maybe he can get paired up with a nice elderly widow, and...." My voice trailed off. *And they'll both live happily ever after.* A little too sugary to say out loud.

"I guess the dating service was a reputable one after all," Wendy said. "They simply told him they couldn't find a match. So next he turned to those newspaper ads."

"Yeah. I guess that would be easier. Still, aren't there some safeguards?"

"Some. You respond to a box number or something, rather than directly to the 'advertiser.' But there's no one to weed out the crackpots—or the golddiggers."

"Is that what happened? Some golddigger answered his ad?"

"Oh, yes. Someone much younger too."

I supposed someone like Tía Dippy would seem much younger to someone as old as Mr. Álvarez. Given her dingaling personality, I wondered if she'd be likely to enter the dating game via the matchmaker ads. Probably not. She seemed to be enjoying her widowhood too much.

Of course I didn't know Tía Dippy very well, since she'd moved to Zapata so recently. But maybe this vacation would give me a chance to see her through Amá's eyes. Before now, I'd always thought of Amá as somewhat of a dingaling herself, but her ditziness paled next to Tía Dippy's.

And even though Ryan joked about his "nutty family," I felt a sudden overwhelming gratitude for them. They were nutty enough to have taken me into their hearts for as long as I could remember. Little everyday squabbles seemed insignificant in light of the deeper heartache Mr. Álvarez's family must feel.

"You seem deep in thought," Wendy said.

"My mind was wandering," I admitted. "How old is this person Mr. Álvarez met?"

"Take a huge breath. I don't want you choking again."

I smiled and inhaled slowly.

"She's thirty-five," Wendy said.

My breath whooshed out like a popped balloon. "Thanks for the warning. Gosh, that's just a few years younger than I am."

"It's the same age as his granddaughter."

"Good lord."

19

"The saddest part is that she's turned him against his family."

"Not too surprising if she's really a golddigger. Is he pretty wealthy?"

"He's well off. But he'll be even richer in a month or so, whenever they finish the probate of his brother's will." Wendy leaned forward. "Sharon, you're a lawyer. Is there any way this little 'romance' can be broken up legally?"

I took another deep breath. "It depends." Stock lawyerly answer. Real answer: Probably not.

"On the surface, there's nothing illegal about using those ads," I said. "You'd have to prove there was intent to defraud, and that can get sticky. Do you happen to have copies of the ads themselves?"

"As a matter of fact, I do. It's so weird. Nobody even knew what Mr. Álvarez was up to till this strange woman just showed up out of the blue. Once Alicia found out how they'd met, she searched through his desk till she found the ads. She made duplicates, then put his copies back."

"Alicia?"

"Mr. Álvarez's daughter. She asked if I'd keep one set 'for safekeeping.' Her own copies mysteriously disappeared."

Wendy went inside to retrieve the ads, then returned with both the ads and a refill of lemonade. She handed me the clippings, both from a Santa Fe newspaper, then sat down again. "Read his 'lady-love's' first."

Her ad was brief and to the point:

BEAUTIFUL LADY
Fun-loving redhead, 35, seeks mature gentleman for companionship, possibly more.

"Well, at least she was up-front about her age," I commented, having no reason at the time to think the ad was anything but a standard come-on.

"I'm afraid the 'mature gentleman' part was all Mr. Álvarez saw. Wait till you read his response."

His ad was a little more flowery:

YOUNG AT HEART
Mature athletic gentleman
enjoys bicycling and horseback-riding
as well as romantic evenings by the fireplace.
Could I be the fun-loving companion you're seeking?

I raised my eyebrows. "My, he's certainly articulate."

"I think he copied that description from someone else's ad. Or else he's living in the past. I've never seen him ride a bicycle, and it's been years since he's ridden a horse. Unfortunately, he's developed a heart condition and does well to take slow walks."

"So the 'Beautiful Lady' wasn't disappointed to find him less athletic than he described?"

"Ha. I think she was relieved. Anyway, Rita—that's the woman's name—Rita fusses over him and babies him and makes him feel young again."

"Has she moved in with him?"

"No, she was smart enough to rent her own apartment. But Alicia says she's over there all the time anyway."

I re-read the ads. "Rita's seems pretty straightforward. From what you tell me, his is the one that's misleading."

Wendy looked so dejected, I felt bad dashing her hopes and tried to think of another loophole. "Wait a minute. You said something about his brother's will in probate?"

21

She nodded. "His brother died several weeks ago. *Very* wealthy. Everything to be divided among the remaining siblings and one or two others."

"Sounds like a number of people."

"Not that many any more. Just Mr. Álvarez and a younger sister and a couple of nephews, I think."

"No problems? Nobody contesting the will, or anything like that?"

"No problems that I know of, but there are some stipulations connected with it. I don't remember exactly. It sounded complicated to me."

"Complicated is good. That might tie it up for a while."

"That's what Alicia's hoping. Her father and Rita are already talking about getting married. We're afraid once he gets his brother's inheritance, they'll move out of state— some big city like Denver—and disappear. Rather, her father will disappear."

"Well, don't borrow trouble." *Wow. Look at the kettle giving advice.* "Believe me, I know how easy it is to imagine the worst. But things are seldom as bad as they seem."

Before Wendy looked away, I caught her rolling her eyes.

I grinned sheepishly. "I'd better shut up before I gag on my clichés."

She laughed then. "There's some wisdom in them. I'll try to keep that in mind."

Chapter 5

That evening we ate fresh trout the fishermen had cleaned and fileted, then grilled over a campfire. While dinner was cooking, Carlos and Omar gave animated descriptions of the fish they'd caught, each boy trying to outdo the other. Digger kept jumping up and down between them, excited as if he'd made the biggest catch of all.

After dusk, we put on our jackets and sat around the fire in our camp chairs. Amá fixed us hot chocolate, and we warmed our hands by wrapping them around our mugs. Spot, having enjoyed his share of the meal, settled himself on Ryan's lap and purred contentedly.

"We need some music," Alana said. "Play for us, Apá."

Pleased to be asked, Apá put aside his cocoa and brought out his accordion. He persuaded his brother to join him on the guitar, and soon the rest of us were singing along. Some of the nearby campers brought their chairs over and either sang with us or simply enjoyed the camaraderie, laughing and sharing stories.

I closed my eyes and immersed myself in the mixture of happy sounds, pushing aside all the worrisome thoughts I'd had earlier.

* * *

We were up early the next morning for a delicious breakfast of fresh peaches, spinach quiche, blueberry muffins, and piñon coffee.

Alana leaned back in her chair and sighed. "Mm. This is wonderful. Wendy, you're the best cook in the world." She smiled at her husband. "Beto, remember when we stayed at that B&B where both 'Bs' were lumpy?"

Beto's eyes twinkled. "Qué sí. How could I forget!"

"A lumpy breakfast too?" Ryan asked.

"We only assumed it was breakfast," Alana said. "I think it was supposed to be oatmeal. Lumps the size of golfballs."

Wendy laughed. "It's good to know my competition!"

* * *

Uncle Javier and Aunt Maribel had their breakfast at The Village Bean, next door to the Chama Station Inn, where they were staying. They joined us afterwards, and we all walked over to the RV Park together.

"I thought Tía Dip—Tía Eppie and Tía Marta would be here by now," Ryan said when he realized they weren't with the rest of the family.

Apá shook his head. "They called last night. Eppie discovered all those casinos around Albuquerque, and forgot all about Santa Fe. Marta said she didn't dare leave her alone."

"Are they coming here at all?"

"Marta said they'd be here this afternoon if she had to drag her sister in by her hair."

I smiled. "I doubt if she'll have any trouble. I think they're both looking forward to the train ride Tuesday."

* * *

"Mom, Spot doesn't like to be on a leash."

"Carlos, we talked about this before we left home."

"I know, but—"

"No buts. Fifteen minutes. He needs some fresh air. And a little exercise."

Neither Carlos nor Spot agreed, but Alana was adamant.

We had all gathered at the RV Park after breakfast. From there, Alana and Amá had taken a tour of Tierra Wools, a co-op where traditional spinning and handweaving are still a vital industry in Northern New Mexico. Others in our group had gone horseback-riding; everyone else had scattered in different directions.

After lunch, Carlos and Omar had found a basketball court near the schoolyard, where they could practice one-on-one. Alana and I were drinking iced tea under a cottonwood tree by the Salazars' Winnebago when the boys returned. They usually took good care of their pets, so Carlos's reluctance to walk Spot puzzled me.

Omar and Digger started ahead, Digger bounding and sniffing joyfully. Carlos trudged after them, pulling gently on the despised leash. Spot slunk behind, ears laid back, expressing his displeasure in a low growl.

Alana rolled her eyes. "I swear. They only have to go to the end of the road and back. You'd think I was sending them to prison."

"Maybe I'll catch up with them," I said. "I'd like a chance to spend some time with my godson—and his cat."

Although I wasn't Carlos's "official" godmother, he'd chosen me to be his *nina* a few years ago, and we had a special bond. By the time I reached them, Carlos had picked Spot up and was carrying him for the duration of their walk.

I put my hand on Carlos's shoulder. "People can't let their dogs run loose here. Spot is really safe."

"I know that," Carlos grumbled, "but Spot doesn't."

"We kind of miss him sometimes."

Carlos looked up at me, his gray eyes wide. "Does Uncle Ryan want him back?"

"No, honey. He always belonged to both of you, and we're glad he's at home with you now."

Carlos didn't respond. Why was he so subdued? I noticed how pale his face looked beneath his freckles.

"Is everything going okay?"

He looked away and tightened his hold on Spot.

"Can you tell me?"

He swallowed. "It's nothin'."

We came to the end of the road and turned back.

"Carlitos," I said softly. "Please tell me."

Again he didn't answer, and I let the silence hang between us.

Finally he mumbled, "I saw La Fea."

My skin prickled. "Where?" My voice was almost as inaudible as his had been.

"At the grocery store."

"Today?"

He nodded. "Before lunch. Me 'n' Omar went with Mom to get some Cokes and stuff."

"Did you tell her?"

Tears began welling in his eyes, and I felt his shoulder stiffen under my touch. Sensing his effort to maintain control, I moved my hand away.

"They didn't believe me, her and Dad."

"Carlos, we all know you don't tell lies."

"They said it was prob'ly just someone that looked like her."

I had the same thought, and was glad I hadn't voiced it. By now we'd come full circle on our walk.

"Carlitos, why don't you let Spot inside. Then we can walk back to where we turned around and keep going down to the river. Maybe it would help to talk about this some more."

He nodded and disappeared inside the RV. After he came back outside, we walked in silence down the road and through the gate. It was a short walk to the riverbank, where we found a log to sit on.

"The thing is," I said gently, after we'd sat there a few minutes, "La Fea's the last person any of us *wants* to see. So we *hope* it was someone else. Does that make sense?"

He gave that some thought. "I guess so."

"What makes you so sure it was La Fea?"

"I just know."

Couldn't argue with that.

"Just for the heck of it," I said, "let's play devil's advocate."

"What's that?"

"Well, it's taking the opposite point of view when you're discussing something. Sometimes it means arguing in favor of someone or something that you don't necessarily believe in."

"I don't understand."

"Okay, here's how it works. I'm going to think of all the reasons the person you saw is definitely Bernice, and you try to prove me wrong."

"That's backwards."

"I know, but let's give it a try. I'll go first. For sure, it's La Fea, because she's driving a red Porsche."

He shook his head no.

"Really? A gold Porsche?"

"Nope. A silver Jaguar."

"Oh. Hmm." I felt the tension ease out of my own shoulders. The car was the only tangible link I could think of. I hoped there were enough differences between the woman Carlos saw and Bernice that he'd decide he'd made a mistake.

"I'm sure she was driving really fast," I continued.

"Nah, she was just sitting in the parking lot with some old man."

"Maybe they were saying the rosary."

This elicited a small grin.

"Okay, I'm sure it was La Fea because she looked like Cleopatra on a bad-hair day."

The grin widened a little. "She had regular hair."

"I see. Orange?"

"No. Kinda like Mom's."

"Her hair now, or before she colored it?"

"Like it is now—kinda dark red."

"So this beautiful redhead has taken up with some old man...."

I felt the blood drain from my face. "Oh, no," I whispered. "This is too much."

Carlos saw the horror in my eyes, and suddenly our roles were reversed. He put his arm around my shoulder and began patting me. "Don't worry, *Nina*. I was prob'ly wrong. It musta been somebody else."

Chapter 6

Don't imagine a coincidence that doesn't exist, I told myself. There has to be some logical explanation.

I looked over at Carlos's worried face and knew I had to pull myself together.

"Carlitos, I just remembered something. Bernice has family in New Mexico—Santa Fe, I think. That's not too far from here. I bet she has a cousin we mistook her for. Sometimes cousins can look more alike than brothers or sisters. You know how sometimes people think you and Omar are twins. I bet it was a cousin—"

I realized I was babbling, and stopped myself. Though it was true that the boys looked alike with their light brown hair and gray eyes. I wondered if this was what Beto— Carlos's dad, Omar's uncle—had looked like at their age.

"Yeah, you're right," he answered slowly, bracing his hands on the log and looking straight ahead.

I didn't know if he was trying to reassure me or himself. In fact, I wasn't sure which of us *I* was trying to reassure. But I realized my scenario wasn't that far-fetched. I vaguely recalled that Bernice had relatives in New Mexico, even though the "Santa Fe" part was just a guess.

"Even if it *is* La Fea," I went on, "there's a warrant for her arrest in Texas. She's probably not any happier about the idea of running into us than we are, so I think she'll keep her distance. After all, she knows we could send her packing off to jail."

The relief on Carlos's face was worth my white lie. In the eyes of the law, Bernice's penny-ante drug-dealing probably wasn't worth the time, money, or manpower it would take to track her down and send her back to Zapata.

In the eyes of our family, she was the epitome of slime. Slippery and devious, she had managed to disguise her attempts at blackmail in such a way they'd be hard to prove. But worst of all, she had terrorized Carlos while pretending to be Alana's friend.

I ruffled his hair. "C'mon, kiddo, we need to get back and see what the others are up to."

We found Tía Dippy and Tía Marta waiting for us when we got back to the Winnebago, and exchanged greetings in a flurry of hugs and chatter. The men had drifted away to exchange tales with other RVers, but Omar and Digger were waiting too. Since boys and dog seemed to have an endless supply of energy, they decided to investigate the wooded area surrounding the RV park.

"Don't be gone long. Remember, it rains every afternoon. And stay together," Alana warned, after hugging all three. "Digger, I'm counting on you to keep an eye on these guys."

Digger thumped his tail happily, then bounded ahead of the boys. Unlike Spot, he didn't mind his leash as long as he could be in the lead.

* * *

"That little girl, always trouble," Tía Dippy said as soon as the boys were out of sight.

"Who? What are you talking about?" I asked. The other children in our group—both boys and girls—had seemed well behaved to me. Besides, their family had gone up to Pagosa Springs for the day and hadn't been around to bother anyone.

Alana pulled another camp chair into the circle where they'd gathered. "Have a seat, Sharon. We'll fill you in."

I sat down next to her and looked at the solemn faces surrounding me. Alana, so beautiful with her deep brown eyes, flawless skin, and smooth shoulder-length hair— auburn, this month, but a shade that suited her. Amá, an older, plumper version of Alana, but with gray hair swept into a French twist. Aunt Maribel, tall and willowy, whose short brown hair was highlighted in gold. Tía Marta, with close-cropped gray hair and thick glasses that tended to make her eyes look larger than they were. Tía Dippy, whose curly black wig was tilted at an odd angle, and whose scarlet lipstick had been aimed more-or-less at her mouth. I bit my lip to keep from laughing, because no one else seemed in a laughing mood.

"Or maybe you can fill us in," Alana continued. "Did Carlos say anything about thinking he'd seen Bernice?"

My shoulders sagged. Was this the "little girl" Tía Dippy meant?

"Yes, he did."

"Well, he seemed in better spirits when you all came back just now. So I'm guessing you handled it better than Beto and I did."

I reached over and held her hand. "I would have told him the same thing if he hadn't told me about your reaction before I had a chance. I know you just wanted to keep him from worrying."

"Unfortunately, it had the opposite effect. He thought we were taking sides against him."

"I think he understands. But more to the point, it sounds like you took him seriously."

Alana looked on the verge of tears. "I'm not sure what I thought. I didn't want to believe she was up here, but I couldn't let go of it."

"Well, *my* ESP has certainly been out of whack. I thought she was nearby when she wasn't. And didn't tune in at all when Wendy told me about someone who sounded just like her."

I gave everyone an abbreviated version of Mr. Álvarez's predicament, as well as my own misgivings. I also mentioned the possibility—that seemed more and more likely when I repeated it—that Carlos could have confused Bernice with a relative.

"Espero que sí," Tía Dippy sniffed, shaking her curls so that her wig slid a tad further askew.

"We all hope so," Alana said. "Let's just assume Sharon is right."

"Bad seed, esa mala," Tía Dippy muttered. "All this tonta psychology. Simplemente excusas...."

My curiosity was piqued. "It sounds like you've known her a long time."

"Qué sí!" Tía Dippy continued in Spanish, as she often did when excited. "I went to school with her parents. Sweet people, both of them. Her mother was one of my best friends. They waited so long to have children, and when Perlita got pregnant, she was so happy, but...." Tía Dippy paused and crossed herself. "Someone gave her the evil eye, and even the *curandera* couldn't undo it."

I was skeptical of such curses, but maybe something had gone wrong in the womb that short-circuited Bernice's development. A little component called "conscience" left out of her make-up.

Tía Marta folded her arms across her chest. "What's past is past. Why are we even talking about this?"

Alana stiffened. "I take it you never knew her."

"No, mijita. I only heard things. But she *is* a human being. Maybe not a very nice one, but she can't be some occult creature my sister makes her out to be."

"You have a point," I admitted, hoping to avoid an argument between the sisters. "Maybe we've given Bernice more power than she actually has. Still, I think it's dangerous to underestimate her."

"She's evil," Alana insisted. "She fancied herself in love with Leo, and when he wouldn't have anything to do with her, she took it out on our whole family."

I'd been disappointed when Leo, Ryan's twin brother, couldn't take time off to join us on this vacation. But if Bernice really was in the area, maybe it was just as well.

"Hell hath no fury...," I murmured.

"What was it she did to your Carlos?" Tía Marta asked.

"Tried to make him think she was going to slash all of us to pieces."

"She did *what*?" Amá sputtered. "You never told me!"

My stomach lurched at the memory. "That's because it's what La Fea would have wanted—to upset you too. That's really her forte—mental torture. I don't think she had any intention of following through. She simply enjoyed seeing our reaction—seeing Carlos terrified."

"So, what do you think she could do to him now? To any of you?" Tía Marta continued.

"I don't know," Alana admitted. "But I'm not sure I go along with Sharon's assessment. I think she's quite capable of physical violence as well."

Tía Dippy leaned forward and addressed her sisters. "Don't you remember, Marta? Ysela? That Easter when she wanted a baby rabbit? She was maybe five or six years old.

Her cousin got one instead, and 'someone' set that little rabbit on fire. It was horrible."

"Me acuerdo. I remember." Amá shuddered. "We were there when it happened. Perlita and her family insisted it had to be an accident. That somehow sparks from the barbecue grill must have blown into the little cage."

"Cage?" I pictured a large hutch.

"A little carrier," Amá said. "All the kids wanted to hold the little bunny, so after a while, one of the grownups said it needed to rest. The carrier was really just a little cardboard box. Anything could have set it off."

"What about all the other kids?" I assumed Alana, Leo, and Ryan had been at the family barbacoa, and wondered if they'd witnessed the incident.

"We didn't see anything," Alana said. "When we couldn't play with the bunny anymore, we must have gone to the other side of the yard. We were still looking for Easter eggs, even though I think they'd all been found by then. Anyway, next thing I knew, Amá and Apá rounded us up and hustled us back home."

"You never knew?"

"Oh, we heard about it later—about the unfortunate 'accident.' I remember crying, but I never questioned it. Who could believe anyone would do something like that on purpose?"

Tía Dippy scowled. "That precious bunny wasn't even close to the grill."

"Did anyone actually see Bernice...?" Somehow the words stuck in my throat.

"We saw her playing with the striker," Amá said. "Someone would take it away from her, and when no one was looking, she'd pick it up again."

"She was right there when the blaze started," Tía Dippy added. "When someone called her name, she ran away. They tried to put the fire out, but it went too fast."

Tears rolled down Amá's cheeks. "Later on, they found the striker in the ashes."

"I remember too," Tía Marta said grimly. "I'm not making excuses. I just think we should focus on here and now."

I looked up at the afternoon thunderclouds as they gathered momentum, mirroring our gloom.

"Maybe it's time," I said, "to surprise Bernice before she surprises us again."

Chapter 7

The next morning after breakfast, I pulled Wendy aside.

"Do you mind if I look at those ads again? The ones between Mr. Álvarez and the fun-loving golddigger?"

"Not at all."

Wendy located the ads and gave them to me.

I re-read them, this time picturing Bernice in the role of the self-described "Beautiful Lady." The thought gave me chills.

"Would you happen to know if Mr. Álvarez's daughter Alicia has a snapshot of the 'beautiful golddigger'?" I asked. "I think she might be someone I used to know."

Wendy's eyes widened. "Rita Méndez?"

"I knew her by a different name, but I have reason to think it's the same person."

"If you're right, I imagine Alicia would like to meet you too."

"And if the picture matches, I might even want to meet Rita. We'll see."

"Goodness! What a strange coincidence! I'll see what I can do."

"We're going to wander down to the bookstore, but I'll take my cell phone with me. If you get in touch with Alicia, would you give me a call?"

She agreed, and Ryan and I began our stroll down Terrace Avenue, the main street. One of the things we loved about Chama was the slow pace. Drivers deferred to pedestrians in the heart of the village, where I'd never seen anyone drive over twenty miles per hour.

"I love these old lampposts," I said, looking at the street lights that lined the sidewalks. "They look like they might have looked over a century ago."

Ryan followed my gaze. "I like the flags too."

Hanging from each lamppost was a small rectangular flag with a stylized version of a train engine imprinted on it. The flags seemed to add a festive welcome.

Unlike enormous "big-city" shopping complexes, the two malls we passed housed only a few shops, where boutiques, jewelry, artworks, and souvenir trinkets could be found. Farther down the street were art galleries, a drug store, and other businesses.

While the commercial part of town was on the main drag, the fire department, post office, and city hall—which housed the library—were located a street or two away.

We took one of our "zigzag" walks, weaving in and out of business and residential areas, and eventually reached The Little Blue Engine. This was a cozy store with a wide variety of books. The owner introduced herself as Deb Williams and offered us hot coffee. Ryan and I sat on a comfy couch with our coffee and read the *Chama Valley Times* to catch up on the local news. When we'd finished, Ryan returned to his browsing while I chatted with Deb.

She was friendly and easy to talk to, so after a while I asked if she knew Rita Méndez.

"Only by sight," she answered guardedly.

"I'm not sure, but I think we went to school together back in junior high."

"Lucky you."

"Does she ever come in here?"

Deb shook her head. "The only time I see her is at the post office. She and Mr. Álvarez walk over there just about every day."

"Interesting. I had the impression they pretty much kept to themselves."

"In a way, they do. Mr. Álvarez used to talk to the folks at the post office—like everyone else in town does—but not any more. They seem to be in their own little world these days. At least he gets some exercise once in a while."

"You say they go every day? Same time?"

"Mm. Could be. I usually stop in before coming to work, but my own time varies."

Ryan brought the latest Michael McGarrity mystery up to the counter and caught the tail-end of our conversation. After paying for his book, we said our goodbyes and left the store.

"Tell me," Ryan said as we started back to the Parlor Car.

"I don't know where to start."

"Does this have something to do with Carlos thinking he saw Bernice?"

"You know?"

"Beto told me."

I took a deep breath. "I'd have told you sooner, but I hated bringing up her name. I knew you didn't want to hear any more about her."

Ryan slipped his hand into mine. "I'm sorry, honey. You're right. I really don't like to. But if something worries you, I want to know about it."

I wound up pouring out the whole story about Mr. Álvarez and the woman who resembled Bernice, as well as the family discussion we'd had yesterday afternoon.

"I feel the same way you do, Ryan. I can't think of anything I'd less rather do than deal with La Fea, but we

38

began to think it was something we ought to meet head-on."

By the set of Ryan's jaw, I could tell what he thought of that idea.

"Why does it have to be you?" he asked.

"It doesn't. I just happened to come up with some ideas."

"So. What do you plan to do? Waylay her at the post office?"

"I don't know. I was kind of hoping Wendy would call."

"Look, Sharon, you know the old saying, 'Forewarned is forearmed.' Well, we're already forewarned. If we accidentally run into La Fea, let her be surprised. It's her turn anyway. We don't need to go out of our way to make it happen."

"The thing is, we don't know if this person really *is* Bernice. I'd like to find out. If we're wrong, then we can put the whole thing behind us."

"And if we're right?"

"That opens another can of worms. As far as our family is concerned, I agree with you. We're forewarned, and we can be careful to stay together. But I'd feel guilty knowing she's latched on to poor old Mr. Álvarez, and I just ignored it."

"And what, sweetheart, can you do? We can't stay in town forever."

"I know that," I went on stubbornly. "But we can stay longer than we first planned. You have a few weeks left before school starts, and I'm only a phone call away if something urgent comes up at work."

Except for the other RV family—who was traveling on to Utah after our train ride—everyone else had decided to extend their vacation here. Another group of campers who played a variety of musical instruments—dulcimers, banjos, guitars—had invited Apá and Uncle Javier to join them in their informal jam sessions every afternoon, either before or after the brief daily thunderstorms.

Alana and Beto's sons had Beto's computer business running smoothly, so there was no hurry to get back. And—except for the possibility that we might run into La Fea again—everyone was having a good time.

"Well, let's hope this mystery woman turns out to be a total stranger," Ryan said. "Then we can get back to enjoying ourselves."

"Believe me, that's exactly what I hope."

Chapter 8

"Sharon, you won't guess what I found out!"

Wendy met us at the door, a stack of clean towels in her arms. "Let me go put these away, and I'll tell you all about it."

Ryan and I sat on the sofa in the living room and looked outside the large bay window facing us. Wildrose bushes along a low wooden fence bordered the sidewalk where tourists strolled by. Wendy returned a few moments later and sat in a cushiony armchair angled toward us, her hands clasped in her lap.

"I talked to Alicia Mondragón, Joaquín Álvarez's daughter, a little while ago. She doesn't have any pictures of Rita, and the odd thing is, she's never seen any around her father's home either."

"Does Alicia go over there often? I thought you said Mr. Álvarez wasn't on good terms with his family any more."

"It's pretty sticky, but Alicia's resigned herself that if she ever wants to see her father at all, she has to do it Rita's way."

"What about Alicia's daughter?"

"Vanessa? She doesn't make any pretense. I think the fur flies whenever she's around, so Mr. Álvarez finally asked her not to come over anymore. It's a mess."

"So Rita—or whoever she is—still calls the shots," Ryan said.

Wendy nodded. "I'm afraid so."

"You don't seem so distressed, though," I said. "Not like the other day."

"You're right." She reached over and put her hand on my arm. "Alicia had an idea, if you're willing to go along with it. I started to call, then I decided to wait and tell you when you got back."

"Sounds intriguing."

"Yes. Well. Alicia told me that Rita gets her hair done every week at the same time. It's one of those places where 'walk-ins' are welcome."

"Hmm. I think I see where this is going. You want me to walk in?"

"How do you feel about it?"

"It might work. I suppose I could get my hair cut—"

"Not too short," Ryan broke in, no doubt remembering a dreadful experience I'd had with an expensive scissor-happy stylist a few years ago.

"Don't worry," Wendy said. "Angie has an excellent staff. You might ask for Jocelyn or Siena."

"I just hope it doesn't seem too coincidental for me to show up at the exact time Rita's there."

Wendy waved away my misgivings. "Everything about this is coincidental. It's a coincidence that you might know her. And more than likely you'd see her someplace or another anyway."

"Just what I was hoping wouldn't happen."

"Oh, Sharon, I'm sorry. I shouldn't have put you on the spot."

"You didn't. I just meant I don't want to get caught off guard. Actually, I'm curious to see her face to face, but I'd rather do it when *she's* least expecting it rather than the other way around. So your idea makes sense."

"I hope so! Alicia hopes you'll find out that she's not who she says she is. It might be exactly what the family needs to drive her away."

"When's Rita's next appointment?"

"This afternoon?" Wendy said in a small voice. "I know it's short notice."

"Actually, it's probably the best time. We don't have any special plans today. Everyone seemed to need a little 'down-time.'"

Wendy's relief was palpable. "About 3:30 okay?"

I could already feel my stomach tightening, but managed a smile. "You bet."

* * *

In our upstairs bedroom, Ryan took off his shoes, removed the down comforter, and stretched out on the four-poster bed, his arms folded behind his head. The bed was so high, there was a small wooden step-stool beside it.

Ryan watched me rummage through the armoire, a look of amusement on his face. "Why are you so concerned about what to wear? You always look beautiful."

I turned toward him and felt a pang of regret that I'd gotten involved in what could very well turn out to be a wild-goose chase. The bed—and Ryan in it—looked much more inviting than the afternoon I had planned.

"I don't know. Some silly feminine conceit, I guess. If it is La Fea, I want her to drop in her tracks from envy. Forget Mr. Álvarez."

"You could waltz in there without wearing a thing, and she still couldn't compete."

"Flattery will get you everywhere. I'll save that particular non-attire for later."

"Promise?"

"Promise."

I sorted through my clothes again. I'd brought mostly jeans and shorts—casual stuff—with only a couple of dressy outfits. I held out a crepe wrap-dress, a birthday gift Amá had bought for me at Neiman Marcus.

"I think I'll wear this one. The opal earrings look good with it."

"Do that. How 'bout the tiara?"

I wrinkled my nose at him. "Aqua does nice things for me."

"Good idea. The aqua dress with eyes to match."

My eyes often reflected the color of whatever I wore, and Ryan never missed a chance to tease me about it.

His expression became serious. "Sharon, be careful. You sure you don't want Alana to go with you?"

I'd told Alana about Wendy's plan and asked if she'd like to be in on it. But after talking it over, we agreed that if 'Rita' did turn out to be Bernice, she might feel ambushed if we both showed up.

"I promise to be careful, Ryan. Besides, she's hardly likely to attack me with a whole room full of people watching."

* * *

I entered the beauty shop feeling overdressed and somewhat conspicuous. Ryan was right: I might as well have worn a tiara.

I'd come early on purpose, and Rita/Bernice hadn't arrived yet. All the beauticians were busy, which suited me fine. I was told Siena could be with me in about twenty minutes.

I sat down and leafed through a fashion magazine featuring rather bizarre hairstyles. Just as I'd fixated on a picture of a model whose head was shaved on one side while the other side sprouted a slew of four-inch spikes, I heard the bell announcing the arrival of another customer.

The hair rose on the back of my neck even before I looked up to see either La Fea or her exact double glide into the room.

Chapter 9

"Be with you in a minute, Ms. Méndez," Jocelyn called as she put the finishing touches on a comb-out.

I had hoped Rita/Bernice would sit down, but she continued standing, tapping the floor lightly with the pointy toe of her Manolo Blahnik pumps. Her coppery skin was nicely offset by a champagne-colored silk dress. A single strand of cultured pearls adorned her slender neck. I felt almost dowdy by comparison. I wondered whom *she* was trying to impress.

I set the magazine aside, stood, and walked over to her.

"Excuse me." Amazingly my voice came out in the well-modulated tone I'd practiced, instead of betraying the shakiness I felt inside. "Aren't you Bernice Peralta?"

She turned to face me, amusement flickering in her eyes. "And who are you, pray tell?"

Her response seemed typically rude, so I gave her a polite smile and continued looking her in the eye.

"I'm Sharon Salazar," I said, without bothering to elaborate.

"Well, Sharon Salazar, I don't know who you are, but I'm not Bernice Peralta."

A couple of customers looked up from their magazines, not bothering to hide their curiosity. I felt my face turning red, a combination of anger and embarrassment. I realized that, short of wrestling her to the floor and choking a confession out of her, I was running out of options, so I changed my tune.

"I apologize," I said softly. "You look like someone I used to know."

She dropped her guard. "And I apologize too. I'm Rita Méndez. It's been a long time since anyone mistook me for Bernice. You caught me by surprise."

"Oh." She'd certainly taken *me* by surprise. "This has happened before?"

"Many times when we were growing up. Even my grandparents got us mixed up sometimes."

"Oh?"

"I'm Bernice's aunt."

"Oh!"

"I know. I'm a few months younger. But her mother was the oldest in a family of eight, and I'm the youngest."

"O-o-oh!"

It occurred to me I wasn't exactly holding up my end of the conversation. I wasn't sure if I believed "Aunt Rita," but I did notice some subtle differences between her and the Bernice I remembered. Rita's eyes were a lighter brown and slightly almond-shaped. Still, contacts and a face lift could account for that.

On the other hand, her make-up was tastefully applied, subdued. Bernice's always looked as though it had been plastered on with an industrial-sized paintbrush.

"Are you ready now, Ms. Méndez?" Jocelyn intervened with a smile.

"In a minute."

Rita turned to me. "Don't go away. I want to ask you about Bernice."

Hmm. Just what I wanted to ask her. Jocelyn was still smiling, but she had one hand on the back of her chair, and the other on her hip.

"I don't want to keep you waiting," I said.

47

Again Rita looked amused. "I take it you're a city girl. No one hurries around here."

Evidently self-centeredness ran in the family.

"Go ahead. I'll stay till you're finished. I'm not in a hurry either."

Which was a good thing. Siena's customer was having her hair highlighted, and still had a lot of goop and foil on her head.

Jocelyn gave me an appreciative look. "You can sit in Carla's chair if you'd like. She's off today." She indicated the place next to hers. "That way you two can visit till Siena's ready."

"Thanks."

I took a seat and watched Rita remove her pearls and let Jocelyn wrap a waterproof cape around her neck. Wearing silk—or an expensive crepe—seemed a little risky, but Jocelyn was a pro.

Following the shampoo, Jocelyn turned Rita to face the mirror, and after some discussion, began trimming her hair.

"Tell me, how do you happen to know Bernice?" Rita asked me while watching the haircut.

I studied Rita's profile, wondering who I was talking to. "There's not much to tell," I hedged. "We went to seventh and eighth grades together."

"You were friends?"

I shrugged. "We hung out with different people. She had her friends, I had mine."

"You didn't like her?"

"I didn't say that. I didn't really know her. But tell me about your relationship with her. Was your family pretty close?"

Rita jerked her head toward me, nearly getting stabbed with the scissors. The steely look she gave me was pure

Bernice. Then her face smoothed into a bland expression as she turned back to the mirror.

"We didn't see each other that often."

But often enough that your grandparents got you mixed up? I bit my tongue. Maybe I should stick to my "ohs." Or find a less direct way to probe.

"Well, that makes sense," I lied. "Bernice's mother—your oldest sister—must have moved away from New Mexico when you were pretty young."

"Before I was born. Only it was the other way around. My sister Perlita is the one who stayed in Texas. Everyone else moved to New Mexico. Then one by one they moved away and started their own families. In fact, I was the only one still at home when my mother got sick. It's why I'm such a homebody, I guess."

Rita seemed to warm to this subject, and I was glad she couldn't see the look on my face. Homebody?

"Poor sweet mami," she went on. "I couldn't bear to put her in one of those awful homes."

"Of course not," I murmured, a little ashamed for agreeing with her. I knew of several excellent nursing homes, and knew it was often a wise choice for people who need 'round-the-clock care.

"After she got Alzheimer's, my brothers and sisters wanted me to do that—make her give up her own home— but I wouldn't hear of it."

"You must be a great comfort to her."

Jocelyn had moved to the side between us, blocking our view of each other. Just as well. I've never managed a good poker face.

"She's gone now," Rita said. "But I miss her. I think that's why I love old people so much."

Bingo. I didn't know if this message was for my benefit or for the wagging tongues that might frequent the beauty shop. In any case, I'd certainly provided her with a soapbox.

"Mrs. Salazar?" Siena touched my shoulder and smiled at me. "Ready?"

More than. I stood and smiled back at her.

"Wait!" Rita said.

I didn't wait but moved to Siena's station, next to where I'd been sitting. Rita and I were still close enough to talk to each other, though it would mean raising our voices a little. Probably a good thing from her point of view.

"Just a sec," I said. "Let me explain to Siena how I want my hair cut." Which didn't take much explaining. A little trim—very little—here and there.

"I'm almost finished anyway," Jocelyn said cheerily.

"Maybe we can get together again," Rita suggested. "Are you visiting, or...?"

"Mm. Yes. For a few days. We're riding the train tomorrow."

"Let's touch base before you leave," she insisted.

"That would be nice."

Did I imagine it, or did Siena wink at me?

"Where can I reach you?" I asked.

Once again, I could feel, if not see, Rita stiffen.

"I'll call you," she said. "Where are you staying?"

"Parlor Car. I don't know the number offhand. We're in and out a lot—mostly out."

"I'll find you."

Innocent words, but they made my flesh crawl.

Chapter 10

I burst into the Parlor Car living room, where Ryan was reading his new book in an easy chair, and blurted out my frustration.

"Ryan, I don't know *who* she is!"

He slipped a bookmark in place. "Slow down. Tell me what happened."

"She's so *Bernice* in some ways, and so *not* in others!"

"You didn't find out anything?"

I began waving my arms in agitation. "I have some things I need to ask Tía Dippy. But I'm not going to mention anything until after our train ride tomorrow. I don't want to get everyone all stirred up again!"

"Who's going to un-stir *you*?"

"Oh, god, I wish I knew."

"Tell you what. Let's go on to Vera's early. We can have a glass of wine before everyone else gets there and talk it over."

We'd planned to meet the rest of the family at Vera's Mexican Kitchen for dinner later that evening, but I liked Ryan's idea of unwinding first. I changed into a peach-colored knit sweater and white slacks; then we drove the short distance to the restaurant.

Over our wine, I gave Ryan a more coherent version of my encounter with Rita.

"Or Bernice pretending to be Rita. I'm still not sure."

"How come?"

"A few things don't jibe. I need to ask you something too."

"Me?"

"Yes, you. Ryan, do you think Bernice was pretty?"

"Is this a trick question?"

"Hey, listen a minute. The last time I saw her she wore so much make-up, I thought she looked grotesque. And I kinda forget what she looked like underneath."

"Underneath the war-paint? Or underneath that?"

"Well, I meant without the make-up. I think we know what she's like inside. You see, this Rita person is very attractive—okay, beautiful—on the surface. She looks the way I think Bernice would look if she hadn't gotten so sleazy. So I got to wondering if Bernice had ever been pretty."

"Like back in high school?"

"Yeah, or even later. Before I came back to Zapata."

"I guess you could have called her pretty. I couldn't stand her, so there were other girls I liked to look at instead."

"Let's not get side-tracked."

He grinned and squeezed my hand. "You brought it up."

I smiled back at him. "So I did. Moving right along...."

"Okay, tell me what this Rita-Bernice person is like 'inside,'" Ryan said.

I took a sip of wine before answering. "That's what has me so baffled. Rita was arrogant and aloof one minute, chatty and friendly the next. Bernice always seemed to operate through a drunken haze, but Rita was very clear-headed. Both very egocentric. They both have—or had—a way of seeming to draw you into their confidence. But I didn't trust Bernice, and I'm not sure I trust Rita."

"Well, even if they're two different people, they might still have some of the same personality traits."

"I guess it doesn't really matter who she is, as long as she's not a threat to Mr. Álvarez. That's what I need to find out, and I'm not sure how to go about it."

Ryan ran his fingers through my short curls. "How often can you get your hair cut before you go bald?"

"Hmm. Are you saying there might be a better way?"

"Uh-oh. Looks like I'll have to help you think of something."

I looked into his deep brown eyes and thought of how much I relied on him—how much I needed him to be in on this with me.

"That's all I need to hear," I told him.

* * *

Early the next morning, Carlos, Omar, and the other kids brought their pets over to stay with Bonsall. Afterwards, we all gathered at the train station, where we boarded a van bound for Antonito, Colorado, forty-seven miles away. The road was curvy, and we climbed two mountain passes, so the ride took about an hour. Ryan and I had fun pointing out trails where we'd cross-country skied.

"Pretend you see snow," I said.

At Antonito we caught the train for the trip back to Chama. Breaking up the six-hour trip was a lunch stop at Osier, where we were served hot meals.

At first the trip wasn't too scenic, but before long we were in canyons surrounded by thick groves of aspen and evergreen trees. The grown-ups appreciated the view more than the kids, but they soon found excitement on their own.

The boys were enthralled with the train itself—one of the few authentic narrow-gauge trains left in our country. But their biggest thrill was spying wildlife along the way.

"*Mira*! Look, everyone!" Omar called. "A bear! A bunch of bears!"

Sure enough, we had the pleasure of a close-up view of a mother black bear and her two rambunctious cubs scuffling not far from the tracks.

Carlos's eyes shone. "I didn't think we'd really see them!"

Beto put his arms around the boys and gave them a gentle squeeze. "This is the best place!"

The kids grinned at each other, then watched the bears till they were out of sight.

They added two bobcats, another bear family, a herd of elk, several coyotes and mule deer, a golden eagle, and quite a few red-tailed hawks to their wildlife count before the trip was over.

As we pulled into the Chama station, we were greeted by visitors who'd come to wave at us passengers, or take pictures, or both. We were waving back when I caught sight of one face I hadn't expected to see among the crowd.

"What is she doing here?" Alana asked in a low voice.

"Who knows," I murmured. "Maybe she comes here every day."

"Do you really believe that?"

"No."

Aunt Maribel, standing next to Alana, whispered, "Is that Bernice? The one Eppie was telling us about?"

Carlos, standing a few feet away, had a frozen expression that told me he'd seen her too.

"Actually," Alana replied evenly, "it's someone named Rita—some relative, I think. Sharon has met her, and they're quite different."

Bless Alana. She knew the magic words to defuse the situation and reassure Carlos.

"She's waving at us!" Tía Dippy said as she made the sign of the cross.

"Oh, people are waving at everyone," I answered breezily.

"*Quizás*. Maybe so." Tía Dippy tossed her precarious curls. "But she's looking right at us."

"Probably remembers meeting me."

I smiled as far as my lips would stretch and waved back with fake enthusiasm.

"*Mírala*! Look what she's wearing!" Tía Dippy continued.

Amá shook her head in wonder. "*Dios mío*! Is that a Donna Ricco?"

Since my boutique of choice was Goodwill, I had no idea of the original price of the almost-new Eileen Fisher and Donna Karan suits I found there. Even so, they weren't cheap. But I doubted that Rita shopped at Goodwill, and knew her dress must have cost a fortune.

"Just the thing for standing by the railroad tracks and waving at complete strangers," Alana said.

I hugged Alana, grateful that she'd given us something to laugh about as we stepped off the train. I hoped that seeing us bunched up together and smiling would discourage Rita from approaching us, but she sauntered over as unconcerned as if we'd sent her an invitation.

Chapter 11

Alana and Beto exchanged looks. Beto, a grim expression on his normally cheerful face, quickly hustled Carlos, Omar, and the other children away from the group and toward Bonsall's to pick up their pets.

A few people in our group drifted away, but Ryan, Alana, their parents, and the tías formed what I thought was a rather formidable unwelcoming committee.

As Rita came closer, some of her self-confidence seemed to ebb. Still, she managed to greet me as if we were old friends.

"I was hoping to see you here. I remembered you were taking the train today," she said. "I hope I'm not intruding on your time with your family."

She swept the group with a bright smile, obviously expecting to be introduced.

I returned her smile, though mine was not as sparkly. "Everyone, this is Rita. Rita, meet my husband, my in-laws, my aunts." I purposely omitted names. Not very polite, but Tía Dippy was already muttering under her breath, and I wanted to cut this encounter short before she began crossing herself excessively. Everyone else nodded and murmured acknowledgment.

"My pleasure," Rita replied graciously before turning back to me. "I wanted to take you up on your offer to get together for pie and coffee."

My offer? Pie and coffee?

"Well, yes. That would be nice...uh...maybe tomorrow?"

* * *

"So what did you think?" I asked Ryan and Alana as we walked to the Parlor Car.

After Rita and I had arranged to meet at The Village Bean tomorrow, she didn't linger. Our "family fortress," having served its purpose, dissolved into family units again, each going its own way.

Ryan shrugged. "She seemed nice enough."

"I guess so," Alana said. "But it did seem kinda strange that she didn't just telephone."

"Neither of you thought it might be Bernice?"

Ryan shrugged again.

Alana frowned, then shook her head. "The resemblance is uncanny. But she seemed too—something—refined?—to be Bernice. For one thing, she didn't flirt with Ryan like Bernice would have."

"Maybe she didn't want to be so obvious with me there," I said, "or with Tía Dippy glaring at her."

"That wouldn't have stopped Bernice. She'd have come on to Ryan in front of God and everybody."

"Hey," Ryan said. "Are you trying to make me throw up?"

Alana linked her arm through his. "No, brother dear. We're simply having a very analytical conversation."

"Well, I suppose she's harmless. But I didn't feel exactly comfortable around her." Ryan put his other arm around me. "And I'm having second thoughts about Sharon getting involved with her."

I was off on a different tangent, turning over Alana's remark about flirting. "I admit I'm not very objective, but Ryan, you're a darn good-lookin' guy."

"Not objective at all," Alana agreed. "But absolutely right."

"You're changing the subject," Ryan said.

"Not exactly," I said.

We'd arrived at the B&B and stopped on the front sidewalk, Alana and I still sandwiching Ryan. I stepped apart, turning to face them both.

"Not exactly," I repeated slowly. "If she has any class, she wouldn't have flirted. On the other hand, she wouldn't have acted as if you weren't there. She barely glanced at you, Ryan."

"Maybe I'm not as irresistible as you think, sweetheart."

But Alana was on the same wave-length with me. "That is puzzling. If it's Bernice, you'd think she'd be curious to see Ryan again."

"Or maybe she was afraid she'd give herself away if she looked at him directly," I added.

"But if it's Rita...hmm...maybe she's just not interested in men."

"Except old rich ones."

"You're making too much out of nothing," Ryan grumbled.

We realized we were blocking the walkway and began walking toward the door.

I stopped suddenly. "There's something else. Something about her voice.... Damn. I can't remember."

Alana thought a moment, then snapped her fingers. "She doesn't talk like us."

"That's it! Now that I recall, I noticed it yesterday too, but it kinda slipped to the back of my mind. I guess I was more caught up in what she was saying than how she was saying it."

"And how do we talk?" Ryan asked.

"You know." I poked him in the ribs. "Like we grew up in Zapata."

It was half-joke and half-truth. We'd been told often enough that people from Zapata had a unique dialect—not just English with a Spanish lilt, but something distinctive beyond that. Even the *güeras* like me picked it up.

"Musta gone over my head," Ryan said.

"It wasn't that noticeable," I had to admit. "Just something else to think about."

"Well, for now at least, my mind's more at ease," Alana said, "So until something more concrete turns up, I don't care if she talks like the Queen of England."

Alana flipped open her cell phone and called Beto. He'd gotten the kids and their pets back safely to the RV park and told us Amá was expecting us over for soup and salad. After our big lunch, a light supper sounded appealing.

We went to our rooms to wash up first. Ryan seemed unusually quiet.

"What is it?" I asked.

"You really want to know?"

"Yes."

"I think we should just pack up and go home, and leave Mr. Álvarez and his family to solve their own problems."

"Okay."

Ryan raised his eyebrows. "Okay? Just like that? You're not going to argue—even a little bit?"

I walked over to the window and pulled the lace curtains aside to look toward the train station and the tourists ambling by. Were they all as happy and carefree as they looked?

"No argument. I'm not being fair to you, Ryan. This vacation was supposed to be fun. I'm making it not fun."

He came up behind me and put his arms around my waist. "The vacation part has been fun, sweetheart."

I leaned against him for a moment, then turned, laid my head on his chest, and slipped my arms around him. "Then let's keep it that way."

"Maybe I'm the one not being fair—backing out like this."

"No, it's not your fault. I'm not trying to make you feel guilty."

"I know that."

"I think I have a glorified view of my part in 'rescuing' Mr. Álvarez."

"Well, you care what happens, that's all. And I didn't mean to set an ultimatum. Let's at least compromise."

"Give me twenty-four hours to play capeless crusader?"

Ryan threw back his head and laughed, then laid his cheek against my hair. "How 'bout if I toss in an extra hour or two? With me as your sidekick."

"It's a deal."

Chapter 12

For everyone else, seeing Rita at the station didn't warrant further mention. I took my cue and gave it a rest. Instead, we enjoyed the supper Amá had prepared and talked about the highlights of our train ride.

So I was surprised when Tía Dippy came up to me at the end of the evening and said she was curious about "that person you were talking to."

"I'm glad you brought it up," I told her. "I'd like to ask you a couple of things too. But I need to get my thoughts sorted out first."

"Mañana?"

"How 'bout right after breakfast. I'll meet you over here."

"Bueno. We can have a 'walk-around' cup of coffee, and talk about it then."

* * *

I'd thought that taking a walk while we discussed Rita/Bernice would afford us some privacy. But keeping up with Tía Dippy was a challenge I hadn't counted on. I was used to seeing her totter around on spike heels, and it hadn't occurred to me she even owned a pair of Reeboks. Breathing deeply, she took quick brisk steps down the path in her new walking shoes.

"I love this crisp mountain air, don't you?" she exclaimed.

Like me, she tended to talk with her hands when she was excited, which meant waving her coffee cup around. Fortunately, the morning air she loved had cooled the coffee somewhat, so it splashed without burning either of us. I finally suggested we sit at a picnic table by one of the unoccupied RV sites.

Once seated, she came straight to the point.

"What is it you want to ask me, mijita?"

The night before, I'd written down gaps in Rita's story that bothered me. Now I was trying to keep the list in my head.

"First of all, Tía, what was your impression when you saw that lady at the station? The one who talked to us. Did you think it was Bernice?"

Tía Dippy gave me a sidelong glance. "At first, yes. Then no. Then yes. Then no. So I wondered what *you* thought."

"I'm not sure either. But I think you know some things that can help me decide."

"I'll do all I can, mijita."

"Okay, didn't you say you'd known Bernice's parents a long time ago?"

Tía Dippy nodded vigorously, sloshing her coffee again. She set her cup on the table, dabbed at the spills with a Kleenex, and readjusted her wig before answering.

"Perlita was one of my best friends, and her husband, Hector, he was a good man."

"I need to know something about Perlita's family. Were there lots of kids? Where did she fit in?"

"She was the oldest. Big family. Their mother was very strict with the girls. The boys—" Tía Dippy rolled her eyes. "Wild, but *muy guapo*. Very handsome. My sister dated one of them for a while."

"Amá?"

"Sí. Ysela. Oh, but she was a pretty one."

I had to digest this. I'd seen their wedding pictures; I knew my mother-in-law was beautiful—and still retained that beauty. But I couldn't picture her with anyone but Apá.

Then my imagination took over. A gorgeous teenage girl riding on the back of a motorcycle with some handsome rebel. I blinked, flicking the images away.

"You should see the look on your face!" Tía Dippy said with a laugh. "You think we were never young?"

I laughed too. "It's not that. I just can't connect Amá with anyone in Bernice's family."

"It was a small town. We all knew each other. Ysela was smart. She broke it off with him before it got serious."

"Thank goodness."

"But it's not Perlita's brother you're concerned about, verdad?"

"No, you're right. It's the lady who talked to us—the one who calls herself Rita. She claims she's Perlita's youngest sister."

Tía Dippy nodded again, more carefully this time. "I thought that might be the case."

"You're not surprised?"

She tapped her forehead with her bony finger. "I've been thinking too. At first, I thought we were just trying to make Carlos feel better. But later, I realized you didn't pick that girl's name out of thin air."

She tapped me on the chest. "You. You must have told Alana something you didn't tell the rest of us."

"And you're wondering why I didn't tell you."

"Sí."

I looked into Tía Dippy's inquisitive face, her bright eyes— kind eyes.

"Well, I'm still not sure who she is," I said. "The whole thing was pretty unsettling, and I guess I was trying to keep everyone else from feeling as mixed up as I was. But I'm glad you asked about it."

After telling Tía Dippy about my meeting with Rita at the beauty shop, I explained why I still had so many questions.

"Are Perlita and Rita really sisters? And when did Perlita's family move to New Mexico? And why did she stay behind? And did Rita and Bernice really look that much alike?"

Tía Dippy fanned herself with her hand. "You do have a lot of questions! Let me think a minute."

"I guess I shouldn't ask them all at once. But they're all jumbled together in my mind."

"No, no—it's all right. They're all connected, but I'm not sure where to start."

She fiddled with her wig as if straightening out the thoughts in her head.

"Bueno." As she brought up old memories, she began speaking in Spanish. "The Zapata you know isn't the Zapata we knew."

"I know that Old Zapata was destroyed when they built the dam."

"I don't mean geography, mijita. I'm talking about hearts. They built us a new town back then—back when I was in high school. But there was no place we could point to and say, 'Here's the house where my best friend lived. Here's where we bought ice-cream cones. Here's the tree where my sweetheart carved our initials.'"

I reached out and held Tía Dippy's hand, noticing how papery it felt.

She smiled at me. "It's not good to live in the past anyway, mijita. But Perlita's parents and grandparents were unhappy with the change, so they decided to make a change of their own, and they left for New Mexico—a little village called Coyote, I believe. They had some relative there who encouraged them to make the move. He had a big ranch, and I think he was looking for Perlita's father to take it over so he could retire."

"But Perlita didn't go with them?"

"No, she and her younger sister Connie went to live with their great-grandparents. They were elderly. Not in good health and not easy to get along with. Moving a few miles to the New Zapata was hard enough on them—they didn't want to go any farther. It was a big help to have the girls with them."

"Rita said *all* her siblings moved to New Mexico, all except Perlita."

"That's odd. Well, maybe not. Connie did move up there, but it was many years later."

Tía Dippy closed her eyes and crossed herself. "That's an ugly story."

I waited for her to continue, wondering if Connie had done something shameful, or had been the victim of something worse.

"You remember I told you about the rabbit that was burned?" Tía Dippy said at last.

I shivered. This must have something to do with Bernice. "I remember."

"There were rumors about other incidents, but that was the only time I was there when something happened. That baby bunny belonged to Connie's little girl, Sylvia. Right after that, Connie and her family packed up and moved. Perlita couldn't bring herself to believe Bernice was the causé of it, and it tore the sisters apart. They never spoke to each other again."

"What about the rest of the family? Did they keep their distance too?"

Tía Dippy thought a moment, then reverted to English when she spoke. "No, I don't think so. They didn't come

down to Zapata very often, but I think Perlita and Hector—
and Bernice, of course—made it a point to go to New Mexico
from time to time."

"So Bernice and Rita did spend time together."

"They must have. I know Rita was a 'late-life' baby, born
about the same time as Bernice."

"Did you ever see Rita, or see her and Bernice together?"

"I might have. If I did, it wasn't anything I gave any
thought to. I probably had other things on my mind." She
paused. "I have a confession to make."

Uh-oh. I felt the muscles in my stomach tighten. I was
beginning to feel I'd already heard more disturbing news
than I'd bargained for.

Chapter 13

"I'm still ashamed," Tía Dippy murmured, her eyes clouding over. "I was not a good friend to Perlita."

What on earth. "Hector?" I whispered.

"Cómo?"

"Did you and Hector...?"

She stared at me a moment, then began shaking with laughter, her dangly silver earrings swinging in rhythm.

"Oh, no. At least I don't have anything like that on my conscience."

The sadness returned to her eyes.

"Perlita hadn't any family left to turn to. The old ones had died. The others had moved. And her friends found it difficult to be around her and that monster child. So we began avoiding her."

"What about Hector?"

"He did what he could. He finally persuaded Perlita they needed help. They took Bernice everywhere—to curanderas, doctors, psychologists." Tía Dippy's eyes narrowed. "For all the good it did. Those tonta psychologists! I think they were afraid of her themselves. All they did was look for blame. Of course there was no abuse, so they had to find something else."

Tía Dippy mimicked the psychologist-quacks disdainfully. "'You're too strict. You're not strict enough. You're too this. You're too that.' Humph. They should examine their own heads."

"This must have taken a toll on Hector and Perlita's marriage."

"I'll say this for them. They stuck it out together...and grew old before their time. Pobrecitos."

I was quiet, locked in one of my "life-isn't-fair" reveries. Tía Dippy was unexpectedly quiet too—unlike her usual buoyant self.

"You couldn't have changed anything, Tía," I said softly. "Don't be so hard on yourself."

"I could have spent more time with her, given her a chance to talk. I was glad when my husband wanted to move to Corpus and I didn't have to make excuses any more. We wrote each other for a while, but even that got harder and harder."

"When was the last time you saw Perlita?"

"When I came back for the boys' graduation—Ryan and Leo's. Bernice was graduating too. She looked pretty from a distance, but up close she had a hard look. To tell you the truth, mijita, I'm not sure I would have recognized her again. I thought that girl by the train tracks was her, but I really wouldn't know, one way or another. I hope you're not disappointed in me." A tear rolled down her rouged cheek, bringing a dollop of mascara along with it.

"Oh, my sweet Tía." I leaned over and kissed her. "You've been a big help. At least I won't be totally in the dark when I see Rita again."

* * *

I decided to dress casually for my afternoon coffee-date with Rita, and wore a denim jumpsuit, a favorite from my haute-couture collection from Goodwill. We'd both made our point—whatever it was—and I'd already given it my all at the beauty shop. Surprisingly, Rita showed up in slacks and a simply tailored blouse. Still expensive-looking, no doubt by a top designer whose label I didn't recognize, but at least more suitable for the occasion.

The lunchtime crowd at The Village Bean had dwindled, but there were still a few customers here and there. We ordered our pastries and coffee at the counter, then chose a small table by a window, where we could look out at the green mountains with gray and white clouds billowing above them.

Plants and colorful wall-hangings adorned the little café. I figured I might as well enjoy the cheerful atmosphere and homemade pie, since it seemed unlikely I'd get any enlightening revelations from Rita with other people around.

It soon became clear that I was the one being interrogated, even though I threw out my share of questions.

"Is this your first visit to Chama?" she asked in a conversational tone.

"No, my husband and I came here last winter to cross-country ski."

"Well, this is a good place for it. You still live in Zapata?"

"We're in San Antonio now. I've been there a long time. How 'bout you? Is Chama your home now?"

She side-stepped the question with a shrug. "For the time being."

"I like it here. I like small towns."

"So why did you leave Zapata?"

I smiled. "Long story. My mother dragged me up to Minnesota when I was in high school, but I came back to South Texas as soon as I could. My grandmother lived in San Antonio, so that's where I landed."

I stirred my coffee and took a few sips. She seemed to remember the excuse she'd used to get me here, and nibbled at her pie. As she patted her mouth with her napkin, I noticed an exquisite turquoise and silver bracelet on her wrist. I had a sudden urge to yank it off to it to see if it covered a small tattoo—Bernice's gecko tattoo. While I was thinking of ingenious ways to accomplish this, she resumed her quiz.

"You must have ideal jobs to have so much vacation time."

Why not give her what she wanted. Maybe she'd be willing to part with a little information herself.

"Well, we are lucky. I'm a lawyer and work pretty closely with someone else in our firm. So we can help each other out when one of us takes time off." I didn't mention that Dave and I kept in touch by phone or e-mail nearly every day. Still, knowing what a workaholic I used to be, Dave was kind enough to let me stretch the leash as far as possible. I was also lucky that Ryan understood the need for me to be "on call."

"Is your husband a lawyer too?" Rita asked.

"No, he's a high-school English teacher."

"Oh, I see. He has all that vacation time."

"He does have several weeks, but not as much as people think. There's always something going on—seminars and one thing and another. Anything to keep teachers from having too much time on their hands," I said lightly.

"But what about you?" I asked before she could come up with another question. "What do you do?"

She stared at me without answering.

"Well, that's a silly question," I babbled, feeling heat rise to my face. "Everybody does something. I meant, what's your career or vocation or...something like that."

She stared at me a while longer, and I decided I'd better shut up before I came right out and asked her what she did besides glomming onto rich old men.

"I'm an LPN," she said, breaking the silence.

"Really? No wonder you were such a help to your mother!"

She rewarded me with a brief smile.

"My brother-in-law is a nurse too," I added nonchalantly, looking at my coffee as I stirred what was left of it.

She didn't rise to the bait. All these questions, and none about Leo? But if she really was Rita, there wasn't any reason to be curious about someone Bernice had been so obsessed with. On the other hand, what *did* she want from me?

"I'm ready for a refill." I said. "How 'bout you?"

"That sounds good."

I rose and took our cups to the counter, then returned with fresh coffee.

"You don't seem like a lawyer," Rita remarked as soon as I'd sat down.

"I hear that a lot. I'm never sure how to take it. What do you think lawyers are like?"

"Well, not like you."

Whatever that meant. "Not like those on TV either," I said. "I'm afraid we get stereotyped unfairly."

"Are stereotypes ever fair?"

"Hmm. You have a point."

"People in this town have prejudged me. Isn't that a way of stereotyping?"

Ouch.

"That's unfair too, Rita. But—whenever you move to a small town, I think you're always considered an outsider at first. It might not be as personal as it seems."

71

"Oh, it's personal."

"I'm sorry."

"That's what I mean about you. You're tactful. You don't pry."

"Well, thank you." I didn't know what else to say. She had no idea how much I *wanted* to pry.

She cocked her head and looked me straight in the eye. "I haven't been entirely candid with you."

"Oh?" No big surprise there.

"I know who you are. I know all about you."

Chapter 14

My tact flew out the window.

"I see," I said icily. "Care to explain?"

She smirked for a second or two, as if deciding whether to comply or to leave me hanging. We stared each other down a few more moments, till finally Rita shrugged and looked away.

"It's really very simple," she said. "When I met you at Jocelyn's and found out you'd lived in Zapata, I called my sister Perlita and asked about you."

"And what did she say?"

"That you'd destroyed Bernice's life."

I was too stunned to answer.

"Well?"

"Well," I said slowly, "I suppose she'd see it that way."

"My sister is heartbroken."

"I'm sure she would be."

"Aren't you going to tell me your side of the story?" Rita demanded.

"I'm not going to get into that. Bernice had a lot going for her. She was smart, talented, pretty. She made a lot of bad choices."

"'Bad choices.' That's the psychobabble buzzword, isn't it? Don't we all make bad choices?"

"You're right. I've made a few of my own," I admitted.

"So?"

"So...what?"

"What were Bernice's so-called 'bad choices'?"

"I'm really not comfortable talking about this. Period."

"You're tough after all." Rita's demeanor changed suddenly, her belligerence diminished. "I mean that as a compliment."

"Thank you."

"There you go, being nice again."

"Even lawyers say 'please' and thank you' sometimes."

I smiled to defuse the sarcasm, but her attention was suddenly focused on something she saw out the window—something that caused her eyes to narrow, something just beyond my field of vision.

"Maybe you could help me," she said slowly.

"Help you?"

"I need some legal advice.... I'd expect to pay you," she amended quickly.

"Oh, dear. I'd really like to help, but I don't know anything about New Mexico law." The regret in my voice was genuine. Although I was glad for a legitimate excuse to avoid a lawyer-client relationship, with all its confidentiality issues, she'd opened a door I didn't want to close. "Maybe I could recommend someone, depending on what you need."

I hoped she'd explain what those needs were, but by now I realized that asking direct questions only put her on the defensive.

"What about something—what would you call it—off the record?" she asked.

"That depends. I wouldn't want to do something that would get either of us in trouble. On the other hand, I might be able to give you some ideas."

"That would work."

I wondered who had outfoxed whom. This might be the opportunity I'd been looking for—a chance to see beyond Rita's façade. But I felt sure she saw it as her chance to suck me into some scheme of her own. We were playing a dangerous game, yet for the first time since I'd met her, I looked forward to the challenge—a curious mixture of excitement and resolve.

Rita looked at her watch. "I have to get back, but I do need to talk to you. Why don't you come by my place in a day or two?"

Wow. I was really moving up a notch.

She wrote down her address and cell-phone number on a paper napkin and handed it to me. I crossed my fingers and promised to be there day after tomorrow.

* * *

My next step was to walk over to the RV park, where I found Tía Dippy sitting under a shade tree drinking Margaritas with a handsome gentleman about her age. They were having an animated discussion, her bracelets clanking as she waved her arms around.

When she looked up at me, her black eyes sparkled. "What is it, mijita?"

I apologized for interrupting, then asked if I could speak to her privately. After we'd moved a few feet away, I told her I needed to get some names from her—for one, the married name of Perlita's sister who moved away after her daughter's pet was burned alive.

"That was Connie. After she came back from college, she married her high-school sweetheart—Sergio Bustamante. Come to think of it, they were both in Ysela's graduating class, so she might know some things I don't."

After a few more questions, I went back to the Parlor Car and sketched out a family tree of sorts.

Ernesto and Juana Méndez

1. **Perlita,** oldest daughter (now about 68?)
    married **Hector Peralta**
        parents of **Bernice** (age 39)

2. **Connie**, next-oldest daughter (now about 66?)
    married **Sergio Bustamante**
        parents of **Sylvia**
            (whose pet Bernice destroyed)

8. **Rita**, youngest daughter (age 39)
        unmarried?

If what Rita said was true, she, Bernice, and I had to be the same age. From what Tía Dippy said, Sylvia was probably a year or two older. I realized that the age of the "beautiful lady" in the matchmaker ad was a good four years younger than stated. That might be another reason nothing rang a bell the first time I read it.

Tía Dippy had given me the names of the other Méndez siblings, but didn't know anything else about them. All I knew was that one of the brothers had dated Amá at one time. I shook my head. That still boggled my mind.

Next I did something I should have done sooner. I made two telephone calls: one to my favorite investigator in San Antonio, Jimmy Romero; the other to Andy Estrada, a Zapata lawyer I worked with now and then. I trusted both men implicitly.

I called Jimmy first. "I need something kinda soon," I told him. "Let me know if that's a problem."

"Hey, Sharon, I can always find time for you. Whatcha need?"

"Everything you can find out about a family in Coyote, New Mexico. Juana and Ernesto Méndez. I think they're both deceased, but I need to know the names and birthdates of all their children, and if any are still living in the area. I'm particularly interested in their daughter Rita. Was she born there? Did she go to nursing school? Where does she live now?"

"Wait a minute. Don't go so fast. I'm trying to get this all down."

I could just see Jimmy, a nice-looking man in his early fifties, scribbling frantically with one hand while running his fingers through his thick gray hair with the other. This habit tended to make his hair stand on end, giving him an innocent startled expression. Like Columbo, he used his rumpled "aw-gosh" appearance to his advantage while his sharp mind ticked away.

"Sorry," I said. "I had to write it down myself so I wouldn't forget. I didn't mean to rattle if off in such a hurry."

"That's okay. Now, where were we after 'family still in the area'?"

I repeated myself more slowly before continuing. "Besides Rita, there's another daughter I'm interested in—Connie Bustamante. She and her husband are both from Zapata, but they moved to Coyote more than thirty years ago." I paused, waiting for Jimmy to catch up. "They have a daughter who had a very traumatic experience when she was six or seven, something like that."

I wondered how that little girl had dealt emotionally with seeing her pet torched by Bernice. I suspected this incident had affected the whole family.

77

"Well," Jimmy said, "some of this will be easy to find from census records and Vital Statistics. I'll have to do some digging on the personal stuff."

"I hope I'm not asking too much."

"Not to worry. I have friends everywhere."

On that note, we ended our conversation, and I turned to Andy.

As we talked, I pictured Andy clearly. No longer the wild-haired clown he'd been in eighth grade, he now wore his black hair neatly trimmed and his shirts buttoned down. Some serious-looking wire-rim glasses framed his jet-black eyes.

After exchanging a few pleasantries about the weather and local goings-on, I explained that I needed his help.

"If you have time to look into this," I added.

"I'll make time."

"Do you know whatever became of Bernice Peralta?"

"Are you serious?"

"Yeah, I know it's kind of an odd question. We've run into someone who looks an awful lot like her. She claims to be a relative, but I'm still skeptical. You know how twins like to trade places and fool people sometimes?"

"You lost me there. Does Bernice have a twin?"

"No. Not literally. But there's someone with a close enough resemblance that they could switch places if they wanted to."

Andy was quiet a minute. "Sharon, don't you think they're a little old—whoever they are—to be playing those kinds of games?"

"Well, when you put it that way," I said. "But I think it's more than a game."

I told him briefly about the possible scam involving Mr. Álvarez.

He whistled. "That's the pits, no matter who's doin' it."

"I know. So far, there's no proof of fraud, either way."

"To get back to your question. It's been a while since I've even thought about Bernice. But my parents know her parents. They might know something."

"You're the only person I can think of who can ask around discreetly. I really don't want to get anyone's curiosity up."

"No, that wouldn't be a good idea."

"I wonder too." I cleared my throat, then asked timidly, "Do you know if her parents blame me because she got caught with drugs?"

"Good lord, Sharon. Whatever gave you that idea?"

"I got the impression her mother was sort of in denial."

"That could be. I'm sure it's hard on her. But I don't think she blamed someone else. And I don't think anybody talks about it any more. It's been three or four years, hasn't it?"

"About that."

"Well, you know how it is—gossip comes and gossip goes. I'm afraid I don't pay much attention."

"And here I am asking you to dig up gossip."

"You've got a good reason. I'll see what I can find out and get back to you."

Chapter 15

Well now, Rita-Bernice, with any luck, I'll soon know all about you, I thought to myself after telling Andy goodbye.

Ryan, Alana, and Beto were on the patio, sitting around a small wrought-iron cabana table with a glass top. They were enjoying Wendy's homemade chocolate-chip cookies and waiting for my report.

I filled them in, then said to Ryan, "I think my twenty-four hours are nearly up."

"That's too bad, isn't it. Just when things are starting to break." Although his tone was teasing, I wasn't sure of the words.

"Twenty-four hours!" Alana said. "What's this about twenty-four hours? I thought we were going to stay another week! I'd already planned to do that fun Laundromat thing tomorrow."

"I gave myself a deadline," I said.

"Why on earth would you do that?" Alana demanded. Then she rolled her eyes. "Never mind. I know my brother. He worries too much."

"Not true." Ryan raised his hands in protest. "I worry just the right amount."

"It's not that," I said. "I want to have it both ways. Be part of this vacation—laundry and all—*and* find out who Rita-slash-Bernice really is."

"Well, I think we're all curious about that," Alana said. "And I know you're worried about Mr. Álvarez and his family."

"Right, but *my* family comes first."

"We know that. It'll all even out."

I looked over at Ryan, but couldn't read his expression. He was studying a bright green hummingbird at the feeder as if it could make a decision for us. He'd tipped his chair back, balancing on the back legs. After a minute or two, he leaned forward with a thump and folded his arms on the table.

Ryan had always been protective of me—even when we were little kids. It was simply his nature. But he wasn't possessive. A thin line maybe, but a definite difference.

When he looked up at me, his face was troubled. "Sharon, I know you're smart—and capable. But you're also too trusting."

"And cowardly. Don't forget 'cowardly.'"

He grinned then. "Okay, let's say 'cautious.'"

Beto spoke up, his gray eyes somber. "Remember when you faced Bernice before. You didn't do it alone."

"Hey, I'll take all the help I can get. I'm not like those heroines in mystery novels who go dragging their broken bones through the muck with the bad guys hot on their heels."

"Don't forget the bullets," Alana said. "Besides the broken bones and crushed-in skulls, they're riddled with bullets."

"You're not helping," Ryan said.

"Relax, sweet brother." Alana leaned over and planted a kiss on his cheek. "We're all in this together. And there won't be any bullets...or mushy skulls."

"La Fea's mind games can be just as bad," Beto said grimly.

I shivered. Beto was usually such an optimist, I was surprised at his dark prediction. Alana was quiet, and I wondered if his comment had crossed all our minds.

"The truth is—as you can probably tell—I run hot and cold about this whole thing. One minute I'm gung-ho. Damn the torpedoes and all that. The next minute I want to turn around and run as fast as I can in the opposite direction."

Ryan laced his fingers through mine. "I've been pretty back-and-forth too. Mostly leaning toward the 'run' part."

"Whatever we do, I like the 'together' part," I said. "Thanks, Alana."

"That, you can count on."

"Then, no deadlines," Ryan said. "Long as you remember the 'cautious' part."

* * *

Early the next morning we all met outside the Salazars' RV to discuss plans for the day over Amá's freshly brewed coffee. Tía Dippy greeted us with what she called a wonderful idea. She'd learned from Charlotte, one of her RV neighbors, that the nearby town of Dulce had a casino.

"*And* a good restaurante. So if we go over there to do our laundry, we can spend the rest of the day having fun."

"Fun!" Tía Marta snorted. "I think doing laundry is more fun than pulling a lever on a loca machine over and over. At least you get something for your money."

"Don't be so pesimista."

"And why are you dressed that way? Are you hoping your gentleman friend will join us at the Laundromat?"

Tía Dippy tossed her head, which bore a different wig today—short straight hair in a rather startling shade of red that matched her short skirt and tall spindly heels. Her older sister, on the other hand, was wearing a nondescript shirtwaist and sensible white oxfords.

Before Tía Dippy could reply, Beto the Peacemaker stepped into the fray. "Dulce has more to offer than casinos, Tía Marta. I'd like to go there myself."

Ryan agreed. "Bonsall's told us a lot about this area. Dulce is the capital of the Jicarilla Apache Nation."

Tía Dippy's eyes widened. "Dios mío! A large city then!"

"No, just a small community, but it is the tribal headquarters. Besides the casino and hotel, they have a market where you can find unique crafts, jewelry, pottery."

"Well," Tía Marta said. "You have the commercial down pat."

"And that's not all!" Ryan said, his brown eyes teasing as he embraced her in a bear hug.

She pretended to brush him off, but looked pleased nonetheless. "And what else, mijo? The Hope Diamond?"

Ryan laughed. "Even better. Several years ago there were rumors that an underground UFO facility existed there."

"Something for everyone, I see."

"Good thing the Jicarillas are so easy-going," Beto put in. "*Muy amable*. They probably take extra-terrestrials in stride along with all the other turistas."

Carlos and Omar were listening intently. Alana had been very adamant about disconnecting them from "all that electronic jazz," as she called it. I figured tracking down little green people would give them something to do while the grown-ups did laundry.

* * *

"That turned out pretty well," Ryan said on our way back. "Clean clothes, good lunch, not too much shoppin'...."

We'd carpooled, Ryan and I with Alana's family, and everyone else with Uncle Javier and Aunt Maribel. Tía Dippy's gentleman friend had shown up, but at the restaurant rather than the laundry. He seemed quite smitten, and offered to bring her home after they'd spent some time at the casinos, which left us free to start back to Chama shortly after lunch.

"More rugged scenery," Alana said, looking out the window. "Good place for UFOs to hide."

"I don't think there are any," Carlos scoffed. "Nobody I talked to ever saw any. Not like Roswell."

"That is disappointing. But you have the whole afternoon ahead of you. Maybe you can spend it r-e-a-d-i-n-g."

"I know what that spells, Auntie," Omar said. "Playing basketball!"

Alana turned around to give him a playful swat, but, since Ryan and I were in the middle seat, Omar was beyond her reach.

"If you kids run out of things to do, you can read the campground rules again," Ryan said.

Carlos leaned forward. "Dr. Johnson told us—"

Omar poked him. "*Cállete,*" he whispered.

Alana's maternal antenna perked up. "Told you what?"

"Oh, he reminded the boys not to let their pets be a nuisance to other campers," Ryan answered lazily.

I looked at Ryan's innocent wide-eyed expression and wondered what that was all about. But I didn't have time to give it much thought. When we arrived at the B&B, we found a folded note by the phone from Wendy telling us that Mr. Álvarez's granddaughter, Vanessa, wanted me to call her as soon as possible. In parenthesis Wendy had written, "Watch out. She can be a little prickly."

Chapter 16

Since it didn't seem like Wendy to comment on our phone messages, I wondered what I was in for. Ryan and I went upstairs, and I called Vanessa on our cell phone.

"Prickly" was an understatement. She began an ear-shattering tirade about how I was supposed to be helping them, and now I was helping Rita, and blah, blah, blah.

"Whoa," I said. "In the first place, I don't even know you. In the second place, I haven't made any promises to anyone. And if you want to talk to me about this, don't scream at me over the telephone."

She lowered the volume a decibel.

I cut her off again. "If you calm down, you're welcome to come over, and we can talk about this in person. Otherwise, if you keep yelling, I'm hanging up."

She kept yelling; I hung up.

"What was that all about?" Ryan asked. "You look a little rattled."

"I *feel* a little rattled."

Confrontations like that always made my stomach knot up.

"Sounds like you held your own," Ryan said.

"Yeah, when push comes to shove, I can shove. I'd just rather not."

Ryan put his arms around me, and I felt some of the tension leave. I wrapped my arms around him, lifted my face next to his, and inhaled the warmth of his skin—the soapy, spicy, musky scent.

"You were made for hugging," he whispered. "Not shoving."

"You too," I murmured. "Know what? I'll call her back, and tell her to wait till tomorrow. It'll probably take her that long to cool down anyway."

Ryan nuzzled my cheek. "Good idea."

I pulled away, picked up the cell phone again, and hit the redial button. "No answer. Damn. She's probably on the way here."

"Well, then, after she leaves...."

I smiled at him. "All the more reason to keep this meeting short."

Vanessa arrived ten minutes later. I'd barely had time to put away the clean clothes and freshen up a bit. Wendy, who'd returned from her errands, ushered Vanessa into the living room and introduced her to Alana and Beto, who were reading up on local history. Ryan and I started downstairs as soon as we heard the doorbell ring and joined the others.

I don't know what I'd expected, but Vanessa didn't fit my preconceived picture. With such a pretty name, I'd somehow assumed she would be attractive at the very least—maybe even glamorous—something to match her volatile personality.

Wendy'd already told me Vanessa was younger than I, but hard lines around her eyes made her look older. Her dumpy frame wasn't enhanced by way-too-tight jeans and tank top. Stringy hair pulled back into a messy bun was more-or-less secured by a chipped brass hairclip. Her only make-up was mauve lipstick, applied well beyond the natural lip line and outlined in black.

"I thought we were going to meet in private," she announced sullenly after Ryan and I introduced ourselves.

Alana pretended to look engrossed in the article she'd been reading. Ryan didn't budge.

"We can sit out in the garden if you'd like," I said.

She nodded agreement, and the two of us moved outside to a sun-warmed day under a lapis-blue sky. We sat on a bench facing a butterfly bush, and I hoped the setting would offer us tranquility as well as privacy.

"I'm sorry you were so upset," I began. "Obviously, there's some misunderstanding."

"Yeah, right."

"Let's start from the beginning. What made you think I'd agreed to help your family in some way?"

I could feel an explosion coming, and placed my hand on her arm. "No yelling. You yell, this conversation is ended."

Vanessa narrowed her beady eyes, apparently mulling over her options.

"Wendy told my mother," she said through clenched teeth, "that you knew Rita was a fraud, and you were going to expose her."

"I don't recall saying that, but since Wendy's involved, let's ask her to join us." Obviously Wendy had said *something*, and I was curious to know what it was, and how it had been misinterpreted.

Vanessa backpedaled. "Maybe not those exact words."

"I see. I need to know the exact words."

"Well, jeezus, what do you think I am? A freakin' tape recorder?"

"Quit stalling, Vanessa. Just tell me what she said."

Vanessa's dislike of me seemed to be growing by leaps and bounds, but she managed to choke down another retort before answering. "Wendy asked my mom for a picture of Rita, because she looked like someone you knew."

"That's true." I stopped short of patting her on the head for giving me such a succinct answer. "But now that I've met her, I don't have any reason to believe Rita isn't exactly who she says she is," I lied.

Normally I'm a terrible liar, but I find it comes more easily when I'm dealing with unpleasant people.

"Now," I said, "what makes you think I'm helping Rita in some way?"

Vanessa seemed to debate with herself about whether or not to explain. Finally, after several dramatic shrugs and careful examination of the black polish on her jagged fingernails, she said, "Rita told me she'd hired you to dig up some dirt on...on our family."

"Oh. Is there some dirt to dig up?"

Vanessa glared, and I backed off.

"I'm wondering why Rita would tell you this—especially since it isn't true. Did you tell her anything about the conversation between Wendy and your mom?"

Vanessa's eyes flashed. "What do you think I am? Stupid?"

I passed on that one.

"Look, Rita didn't hire me to do anything," I said. "We chatted over a cup of coffee, that's all. She didn't tell me her problems, if any. And your name never came up." All that *sturm und drang* for nothing. "Feel better?"

She studied me a few moments. "I don't trust you."

"And I don't trust you," I said, returning her gaze. "I guess we've said all we have to say."

I stood up, and she grabbed my arm, trying to pull me down again.

"Don't act so high and mighty with me!" she screeched.

Bonsall appeared from around the corner of the house. "Afternoon, Sharon, Vanessa. Is everything okay? I thought I heard someone yelling."

Vanessa shot a daggered glance at Bonsall, snatched up her ratty purse, and flounced off. I took a quick peek at my bruised arm, relieved to see that her nails hadn't left any puncture wounds.

Bonsall scratched his head. "Something I said?"

"Yes, and thank you."

His brown eyes twinkled. "She's a handful, isn't she."

The Johnsons seemed given to understatement. Or, more likely, they were simply being kind.

I smiled at Bonsall. "I'm just going to sit here and count butterflies till my heartrate goes back to normal."

He turned away with a grin and a wave, calling over his shoulder, "Let me know how many there are."

Chapter 17

The next morning, over a breakfast of Belgian waffles and fresh strawberries, we sketched out plans for the day. Apá and Uncle Javier had asked about fishing permits at the Jicarilla Visitor Center and were off to Mundo Lake with Omar and Carlos. Amá, her sisters, and Aunt Maribel planned to alternate between shopping and playing cards. Beto, Alana, Ryan, and I looked forward to hiking the trail at Trujillo Meadows.

After helping Wendy in the kitchen, Bonsall joined us at the table. "It'll be interesting having the kids here tomorrow."

"I hope you don't mind," Alana said. "They think just because they love animals, that's all it takes to be a veterinarian. This might be an eye-opener for them."

"I'm glad to do it. Not that it's ever the same two days in a row. Anyway, I think you'll be pleasantly surprised. They take good care of their own pets, and they were very serious when they asked me if they could help out."

Wendy came into the dining room, her face flushed as she refilled our coffee cups. "I'm really sorry about yesterday, Sharon. I'd hoped you'd meet Alicia before you had to tangle with Vanessa."

"It's not your fault," I reassured her. "Besides, we got untangled."

Wendy set the coffeepot on a trivet and sat down with us. "Alicia is a good friend and a good person."

"I'd like to meet her."

"I'll see if she's free this afternoon when you get back from your hike—if you don't think you'll be worn out."

"Late afternoon would be fine."

"Vanessa—well, I guess you're used to confrontation in the courtroom, but I get the impression you don't enjoy it."

"You guess right. The part I like is talking to our clients and doing research on their cases. I team up with someone who's a brilliant litigator, so he gets to do the courtroom part."

"He shares the honors, whenever he can talk you into it," Ryan said.

"True, and I suppose the challenge is good for me, but I'm really happier in my own quiet little niche."

"Now you've done it," Beto said with an exaggerated sigh. "Gone and shattered all our illusions. I guess we'll never get to see you on *Court TV*."

We laughed with Beto as we finished our coffee, then began our day.

* * *

I enjoyed our hike among the quaking aspens and Ponderosa pines, the chattering of the magpies. At the same time, I missed the silence of the snow, the rhythmic "swoosh, swoosh" of our skis the only sound. The deep blue of the New Mexico sky must be the only constant, I thought. That, and the fresh air.

At least the combination of clean air, exercise, and the scenic view helped clear my mind of worrisome thoughts. We were ravenous by the time we returned to Chama, so stopped at Patsy's Restaurant for Navajo tacos.

When we got back to the B&B, I spent time in the upstairs library, laughing out loud at Jean Shepherd's short stories, until the doorbell announcing Alicia's arrival brought me back to reality. Although I was curious to meet Alicia, I hoped yesterday's encounter with her daughter wouldn't raise a barrier between us.

I came downstairs to the living room, where Wendy had already set out a plate of tangy orange cookies and a pitcher of iced tea. After introducing us, she hesitated, as if unsure whether to leave us alone.

I had a feeling both Alicia and I would feel more comfortable if she stayed, so I motioned for her to join us. Then we pulled our chairs into a little triangle.

Unlike Vanessa's bird's nest, Alicia's gray hair was pulled back into a tidy bun. She was wearing a simple pale-green dress. Her pleasant round face held a sad expression, and her shoulders slumped. I wondered if she was burdened more by her father's behavior or by Vanessa's.

We chatted about the train and some of the events in town before Alicia finally broached the subject of her father and Rita.

"He seems happy, and she seems to treat him well, but there's something about her that just doesn't ring true." Alicia paused. "This might seem like a little thing, but my father had a beautiful long-haired black-and-white cat. That cat was his constant companion even before my mother died. Rita said she was allergic. I got the impression she just didn't like cats. Max—that's the cat—Max certainly didn't like her. Hissed and slunk out of sight whenever she was around. I don't have any real reason to think Rita would mistreat Max, just an uneasy feeling. Anyway, I told my father I'd bring Max home with me till Rita's allergies cleared up, or something like that."

"Your father didn't mind?"

"He asks about Max now and then. But I guess this—this *stranger*—is better company."

"So you don't know anything about Rita at all?"

Alicia gave a half-hearted shrug. "I tried to check as best I could. Rather, my boss checked."

"Your boss?"

"Dan Oliver. He's a CPA here in town, and I'm what they used to call a 'girl Friday.' I think the politically correct term is something else—something more 'la-de-da.'" Alicia smiled, erasing the plainness from her face. "I answer the phone, file things, send out statements—whatever needs to be done around his office."

"You like your job?"

"Very much. Dan's always been very supportive—he even hired my daughter for some part-time work." Alicia stopped short, pressing her lips together.

Dan must indeed be a jewel to take on Vanessa. My curiosity was up, but Alicia looked uncomfortable, so I put it aside for now.

"So you say Dan—Mr. Oliver—checked on Rita for you?"

"He knows the former principal of the high school where she said she graduated, and he knew enough about Rita that her story seemed to add up. He told Dan she went on to St. Victoria's Nursing School in Santa Fe, just like she'd said. He even faxed Dan a picture from the high-school yearbook. Well, after twenty years, it wasn't an exact match, but it looked close enough."

It seemed like a pretty sketchy "investigation" to me, but hiring a detective probably seemed both expensive and unnecessary to Alicia, now that she had Dan's help. Mr. Álvarez might have been wealthy, but I had no idea what Alicia's financial status was. I suppose it would have been a little tricky for her to borrow money from her father in order to discredit his fiancée.

"I don't want to burden you with this," Alicia said. "But when Wendy said you thought Rita looked like someone else, it got my hopes up."

I spread out my hands in a gesture of helplessness. "I'm sorry I've disappointed you."

Alicia was quiet a moment. "Vanessa thinks Rita has you fooled."

"She might be right."

Alicia's eyes widened. "But you're still working for her?"

I shook my head. "I don't know where Vanessa got that idea. Maybe Rita said something just to push her buttons. Do you know if Vanessa told her I was helping you?"

Alicia looked taken aback. "Why would she do that?"

I shrugged. "Why would my name come up?"

Alicia gazed down at her hands, folded in her lap, and said nothing.

"About that yearbook photo...." I paused and exchanged puzzled glances with Wendy. It seemed curious that Alicia had told Wendy she didn't have any pictures of Rita. I tried to think of a way to ask about it without making it sound like a cross-examination.

Before I could say anything else, Alicia looked up, her face impassive. "That photo 'vanished.' Along with the copies of the matchmaker ads."

"Have you missed anything else?" I asked. "Any other personal belongings?"

She shook her head. "No. Just those things. In a way, it seemed rather odd. It was so obvious. One day they were in a folder in a kitchen drawer. The next day the empty folder was on the kitchen table." Alicia reddened. "I know I should have locked my doors—it just never occurred to me before now."

I thought this over. "That is odd. What seems even stranger is that all those things could be so easily replaced."

"That's true. I already had extra copies of the clippings." Wendy nodded. "The ones you gave me."

"I couldn't see much point in getting another outdated yearbook picture." Alicia said. She grimaced. "Maybe Rita is pushing *my* buttons."

Or maybe Vanessa had taken the clippings, knowing suspicion would fall on Rita. I couldn't believe Rita would be so careless—or so transparent.

"I know you're worried," I said gently. "And I honestly wish I could help, but I don't want to raise any more false hope.

"I understand. But will you let me know if you do find out anything—anything that will help?"

I smiled at her. "Of course. I'll see her again tomorrow, and if something happens to change my mind, I'll let you know."

Chapter 18

I had never been in a place so devoid of personality as Rita's. According to Alicia, Rita had come here a little over three months ago—and it seemed obvious she didn't intend to stay long enough to make it a home. Maybe she'd already been here longer than she'd planned.

The small complex was definitely at odds with Rita's expensive tastes. Originally a low-budget motel, the "refurbished" apartments appeared to contain the same low-budget furnishings. The carpet, drapes, and armchairs were all a dingy tan overlaid with darker brown and green blobby things. Except for a generic-type landscape on the wall, there were no other pictures. No smiling faces of parents, siblings, or friends. Not even a picture of Rita herself.

I had arrived Saturday afternoon, as promised, and was already having a few regrets. Rita, wearing an elegant pale-blue lounging outfit that could easily have doubled as cocktail attire, motioned for me to sit in one of the faded armchairs while she prepared a pitcher of sweet tea. Since she didn't invite me into her kitchen, I was left to wonder if it was as impersonal as the living room.

I also wondered what ingredients were going into the tea.

Rita set a tray on a TV table between us, and poured tea into frosty glasses already filled with ice. I swirled the cubes around before taking a small sip. I was relieved not to notice any unusual taste, but contented myself with doing more swirling than drinking.

Rita leaned forward. "I'm sure by now you've heard about my relationship with Joaquín Álvarez."

So much for small talk. I had already decided to tell Rita up-front that I'd met both Alicia and Vanessa; I'd just skew the timeline a little and be as vague as possible. I still didn't know what Vanessa might have said to her, but figured—hoped—it would be easy enough to shrug off, given Vanessa's personality.

"That old grapevine!" I said. "After I ran into you at the beauty shop, I told everyone over breakfast how surprised I was to meet someone related to Bernice—small world, and all that."

"Mm hmm."

"It's a little embarrassing." My face reddened, as if on cue. "Wendy mentioned it to Alicia and Vanessa, and they were curious to meet *me*."

The hostility in Rita's eyes was so like Bernice, a chill ran up my spine.

"And?" she said.

"Nothing really. Alicia told me you were seeing her father."

"I'm sure she told you she disapproved of me."

"I think it's natural for his daughter to be protective. As for his granddaughter...." I rolled my eyes.

She smirked, and I laughed as if we were sharing some kind of joke.

"It's Vanessa I need to ask you about," Rita said.

My heart leapt to my throat. "Oh, dear." *Had Vanessa told Rita I'd asked for her picture?*

"She's been stalking me."

"Stalking?"

"Well, following me around."

97

My heart settled down again. Rita seemed more irritated than worried. And apparently this had nothing to do with me. I also figured I could forget worrying about the tea if Rita needed to use me for something.

"No matter where I go, she's there," Rita continued. "The other day when you and I were having coffee, I looked out the window and saw her standing across the street, just staring at the café."

"Did she follow you when you left?"

"Not in my footsteps, no. But she was skulking behind a neighbor's tree when I got back. Like she could find a tree wide enough to hide behind. I told her to go away, and she said it was a free country and she had permission to be there."

"She wasn't actually on your property?"

"No. I didn't step foot on the neighbor's either. But I did get close enough to tell her I'd found out about her sticky fingers and shoplifting, and I'd hired a lawyer to put a stop to it."

"Good idea! I didn't know you already had a lawyer."

"I don't. I just said that hoping she'd back off—not that it seemed to work."

"I take it you weren't bluffing about the shoplifting."

"No. That part's true—or used to be true at any rate. Joaquín told me. She was a juvie at the time she was caught." Rita's eyes narrowed. "Evidently he pulled a few strings and got her off the hook."

"If she knows there's always someone to bail her out...hmm. Do you think it's still going on?"

Rita tapped her fingers on the table impatiently. "I really don't give a damn about that. All I want is for her to leave me alone. I'd hoped to scare her, but she's still hanging around. Maybe I should get a restraining order or something. What do you think?"

"I think you need an attorney to answer that. One who practices in New Mexico. But—playing devil's advocate for the moment—here's something to think about before you hire someone. In a town this small, where you're likely to run into the same people over and over, it might be hard to prove your case."

Rita thought this over, then nodded.

"More tea?" she asked, topping my almost-full glass without waiting for my answer.

I smiled politely. "Thanks."

"She thinks—they think—she and her mother—that I'm after Joaquín's money. That's a joke. I haven't touched a cent of his money. I have plenty of my own from my parents' estate."

A sad, faraway expression crossed her face. Maybe she really did miss her parents, and maybe she really did care about Joaquín Álvarez.

"It's Vanessa who's after his money," Rita continued softly. "He's been doling it out to her for years. Lately he's cut back. She blames me, of course. What she's really worried about, he's threatened to cut her out of his will."

That would definitely set Vanessa off, not that it would take much.

"If her behavior escalates," I said, "you should see a lawyer for sure."

"I guess." She paused. "It's nice to be taken seriously."

Her eyes clouded over, and for a moment I thought she might start crying. It occurred to me that I'd never credited Rita with having any feelings before now. It must be hard to live in this town without having anyone to confide in. I supposed she had phone conversations with a friend or one of her sisters, but that wasn't the same. Maybe her sense of isolation was what made her so defensive.

Here I go again, I thought—playing devil's advocate all over the place. I certainly didn't want to volunteer to be Rita's friend. Still, she'd made me see the situation in a new light. I could easily believe everything she told me about Vanessa, and wondered how far Vanessa would go to protect her interests.

Rita gave her shoulders a tiny shake, as if the physical action shook off her mental state as well.

"Would you like to meet Joaquín?" she asked.

Both the question and the abrupt change of subject surprised me, but I answered without hesitation. "Yes, I'd like that."

"Alicia goes over in the mornings on her days off. She fixes his lunch, and then he takes a little nap."

Rita glanced at her watch, then stood up. "He should be awake by now. You can come over there with me if you want to."

"Good. I'll follow you in my car."

I could give Ryan a call on my cell phone on the way, and let him know that I'd not only survived my visit with Rita, but was actually making some progress.

Chapter 19

I don't know what I expected Mr. Álvarez to be like—
feeble and passive, I suppose. Although he was resting in a
recliner, with a small pillow behind his head and a
multicolored afghan across his legs, his black eyes were
alert and his voice strong when Rita introduced us. His white
hair was surprisingly thick for someone his age.

His southwestern living room was as elegantly furnished
as Rita's was sparse. The luxurious carpets and sofas were
defined in earthtones accented in shades of turquoise, and I
found myself surrounded by expensive artifacts. A glass
cabinet along one wall held Santa Clara and Jémez pottery.
Several original paintings by Alice Valdez, R.C. Gorman, and
Edward Gonzales graced the thick adobe walls.

Alicia was still there when we arrived, and the tension
stretched between the two women like an invisible current. I
felt as if I were caught in the current too. *Meet Sharon
Salazar, double agent, pretending to be everyone's friend.*

"Mucho gusto, pa' servirle," I said instead, managing a
faint smile.

"The pleasure is mine," he replied with equal courtesy.
"But you don't need to speak Spanish. Rita doesn't."

My eyes widened. "Really?"

She shrugged impatiently. "I understand it, and I know a
few words. But my sister insisted this was an English-
speaking world, and that's what we spoke at home."

I decided to forego my soapbox on the advantages of
being multilingual.

Mr. Álvarez gazed indulgently at Rita before pinning Alicia with an angry scowl. What brought that on, I wondered.

"I thought you'd be gone by now," Rita addressed Alicia. No words minced there, in any language.

"My father became ill," Alicia retorted. "I didn't want to leave him alone."

Rita went over and gave Mr. Álvarez a perfunctory kiss, fluffed his pillow, and straightened his afghan in quick jerky motions. "What's the matter, dear? What can I do for you?"

I felt her animosity was directed at Alicia rather than her lover, but the brittleness in her voice belied her concern.

Mr. Álvarez leaned forward. "I'll tell you what's wrong—" he began, even as his face grew flushed and an angry vein throbbed in his forehead.

Clearly alarmed, Rita pulled up a chair beside him and stroked his hand. I felt my own anxiety rising and wondered if we should take him to the clinic.

"Did you remember to take your blood pressure medicine?" Rita asked him.

"He took it earlier," Alicia replied, her own face white with worry. "But his blood pressure still went sky high, and his stomach was upset. Maybe the dosage needs to be changed."

"*Qué tontería!* That's not the problem. The problem is that daughter of yours!"

"That daughter of mine is also your granddaughter. Have you forgotten that?"

"She's a troublemaker, that's what she is. Comes here uninvited—" Mr. Álvarez began coughing and wheezing, the redness in his face becoming more pronounced.

"She was here?" Rita glared at Alicia. "Why did you let her in? You know how it upsets Joaquín."

Alicia seemed to be fighting back tears. "Vanessa might be difficult at times, but she *is* family, and she shouldn't be shut out."

Then, as if realizing that calming her father was more important than winning an argument with Rita, she came over and put her arm around his shoulders, bending down to rest her head briefly on his.

"I'm sorry, Papá. She had promised not to start something, and I wanted to give her another chance. I should have known...."

But Mr. Álvarez wasn't pacified. "That's the trouble. One chance after another. She never appreciates—"

"I know. I know. It won't happen again."

Alicia turned to me. "I'm sorry, Sharon, that you had to come over in the middle of this. I'll be on my way."

"No need to apologize. I should probably be on my way too."

"Don't go, Sharon," Rita said sharply. Maybe she was afraid Alicia and I would compare notes if we met up outside.

Alicia didn't wait to see what I would do, but walked briskly through the door, almost—but not quite—slamming it behind her.

Mr. Álvarez seemed to have regained his composure, although his face was still somewhat mottled. "Please stay, señorita. Join us in some tea."

Rita's demeanor changed too, now that Alicia was gone. She gave Mr. Álvarez a warmer hug, and they exchanged some goo-goo words. Now that I'd seen what Rita had probably invited me to see—how much "in love" they were—I was ready to leave. But it seemed awkward to leave too abruptly.

"Maybe for a few minutes. We have plans later on tonight, so I can't stay long."

Rita arched her eyebrows. "Oh? What's going on tonight? I thought this town rolled up the sidewalks before dark."

I ignored the slur. "We're going to the chuckwagon supper at the Elkhorn. Have you ever been? We've heard it's a lot of fun."

Rita ruffled Mr. Álvarez's hair. "Would you like to go sometime, Sweetikins?"

"It is fun," he said. "Alicia took me one time before—"

"Before I came? Well, we'll just have to go again, won't we."

Not tonight, I prayed, wishing I'd kept my mouth shut.

"I'd ask you to join us," I said, hoping my insincerity wasn't too transparent. "But our tables are already filled."

Wrong thing to say. Now that I'd tried to discourage her, Rita seemed determined to make it happen.

"Well, we wouldn't have to sit at your table. I imagine there's room for lots of people."

I smiled the fake smile I'd practiced on the way over. "Maybe we'll see you then. I really do have to go back now."

I took Mr. Álvarez's hand. "I'll take a raincheck on that tea in a day or two."

Seeing the flash of dismay on Rita's face, I smiled a real smile. I was still in the game.

Chapter 20

I was glad to have a few hours to unwind between Rita-time and dinnertime. Ryan, Beto, and Alana were waiting for me on the patio when I returned. I was reluctant to "tell all"—part of my legal training, I suppose. At the same time, I wanted feedback from the others, so I gave them a condensed account.

"I don't believe for a minute she's not interested in Mr. Álvarez's money," Alana stated. "If she really wanted to impress the family with her financial independence, she wouldn't live in a dump."

"Well, it's not exactly a dump. Shabby, maybe, but very clean. And she does drive a pretty high-powered car—a new Jaguar. I got to follow in its wake on the way to Mr. Álvarez's."

"Maybe she thought she'd have Mr. A. out of town by now," Beto said.

"Hmm. That makes sense," I said. "She probably thought his brother's will would be settled sooner. That must be the only reason they're still here."

"Did you catch her lapsing into 'Zapata-talk'?" Alana asked.

"No. But something odd. She insisted she speaks only English."

"That's interesting," Ryan said. "If she's lying about that, it would be easy to trip her up."

"Why would she make an issue of it?" Beto mused.

I shrugged. "Maybe she's telling the truth."

"And maybe," Alana said, "that's the accent she can't hide."

Ryan grinned. "You're really hung up on this accent thing, aren't you."

Alana gave him a sisterly bop on the head.

"Do you really think they'll show up at the supper tonight?" Beto asked. "I don't want Carlos caught off guard."

"Even though he knows it's probably not Bernice," Alana explained, "just seeing her double could be unsettling."

"To tell you the truth, I'd be surprised if they came. Mr. Álvarez has had a pretty strenuous day," I said. "But it might be a good idea to warn Carlos in a general way."

"General. What's that?" Ryan asked.

"Well—you know. She could show up anywhere at any time."

"We've already talked that over," Alana said. "In a way, I think it's helped that you've gotten together with her, Sharon. If she'd given you the heebie-jeebies, Carlos would have picked up on it."

"Just the heebies."

"Speaking of Carlos," Ryan said, "here come the boys now."

Both boys spilled out of Bonsall's mobile clinic and bounded over, full of energy, their gray eyes shining. I'd thought spending the day caring for sick animals would be pretty intense, but sometimes I forget that kids never run out of steam. They gave us all big hugs, and I felt some of their exuberance rub off on me.

They started talking at once, till Beto told them to slow down.

"One at a time."

They looked at each other a fraction of a second before Omar took the lead.

"This big dog came in with a bunch of porcupine quills all stuck in his face!" Omar said.

"There were so many, Dr. Johnson said there must be a bald porcupine out there somewhere," Carlos added.

"Dr. Johnson had to give the dog a shot so it wouldn't hurt when he pulled 'em out."

"It took a LONG time to get 'em all out. Dr. Johnson said you have to be real careful not to make it worse."

"One time he had to go out to this ranch to take quills out of a horse's nose. And this burro kept getting in the way."

"Like it wanted to see what was goin' on."

"He said burros are curiouser than cats."

"Well, it sounds like you all got a pretty good idea of what it's like to be a veterinarian," Alana said before shooing the boys back to the RV park to take care of their own pets. "You can tell us more about it over supper."

* * *

We arrived at the Elkhorn Lodge a little early so we could lay claim to tables surrounded by other guests, satisfied that Rita and Mr. Álvarez couldn't find room near us even if they did happen to show up.

The lodge and adjoining cabins among the pine trees seemed the perfect setting for a mountain retreat. Between the lodge and the Chama River was a pavilion where picnic tables with red-checkered tablecloths were set up for the tasty barbecue the Lanes had prepared.

Tía Dippy had invited her gentleman friend, giving us an opportunity to size him up and decide if we approved—as if she needed our approval. He was pleasant and witty and seemed to dote on Tía Dippy.

Before dinner was over, we found another treat in store for us. Wiley Jim entertained the crowd with a lively rendition of Western tales and tunes, accompanied by guitar, banjo, or harmonica. Even Uncle Javier, who considered himself a pretty good guitarist, said he couldn't always keep up with the lightning pace of Wiley Jim's fingers. Omar and Carlos decided then and there they wanted to learn how to yodel.

Afterwards, we were chatting happily on the way out of the pavilion when Alana nudged me.

"Look over there," she whispered.

I turned, expecting to see Rita and Mr. Álvarez. Instead, at one of the back tables—almost out of sight—Vanessa was sitting with a scuzzy-looking man. Her boyfriend? Could she be tailing me too? Far-fetched as the idea seemed, I felt the little hairs rise on the back of my neck.

* * *

Midnight, and I was still wide awake. I slipped quietly out of bed and took my laptop into the small library across the hall from our bedroom. I was more confused than ever about whatever was going on with Mr. Álvarez, and needed to pinpoint my thoughts in writing.

♦ Who is Rita? Is she really Bernice? If not, how much are they alike (besides in looks)?

♦ I need to find out more about "the real" Rita and her family. (Note: Call Jimmy Romero again to see what he's learned.)

♦ Where has Bernice been the last three-and-a-half years? Where is she now? (Call Andy Estrada again. Check with anyone else in Zapata?)

♦ Rita was genuinely worried about Mr. Álvarez's episode this afternoon. Is this concern for his health? Or concern that he'll die before he changes his will—or before they get married?

- Vanessa: The same question in reverse. Is she concerned that he WON'T die before changing his will, etc.?
- If either (or both) of these conclusions is true, Mr. Álvarez is in danger.
- What caused Mr. A.'s sudden illness? Vanessa was there earlier in the day. Had she doctored his food or medication? On second thought: Unlikely. Her mere presence is enough to raise anyone's blood pressure.
- What does Vanessa have to gain by shadowing Rita? (Or me.) If that's what she's doing. Is it simply a mind game?

The center of all this, of course, was Mr. Álvarez. Now that I'd met him—now that he was a person and not just a name—I felt more involved than ever. "Mind your own business" was a motto that seemed to elude me.

Chapter 21

As if reading my mind, my lawyer-friend Andy Estrada called the next evening while our family was relaxing around the campfire. We were singing Tejano tunes along with Apá on his accordion and Uncle Javier on his guitar when my cell phone rang.

"Hope I'm not calling at a bad time," Andy said. "I'm going up to Austin early tomorrow morning and wanted to catch you before I left."

"No, this is fine. Hang on a minute while I go inside."

"Sounds like a party."

"Just our usual boisterous group," I said as I went into the quiet of the Salazars' Winnebago. "What's up?"

"Well, there seem to be as many Bernice-sightings as Elvis-sightings."

"That many?"

"Just about. I'm going to turn the phone over to Melody so you can hear this third- or fourth-hand instead of fifth."

I liked Andy's wife, Melody, with her strawberry-blond hair, lightly freckled face, and wide grin. A moment later, she greeted me. "Hey, Sharon. I hope all this gossip is helpful."

"It sounds like there's been a lot."

"Not exactly. A few things came up—a long time ago— that caused a stir for a day or two, but died down about as quickly. Until Andy asked his mom and me."

"He said something about people seeing Bernice?"

"Supposedly. Just a few months after she 'disappeared,' my sister said she saw her in Laredo. But that was it. Since my sister wasn't sure, and since no one else mentioned seeing her...."

I could almost picture Melody shrugging.

"I'd forgotten about it," she continued, "till Andy's mom confessed seeing her too. She hadn't said anything till now, out of respect for Bernice's mother."

"Andy said they were friends."

"Well, Mom swears she saw Bernice—she can't remember when. But from what she said, it was about the same time my sister saw her. Still, the details were pretty skimpy. Then Mom—rather reluctantly—told us something Cici had said. You remember Cici."

"Yeah."

She gave a short laugh. "Okay, so you know how Cici likes to dramatize things and make herself sound important. This is exactly the kind of thing Andy would normally blow off. But he felt you ought to hear it and decide for yourself. Maybe he should tell you this part."

My skin began tingling. Andy, skeptic that he was, must have good reason for thinking this was something worth passing along. I heard a mumbled conversation between them; then Andy got on the extension, and they took turns filling me in.

"Cici claims she came face to face with Bernice about three years ago, sometime *after* Mom & Melody's sister thought they saw her," Andy began.

"In Tucson, Arizona, of all places, in some big mall," Melody added. "She said Bernice was dressed to the nines and hanging on the arm of some elderly man."

Andy must have heard my startled gasp. "That got my attention too," he said.

"That's not all. Cici said she spoke to Bernice, but Bernice ignored her," Melody continued. "Worse than that. When she saw Cici, she spun that poor old man around in the opposite direction. I guess 'spun' is an exaggeration. He wasn't that agile, and she had to practically shove him to get his feet moving."

"All this is Cici's version, of course," Andy said.

"If Cici was telling everyone," I put in, "I wonder why my family missed it."

Even if they hadn't believed it, the coincidence would have kicked in once they knew about Mr. Álvarez.

"I missed it too," Melody admitted. "The first I heard was when Mom told us. And she never would have said anything if Andy hadn't told her it was so important. Apparently Cici made the mistake of telling her and some of her friends over coffee. They all came down on her pretty hard—told her it was cruel, that it would hurt Bernice's mother if she got wind of it."

I shifted the phone to my other ear. "So the story didn't get any further?"

"I don't think so. Cici's gossipy, but she's not stupid. She must have figured out that her 'big news' wasn't winning any popularity points."

"Do you know if Bernice ever got in touch with her mother?"

"No," Andy replied. "She hasn't."

"How sad. Especially if she *has* come back. You'd think she'd at least send her a post card letting her know she's okay or something."

I felt a stab of conscience the minute my words were out. "Not that I write my own mother that often," I added.

Melody overrode my misgivings. "At least she must know where you are and how to get in touch with you."

"More or less. She assumes I'm in San Antonio right now, 'playing Doña Quixote,' as she puts it."

"Well, how often does *she* write?"

"You know my mother?" I tried to keep my voice light, wondering how this conversation had somehow turned to me and to my mother's indifference. "She keeps herself busy researching her family tree. I think she finds her ancestors more interesting than her offspring."

Offspring, singular.

"Gee, Sharon," Andy deadpanned. "You never told me you had ancestors."

"Vikings, according to Astrid—that's my mother." It was a story I'd told before. "They had names like 'Harald the Tall and Handsome' and 'Edvard the Strong and Brave.' Then along came my dad—he's Welsh—to muddy the gene pool. So here am I—'Sharon the Short and Tainted.'"

Andy laughed and left Melody and me to finish chatting about other things. I was glad our call ended on a less serious note. But afterwards, my mind went back to the original purpose. What was left after adding it all up and slicing through Cici's flair for melodrama?

Three different people—on three separate occasions—claim to have seen Bernice back in the States.

She might have taken up with an old man.

How many lonely old men? And where was she now? My own imagination left Cici's in the dust.

Chapter 22

The next morning I decided to brave Rita's displeasure and visit Mr. Álvarez again. I called first and Rita answered his phone, which didn't surprise me.

"I have plans this afternoon," I told her. "And I really can't stay long this morning. But a promise is a promise."

Not that I'd promised anything, but she let it go. Apparently she couldn't find an excuse to keep me away, or maybe decided it would be easier to get my visit over and done with than to have me keep pestering. And the "can't stay long" might have sealed it.

* * *

As I drove up to Mr. Álvarez's home, I kept a lookout for Vanessa-the-Stalker. Sure enough, I spotted her parked next door, slunk down behind the steering wheel of her dark-green Aztek. I started up the walk, making it a point to turn and wave at her.

She started the engine and peeled off, skimming by my car with only inches to spare. I turned my back and continued toward the house, hoping she couldn't see how jittery her reaction made me, hoping I wouldn't regret antagonizing her.

Rita met me at the door and ushered me into the living room. Sitting in his recliner, but without the blanket and pillow today, Mr. Álvarez looked quite thin. His ivory-colored cotton shirt hung loosely from his narrow shoulders, and thick brown suspenders clasped his baggy dress pants. His shoes were brightly polished, and I hoped that meant he and Rita were planning to take their daily walk to the post office later this morning.

Rita, of course, was dressed for an evening at the opera, in a sleek black Donna Karan number, enhanced only by a small ruby pin and matching earrings.

I, of course, was dressed in the same denim jumpsuit I'd worn when we had coffee at The Village Bean. Thanks to our trip to the Laundromat, it was crisp and clean again.

Mr. Álvarez thunked the footrest to the floor and made a shaky effort to stand.

"Please don't get up," I said, quickly seating myself in the plush armchair Rita had indicated. She pulled up a straight—lighter-weight—chair for herself on his other side. My chair was angled so that I was more-or-less facing both of them.

I'm not sure he even remembered me or the "raincheck" I'd extracted from him. I was concerned that reminding him might also remind him of the blowup with Vanessa. No need to worry. He was following his own train of thought.

"Now tell me," he said. "How is it you and Rita know each other?"

I looked at Rita, and her eyes narrowed.

"I told you, Sweetikins," she said. "She knows some of my relatives in Texas."

"Oh? I didn't know you had relatives in Texas."

She forced a laugh. "You just forgot."

He accepted that and made some joke about his memory. "Well, tell me again."

I hoped my expression didn't give me away. I was practically gloating that Mr. Álvarez might succeed where I had failed in worming information out of Rita.

She sighed. "I don't keep in touch with any of them."

I raised my eyebrows. Had she forgotten her call to Zapata to check me out?

"Except Perlita," she amended, seeing my expression. "But only once in a while."

"That's a shame. *La familia* is very important," Mr. Álvarez said, ignoring his own estrangement from his daughter and granddaughter.

"Well, at least you're on good terms with Perlita," I said to Rita, pretending to be helpful.

"You should invite them up here," Mr. Álvarez cackled. "You know mi casa is everybody's casa."

I wondered at his mood change. Was this typical when Alicia and Vanessa weren't around to agitate him? Or did it have something to do with his meds?

Rita chose to ignore his comment, and I tried to think of ways to get the conversation rolling again.

"You're lucky to come from a big family," I said to Rita.

"You came from a big family?" Mr. Álvarez asked.

"I told you, dear," she said testily.

"I always wished I had lots of brothers and sisters," I prodded.

She was silent a few moments, then, "It wasn't that great. The next-youngest—Rafael—was fifteen years older, and most of the others had already left home."

"I bet you were the princess!" Mr. Álvarez said, beaming.

Her expression became guarded, and I had the impression she was choosing her words carefully. "No. Not for long. A few years maybe. Then my sister Connie and her family moved in with us. We lived on a big ranch. There was lots of room."

"Did Connie have kids?" I already knew the answer as well as the reason Connie had moved back, but was curious to hear Rita's version.

"Oh, yes. Yes indeed."

"That must have been fun. Like having a big family again." I said.

Rita looked at me quizzically, as if searching for signs of sarcasm. But I had my bland fake smile in place.

"My sister Connie was—probably still is—nutty and neurotic. She was loud and controlling and ran the house as if my mother wasn't even there. There was only one kid—Sylvia—and she had the personality of a mothball.

"Was she your age?" I asked.

"A year older. Connie home-schooled us, didn't trust the outside world. I was smarter than Sylvia, and that seemed to bug Connie. She was always finding fault with me, but she treated Sylvia like she was made of glass."

"I'm sorry." My dismay was real. The effects of Bernice's malice had extended even further than I'd imagined. I was surprised that Rita had divulged so much about her home life. If she was telling the truth, it would explain a lot about her own personality, the chip on her shoulder that kept cropping up.

"What kind of man was her husband!" Mr. Álvarez said indignantly. "Not a man at all!"

"I barely remember him," Rita said. "I guess staying busy with the ranch kept him from having to deal with Connie."

"How long did this go on?" I ventured to ask.

Rita stiffened, and I realized I'd probably overused my quota of questions.

But Mr. Álvarez had no such quota. "You went to school finally, true?

"Yes."

"How did you get away from this tyrant of a sister?" he persisted.

"They finally moved. I don't know where they went, and don't care."

"I don't blame you," I murmured.

Maybe because I didn't question—or judge—her actions, she took up the story again.

"I'll say one thing for Connie—she was a good teacher. When I started high school, I sailed through my classes and earned a scholarship to St. Victoria's in Santa Fe. Became a nurse. Met my Sweetikins."

She leaned over and patted Mr. Álvarez's cheek. "And now you know everything."

Then she turned to me. There was something almost triumphant in her smile, as if challenging me to mention that she'd left out significant chunks of her life history.

Chapter 23

Rita made a point of looking at the wall clock—the clock whose face was made of aged wood, whose thin gold hands pointed to turquoise stones in place of numbers. I looked at my own Minnie Mouse wristwatch, the one Carlos had given me one Christmas. Big hand on the three; little hand on the ten. Yep: 10:15.

I rose and smiled at Mr. Álvarez. "I'd better go now. I don't want to wear you out."

"But you just got here!" he protested.

Despite my excuse for leaving, I noticed that he seemed somewhat invigorated. I wondered how often he got to interact with anyone besides Rita—not counting the confrontations with Vanessa. I suspected that Alicia and Rita both provided mostly hen-clucking. But what did I know? Maybe they all discussed the classics and politics and other stimulating subjects.

Rita was already guiding me toward the door. "Sharon has a busy day ahead of her," she told Mr. Álvarez over her shoulder. "And we're going to the park, remember?"

"You'll come again, won't you?" he called out.

I ground to a halt, stopping Rita mid-shove, and looked back to see him struggling to his feet. I hadn't the heart to tell him my welcome had an expiration date.

"I'll do the best I can," I promised.

* * *

Vanessa hadn't returned—or maybe she had. A black Chevy pickup parked farther down the street pulled slowly away from the curb just as I did. I made a few turns, then pulled into the post office parking lot. The pickup followed me the short distance, then drove on by. Its windows were tinted, so I couldn't see who was inside.

I thought of my earlier advice to Rita and scolded myself for blowing things out of proportion. After all, this was a small town. There weren't that many residential streets, so it was hardly unusual for two or more cars to be using any one street at the same time.

Besides, hadn't Wendy said that Alicia and Vanessa lived near Mr. Álvarez? Where was "near"? Next door?

On impulse I drove to Dan Oliver's office, where Alicia worked. It was only a couple of blocks from the post office, and not that far from Mr. Álvarez's. I would rather have walked to begin with, but I'd been trying to save a little time. My original plan was to leave directly from Mr. Álvarez's and meet up with the rest of the family at El Vado Lake. Now, here I was sabotaging my plan with this side-trip. It couldn't take too long for Alicia to answer a few questions, I told myself, and then I'd be on my way.

Alicia introduced me to Dan, her manner polite but cool. After the standard amenities were observed, Dan went back to his office.

"You know something, Alicia?" I said, trying to keep my annoyance in check. "You want me to find out something about Rita. Yet every time you or Vanessa see me with her, you get your backs up."

Alicia's cheeks turned pink, but her gaze was steady. "I guess we thought you could tell right away who she was—or was not. Apparently you told Vanessa you believed Rita. So what is there to find out? We don't understand why you're still friendly with her."

There was so much to refute, I hardly knew where to start, so I began with the most insulting.

"Are you saying I'm not allowed to be friendly with people you don't approve of?"

Alicia's flush deepened, and she lowered her eyes. "Of course not."

I softened toward her. "I know you feel caught in the middle, and it's natural that you want to defend Vanessa. But she does misinterpret things sometimes."

Alicia nodded, a trace of resignation, or perhaps dejection, in her face.

"As for Rita," I said, "I'm still trying to figure her out. I thought you might like an outsider's viewpoint. Once I have one."

"I just hope it doesn't come too late.

"Don't sell your own observations short. You live next door to your father, don't you?"

"No, on the next street. Our house backs up to his."

I raised my eyebrows. "Oh? I thought I saw Vanessa parked next door. Maybe it was someone else. Does she have a black pickup?"

Alicia seemed wary again. "No."

"Her boyfriend?"

"Why are you asking all these questions?"

Why indeed? Because I don't trust your daughter?

"Never mind. It's not important."

Alicia managed a smile, and my impromptu visit ended on a pleasant note, if not an enthusiastic one.

* * *

I decided that adding five more minutes to my already delayed trip wouldn't make that much difference. I drove to Mr. Álvarez's house on Spruce Avenue. Most of the houses in Chama were either frame or stucco, all topped by steep metal roofs designed for the heavy winter snows to slide down. An adobe house like his was unusual. Still, it had a pitched roof rather than a flat one.

I circled the block where he lived, hoping to catch sight of either the Aztek or the pickup. I had counted four houses between Mr. Álvarez's and the corner, then counted four from the corner on Alicia's street.

Not as straightforward as I'd thought. No two lots were the same size, so they didn't match their counterparts the next street over. I couldn't see past the dense foliage of wild rose, lilac bushes, and ponderosa pines that separated the back yards. Couldn't even catch a glimpse of a pitched roof. I had no idea where Alicia's lot met her father's, so could only guess which house was hers.

With nothing else to go on, I slowed down when I came to the fourth one and peered into the carport. Only a maroon Ford van there. Two doors down, parked in the driveway of a small house with an attached garage, I finally spotted the black truck. Rather, "a" black truck. I stopped in front of the house so I could jot down the license number, just in case.

I looked up to see a couple of slats in the blinds being separated. Then the slats fell back in place. I continued staring at the window, hoping whoever was watching me would open the blinds a little wider. While I was studying the window, someone evidently slipped out the side door. The next thing I knew, the truck was pulling out of the driveway.

Instead of driving off in the opposite direction as I expected, it backed up in front of me and parked. I started to back up too, then saw that the maroon van had closed in behind me, virtually boxing me in. What had I gotten myself into?

The man I'd seen with Vanessa the other night slammed out of the black Chevy and staggered over to my Honda. In broad daylight, he was even less appealing, wearing a stained undershirt and an ill-fitting pair of greasy jeans, with greasy black hair to match. He glared at me through bloodshot eyes.

Out of big-city habit, I'd locked the doors earlier, but I rolled the window down a quarter of an inch—just enough to hear what he had to say. When he couldn't get the door open, he placed his hands on the roof of the car and put his face right up against the window, his nose leaving moist breath spots on the pane. Even with the glass between us, the strong smell of alcohol assailed me.

Vanessa left the van and rushed to his side, then began her usual harangue. He snarled at her to shut up. She turned on her heel and stomped into the house, leaving me still hemmed in.

Between my karate skills and his apparent inebriation, I could probably have flattened this guy in no time at all. However, one of the first things I had learned—in and out of the courtroom—was never to underestimate my opponent. Besides, all I really wanted was to extract my car and get to the lake. That was challenge enough.

"You're trespassin', *pendeja*," the creep told me, his voice slurred.

"Oh, dear. I'm sorry," I said, trying to sound contrite. "Am I at the wrong house? Isn't this where Alicia lives? I'm supposed to meet her here."

"*Mentirosa*." He spat the words, leaving a trail of saliva on the pane. "Liar. Che's workin'. You chood know that."

Mentirosa I was, and I dug myself even deeper. "I must have misunderstood. I thought she said for me to wait here. She has something to give me. I guess I should go to where she works."

He backed away from my car momentarily and scratched his head. I half-expected bugs to come flying out.

"I'm gonna call her," he said with a sneer, leaning toward me again, confident that he'd called my bluff.

Rather belatedly, I thought of the cell phone in my purse, which I'd shoved under some beach towels in the back seat. I'd like to make a few calls of my own.

"That's a good idea," I said. "And if she tells you I'm lying, you can phone the sheriff."

My own bluff must have worked. Creep stumbled backwards a step or two. Of course, he had to have the last word.

"Get outta here, *beech*," he yelled, waving his fist.

Glad to oblige. I figured this wasn't a good time to correct his pronunciation. Instead, I nodded and thanked him as if he'd done me a great courtesy by allowing me to leave. He swaggered to his truck, started the engine, and moved forward with a noisy jerk, flipping me off as I passed by.

I tightened my hands on the wheel, resisting the urge to respond in kind, and started toward El Vado.

Chapter 24

When I unclenched my hands, they began shaking, and I knew I needed to take time out. I drove to the B&B, then got my purse from the back seat, pulled out my cell phone, and called Ryan.

"I'm running a little late," I told him.

"What's wrong?"

No matter how hard I try to sound nonchalant, Ryan can always see—rather, hear—right through me.

"Nothing important. I had a little run-in with Vanessa and her main sleaze, that's all."

"Sharon, I should never...."

He carried on for a few moments about not letting me out of his sight.

"Ryan," I interrupted. "I love you. I promise, I'll be very careful. I'll be there as soon as I can. But I need to go to the bathroom and get a drink of water before I start out."

There was a short pause before he said, "Permission granted."

I was glad to hear the smile in his voice.

"And I'll call while I'm on the way," I continued, "so you'll know exactly where I am."

"I overreacted?"

"A little. But it's okay."

* * *

Just north of the turnoff to Tierra Amarilla (or "T.A." as some of the locals called it), I turned west toward El Vado Lake. People going there had already arrived, and it was too early in the day for anyone to leave, so the twenty-five-mile stretch to the lake was pretty deserted. Maybe I was the one overreacting, but I was glad to keep in touch with Ryan via cell phone.

I could feel myself relax as soon as I located our group. I felt even better in the warmth of Ryan's hug. I had changed clothes at the B&B. Now I slipped out of the shorts and shirt I'd worn over my swimsuit and tossed them into the car. Next I exchanged shoes and socks for flip-flops, and donned a white poncho.

Carlos, Omar, and Digger were playing a lively game of keep-away with a red-and-yellow striped beachball. I took a Dr. Pepper out of the ice chest, and joined everyone else under a large beach umbrella. Everyone, that is, except Spot, who had stayed behind in the RV, where he didn't have to deal with the heat or the leash.

"Digger has a temporary reprieve from his leash," Alana said. "But not from the pooper scooper. One of life's little realities."

Although Amá was wearing a flowered swimsuit under her terry poncho, her sisters weren't in swimwear. Tía Dippy was dressed in hot-pink shorts and halter. Fortunately, she was wearing the black wig, so there was no clash with the red one. To my surprise, Tía Marta was actually wearing shorts, albeit gray Bermudas that came down to her knees, and a polo shirt. The guys were all wearing loud patterned board shorts.

Thanks to the abundance of storage space in the Salazars' Winnebago, we'd brought all sorts of water-fun paraphernalia, including water-skis and fold-up beach chairs with stubby legs. I'd no sooner sat down when boys and dog came racing over and plopped down beside me.

First, Digger had to shake himself vigorously, then give me a welcoming lick. I wrapped my arms around his neck and buried my face briefly in his fuzzy ruff.

"It's a good thing you came over before I'd smeared myself with sunscreen, silly dog, or I couldn't have hugged you!"

"Can we eat lunch now?" Carlos asked. "Mom said we had to wait till you got here."

I ruffled his hair. "Oh, wow! I'm glad to see you too!"

He grinned, and I put my arms around both boys.

"I'm not hungry," I teased. "Let's just skip lunch today."

"Good idea," Alana agreed, closing her eyes and pulling her floppy hat down over her face.

"Mo-om!"

Alana pushed her hat back and eyed the boys. "Well, I suppose the hungriest people can bring the ice chest over to the picnic table and get everything set out."

Carlos and Omar jumped up and practically collided with each other in their race to get lunch on the table.

"Wash your hands!" Alana shouted after them.

* * *

Lunch finished, it was time for another round of water-skiing. Beto had rented a boat so he could tow the skiers, and everyone but Tía Marta and Tía Dippy had given it a try. I gave it a couple of rounds, but even slathered with sunscreen, I could feel the sun scorching my wimpy tan-resistant skin.

I toweled off and joined the tías under the beach umbrella again.

"Mira," Tía Dippy said with a smile as she gazed out at the lake. "Look at Ysela and Ric on those skis. They think they're young again."

Tía Marta shook her head. "They'll think 'young' tomorrow." Then she smiled too. "Good for them."

Tía Dippy turned to me. "Tell us about your morning, mijita. What happened to make you so late?"

"Well, everything started off well. I had an interesting visit with Mr. Álvarez and Rita. Then I made the mistake of doing some 'sleuthing' that wound up mostly a waste of time."

"Why is that?"

I looked at the two aunts, at the concern in their eyes, and realized they weren't any more fooled than Ryan was. I also realized I'd like to pour out the whole story enfolded in their sympathy.

I told them about going to Alicia's office, then to her home. "If it *was* her house. I think I was in front of Vanessa's boyfriend's place. Alicia's is probably where I saw the maroon van parked. I didn't see Vanessa's Aztek, so I'm guessing she parked it in her boyfriend's garage. And the thing is, I don't know why they're bulldogging me."

"That scares me, mijita," Tía Dippy said.

"It's a little unnerving," I admitted before giving her hand a gentle squeeze. "But maybe we're making too much out of it. Maybe they just don't have anything else to do besides pick up their unemployment checks."

"Now, Sharon," Tía Marta admonished me. "This is nothing to be flippant about."

"I know," I said, squeezing her hand too. "And to tell you the truth, I'm glad you take this seriously. I guess being flip is my way of whistling in the dark."

"Tell us more about seeing Rita," Tía Dippy said.

"Oh, that! It was both strange and pleasant. Mr. Álvarez is a dear, and I hate to think of anything happening to him." I filled in the details of my visit.

Tía Marta raised her eyebrows and peered at me through her thick glasses. "That was different—Rita telling you so much about herself."

"I wish I wasn't so suspicious. I don't know if she was really being candid, or if those little tidbits were carefully chosen for my benefit—or maybe Mr. Álvarez's."

I leaned forward excitedly. "But I do have an idea, and you all can give me a hand, if you'd like."

Tía Dippy answered without hesitation. "Qué sí,"

Tía Marta didn't say anything, but listened expectantly.

"There are a few things I want to do before time runs out." And time seemed to be dwindling away. Uncle Javier and Aunt Maribel had already started back for Zapata.

"For one thing," I said, "I'd like to go to Santa Fe and check out this nursing school where Rita went."

Tía Marta folded her arms across her chest. "You think she's lying?"

"Not about going there. I'm sure the 'real' Rita went there. But I'd like to talk to staff members who were there back then, and find out how she came across—to them and to the other nursing students."

"Ah," said Tía Dippy, nodding. "To see if the personality matches. But don't you think it would get back to her?"

"That I've been snooping around? Probably."

Tía Dippy frowned. "It could be dangerous."

I gave that some thought. If Rita found out, it would definitely cut off any opportunity I had to see Mr. Álvarez again. Worse, she might decide not to wait any longer to follow her plan—whatever that was.

"Okay, I have another idea that's less risky. I'd like to drive down to Coyote. Rita's family used to live on a ranch near there. This is where you all come in. Amá too, if she's interested. You all could say you're trying to locate your old

129

friend Connie Bustamante. If we're lucky, someone will talk about the family, and we'll learn something about Rita without having to ask any direct questions."

Tía Dippy's eyes lit up. "I really would like to find out what happened to Connie. So I won't have to pretend anything. This just might work!"

Chapter 25

We gathered at the Salazars' for supper. Despite our big picnic lunch, all the exercise had made us hungry—and more than a little worn out. Ryan offered to fix "surprise" omelets for everyone. For once, Amá didn't protest having someone else take over her kitchen.

"What's the surprise?" Omar asked.

"Whatever I can find to put in it," Ryan said, moving things around in the fridge. "It'll be a surprise to me too."

"Can we help?" Carlos asked.

"Yeah, but—" Ryan looked down at their hopeful faces. "Tell you what. There's not a lot of room for all of us to be dodging each other in the kitchen. Why don't you guys sit at the dinette, and we'll find a way to make this a family project."

I sat with the boys while we watched Ryan pull out utensils and a variety of ingredients for his mysterious concoction.

"No omelet pan, but that won't stand in our way," he said cheerfully, pulling a large skillet from under the stove. "I'll heat up some tortillas too."

Spot, glad to have us home again, settled himself between the boys so he'd be available in case Ryan included some tidbit that might interest him.

Ryan handed Omar a large bowl and two cartons of eggs. "Okay, pardner, your job is to crack these without getting any shells in the mix."

Carlos was assigned to chop onions into very fine pieces for me to sauté.

I began to think we were being Tom-Sawyered, but Ryan was busy too, whistling as he greased the skillet and set out salt, pepper, milk, grated cheese, a small can of mushrooms, and—most important—Merlie's Blue Ribbon Chile, to be added at the right time.

The boys took turns beating the eggs, then Ryan took over, coordinating the mixture, which he slow-cooked.

The mouth-watering fragrance of green chile and Amá's warm homemade tortillas filled the RV and floated out to the others, who gravitated toward the picnic tables.

Alana spread out tablecloths patterned with daisies and asters, then finished setting the tables. Finally ready, Ryan's "surprise" took much less time to polish off than it had taken to prepare, but we chefs were just as hungry as everyone else, so had no complaints.

Pleasantly full afterwards, we sat around the campfire, happy to simply do nothing but look at the stars. Even Digger and Spot had wound down. After finishing their own dinner, they curled up together and snoozed.

I wished I could shut my mind off so easily. Much as I wanted to quit thinking about Rita and Mr. Álvarez, I mentally began making plans for tomorrow.

* * *

Over breakfast at the Parlor Car the next morning, I brought up my plan to go to Coyote with the tías and Amá.

"Well, I guess there's safety in numbers," Ryan said. "But why don't you call your investigator friend Jimmy Romero first. He might know which of Rita's relatives still live there—if any."

Alana winked at me. "Beats wandering around town hoping to run into people who knew the Méndez family."

"Yeah. I guess I got a little carried away with the idea," I admitted. "I didn't think to call Jimmy because—I don't know—I guess I just figured he'd have called me by now if he knew anything."

"Call him, honey," Ryan said, seeing the disappointment in my face. "I bet he can help."

* * *

"Right now, all I got are statistics," Jimmy told me when I phoned him after breakfast. "I was hoping to pin down some other stuff before I got back to you."

"If you've found out *anything*, that's a head start."

"Okay, here goes. Ernesto's parents lived with them—that would be Rita's grandparents, Bernice's greats. They outlived Ernesto, who died fairly young. Rita would have been about thirteen, just starting high school."

"What about Rita's mother?"

"Juana developed Alzheimer's. Died in a nursing home a few years ago."

"A nursing home? Are you sure?"

"Peaceful Pines in Española. I can give you the exact date if you'd like."

"That contradicts what Rita told me. Hmm. Go ahead and tell me all the dates you have."

I jotted down the numbers Jimmy gave me.

"Most of the brothers moved to Colorado or Texas. One moved back to Coyote after their dad—Ernesto—died, but he's in Texas again. Connie and her family moved to Montana a few years after the brother moved in."

My head was spinning. Now I knew how Jimmy felt when I'd swamped him with information earlier.

"One brother can't seem to stay out of prison from one day to the next. Right now he's supposedly in Mexico, but who knows which side of the law he's on down there. Anyway, that takes care of everyone...except...."

"Except who—what?"

"There is one brother who still lives in New Mexico. Kiko. Something of a recluse, from what I hear."

"Is he still in Coyote?" I asked hopefully.

"Nope. Tres Piedras."

"That's not far from here at all! Do you think he'd be willing to talk to me? Rather, to Ryan's aunt? They grew up together."

Jimmy hesitated, and I could almost hear his gray hair springing out of his head as he combed his fingers through it.

"I couldn't tell you, Sharon. Wouldn't hurt to try, I suppose."

"You don't sound very optimistic."

"There's just something about the missing pieces that bugs me. I'm working on another angle. I'll let you know how it turns out."

"Jimmy, I hope this isn't getting to be a headache for you. You've done quite a bit already."

"Don't you worry about that. If I didn't like puzzles I wouldn't be in this business. This one intrigues me, and I'd like to see it through."

"Well, let me know how much—"

"Sharon, I'm gonna get really mad if you say another word about that!"

I laughed. "Okay. I just don't want to take advantage of you."

"I'd have to work on this night and day for a thousand years before we'd be even."

Tears pricked my eyes at his generous response. We'd helped each other out so much over the years, we'd probably both lost track. Payment had long been forgotten.

We ended our call, and I reported his news to Ryan, already sketching out "Plan B" in my mind.

Chapter 26

Ryan and Alana lagged behind Beto and me on the way to the RV park.

"I thought I was in good shape," Alana groaned, trying not to limp. "But I guess I overdid it yesterday."

"I think we all did," Ryan agreed, his own gait a little stiff.

Beto's eyes twinkled with mischief. "Not us unathletic types. Nothing to get out of shape in the first place, verdad?"

I chuckled. "Good thing I quit when I did. I've got a BUSY day ahead."

This time, Ryan groaned. "I'll leave it to you and the peppy people."

Once we arrived at the RV park, I told the others about Jimmy Romero's report. Then I asked Tía Dippy if she'd mind phoning Kiko Méndez. "He'd probably remember you, and he'd be more likely to talk to you than a stranger. His number's unlisted, but Jimmy unearthed it for me."

"I'd be glad to," she answered. "I always liked Kiko. Sweet boy."

After talking to him, she shook her head. "I told him we'd like to come see him and catch up on old times. A little *plática con amigos*. He hemmed and hawed, and I pretended not to notice until he finally gave in. But I tell you, he doesn't seem the same."

"Well, of course not! What do you expect?" Tía Marta said scornfully. "You both got *old*!"

Tía Dippy's eyes snapped. "Speak for yourself. Are you going with us or not?"

"Sharon's friend said the man wanted to be left alone, so that's what I intend to do—leave him alone."

Amá begged off too. "I'm very achy from yesterday at the lake. I'm sorry, mija. I just don't feel up to it."

Ryan put his arms around his mom and me. "You and Tía—uh—Eppie go on ahead before it gets any later. We'll just hang out here and commiserate with each other."

"You're right. We'd better get started. I'd like to get home before the afternoon rains start."

Tía Dippy had already gotten her purse. "I'm ready. Where's the car?"

"We walked over. Thought it would help get the kinks out. I'll go get it, then come back and pick you up."

"Walking's a good idea, mijita. I'll go with you."

I smiled, glad she was excited about our venture. I also wondered what Kiko would think seeing his old friend in her unlikely black wig, lime-green tights, and psychedelic tunic.

* * *

"How did you find me?" Kiko asked after he'd greeted us and ushered us into his kitchen, where he was brewing coffee. "Sit, sit."

While he took down mugs from the cabinet, I made a quick survey of the kitchen, wondering if he was one of those hermits who collect stacks of newspapers and dirty dishes. I was relieved to find the room clean, though a little confining. If he collected anything, it was a wide array of plants parked in every conceivable space and hanging from numerous hooks in the ceiling. It reminded me of one of those sci-fi movies where the green vine from hell slithers through cracks in the wall and chokes the heroine in her sleep. I shook off the image as Kiko turned back toward us, waiting for his answer.

"We ran into your sister Rita in Chama," I said, hoping that was explanation enough.

Kiko's black eyes bore holes through me. "Rita doesn't know where I am."

Tía Dippy came to my rescue. "She didn't tell us where Connie is either. Rita seemed very, hmm, evasive? So—" She nodded and tapped her forehead with her forefinger, as if deep secrets resided in her brain. "I have this friend who can find out things. Connie is in Montana, no? And here you are!"

Kiko smiled, his expression softening. "And here you are too."

He didn't fit the imaginary "hermit" picture I'd formed earlier of a shriveled-up mole-like creature with very little hair and even fewer teeth. His white hair was thinning, but his teeth were strong and even. Tanned and muscular, he appeared to take care of his health.

Kiko brought the mugs, sugar, creamer, and spoons to the table, then took the carafe from the coffeemaker.

"Our family was dysfunctional before the word was even invented. Coffee?"

I nodded, too startled by his bluntness to say anything.

"Oh, sí. I can always use a good cup of coffee!" Tía Dippy answered, as Kiko filled our mugs. "Tell me about your family. Why do you say that?"

I saw once again how her open curiosity, her kookiness, were overshadowed by her innate kindness. Kiko was drawn into it, but dodged her question. Still, they were soon talking together comfortably. They automatically slipped into Spanish—rather, the "Zapata patois" we all spoke.

Kiko stopped himself and glanced at me over half-rim glasses. "I'm sorry, I didn't mean to leave you out."

I smiled. "You didn't. I grew up in Zapata too."

"Oh, that's good," he said, relief in his voice. "I hope you don't mind if we talk about old times."

"Not at all. I find it interesting too."

Tía Dippy beamed at me. "Not everyone listens to my old stories. But Sharon, she's a good listener."

From then on, they included me with occasional nods and smiles, but I mostly smiled and nodded back. I hoped we'd find out something about Rita before long, but left it to Tía Dippy to bring up the subject.

In the meantime, I learned that Kiko's two sons lived in Houston, and that he was a master electrician whose wife had left him a few years ago for a young but penniless musician.

At last, after telling him something about our family, Tía asked about his again.

"Well, let's see. My brother Neto turned out to be pretty normal—once he quit carrying the torch for your sister," Kiko said with a twinkle in his eye. "He moved to Colorado, got married, had a bunch of kids."

"And the others? José? Rafael? Flavio?"

"José decided to be an Anglo, changed his name to Neville Wentworth, and moved to Dallas. He joined some strange religion, and now he goes around telling the rest of us we're going to hell. Rafael finally 'came out of the closet'—but at least he's honest about it, and a damn sight pleasanter to be around than José. Flavio—" Kiko's shoulders sagged. "Flavio keeps winding up in prison."

"I'm sorry," Tía Dippy murmured. "But what about your sisters? What about Connie?"

A closed look came over Kiko's face, and he didn't answer right away. Finally, "Both Perlita and Connie had difficult pregnancies, so they got to be very protective—too protective—when their kids were born. It might not have been so bad, but...you were there that Easter, weren't you?"

Tía Dippy and I knew exactly which Easter he meant.

She nodded, smoothing her wig as she spoke. "Everything happened so fast. It didn't seem possible it happened on purpose."

I was impressed with her tact, since I knew she had very definite opinions to the contrary.

"Did you see it?" she asked Kiko.

"I still see it," he answered heavily, staring into space. "We were in Sergio and Connie's big back yard. Beautiful day. Everyone happy. Kids all playing and making lots of noise. I noticed that Bernice didn't join in their games. She was quite the manipulator, and she tried to bully Sylvia into letting her hold the little rabbit. Sergio's mother thought she put an end to the problem by telling the girls to put the bunny in the carrier for a while. Then someone else tried to distract Sylvia by calling her over and making a big fuss over her new dress.

"For some reason, I found myself watching Bernice. I saw her sneak over to the carrier and reach inside. I heard the bunny squeal, but she pulled her hands out real quick. I didn't think much about it at first. Then after—afterwards, I figured out she must have broken its neck. It never made another sound."

Tía Dippy and I listened in horrified silence. Although we knew what was coming next, I had the absurd hope that we could rewind the tape and come up with a different ending.

Kiko swallowed hard before continuing. "If she'd just left it at that, we'd have all probably thought it really was an accident. I don't know why I kept watching her, but something about her just didn't seem...right. I saw her pick up the little carrier when no one else was looking and take it over toward the barbecue grill. Sergio was cooking hamburgers there, and I thought maybe she was going to ask him something, like could she play with the bunny again. I never in a million years thought...."

Tía placed her hand on his arm. "Of course not! How could anyone have guessed."

"Bernice pointed to something, and Sergio looked away. I saw her pick up the striker, but then I lost sight of her. Evidently she set the carrier right next to the grill and lit it there. It was just a flimsy makeshift thing. The next thing I knew, it had gone up in flames, and Bernice was nowhere around. Everyone went to see what had caught fire. By the time I got there, the fur had begun to singe, and the smell was pretty sickening."

The lines in Tía's face deepened. "I remember there was a lot of chaos."

"I don't know how Connie knew—mother's instinct, I guess. She blamed Bernice right away, and Bernice cried when Connie screamed at her. But as soon as Perlita intervened and insisted it was an accident, the tears stopped."

"At least someone kept little Sylvia from seeing anything," Tía said. "Connie—pobrecita—she just went to pieces."

"So did I, but in my own way." Kiko took out a handkerchief and wiped his face, which had turned ashen. "I was a grown man, and I'd gone hunting with my dad and brothers, but this was different. I barely made it into the house in time to vomit my insides out. I never said anything. There wasn't anything left to say."

Chapter 27

"Let's go outside," Kiko said. "We could use the fresh air, and I'll show you my garden."

I had begun to feel a little queasy myself, and all the indoor plants seemed to be closing in on me. I hoped Kiko's garden wouldn't turn out to be a jungle.

Fortunately it was laid out with plenty of space between the rows of vegetables and flowers. Vivid orange poppies contrasted with blue and yellow columbines. Hollyhocks—ranging in color from purple so deep it looked black through various shades of red to stark white—lined the back wall. Kiko also grew a variety of vegetables—squash, cucumbers, pinto beans....

As we wandered down the rows of produce, I thought about what Kiko had just told us. No two people see things exactly the same way, but his version of Bernice's cruelty was fairly close to the one I'd heard from Amá and her sisters. Still, I wondered what connection it had to Rita.

"I don't want to keep dwelling on this," I said as we paused to admire the sturdy tomato vines, "but were your parents and Rita there when...when it happened?"

"No. They had come down at Christmas and didn't want to make another trip so soon. At least that's what my mother said. Since then, I've wondered if it had something to do with Bernice."

"So Rita didn't know about the fire?"

Fire—euphemism for the whole tragic incident.

Kiko peered at me over his glasses again. "You seem very curious about Rita."

I felt heat rise to my face, but kept on. "Yes, I am. She seemed so...secretive."

Kiko shook his head and picked a couple of shiny red-orange tomatoes. "I hardly know Rita. What is she now? Thirty-five? Forty? I moved to Albuquerque a few years before she was born. There were only two brothers still at home, and they moved on once they started college. My father was unhappy that none of us wanted to carry on the ranch. Let me tell you, ranching is hard work."

"So you never saw them again?" I asked before he could get further side-tracked.

"No, I saw them a lot at first. I was married with two little boys, and we'd load up the station wagon and drive over to Coyote every two or three weeks. Here, help yourself to some tomatoes. They're at their peak right now."

Kiko went back to the kitchen for paper sacks, then rejoined us. The three of us began threading through vines bulging with ripe fruit.

"I guess the kids all got along?" I said.

"Who?"

"Your boys and Rita—back then."

"Oh, that. Yes. Everything was fine till Connie moved in."

He had a faraway look on his face, and I had the feeling he was ready to tell us more. I put another tomato into my sack and kept quiet.

"Connie wasn't all that easy to get along with, and my wife couldn't stand her," Kiko said at last.

"Had Connie been like this before the fire?" I asked softly.

"No, I wouldn't say so. She was always a little self-righteous. Then she went off to college and got a degree in psychology and was even worse. But she didn't go off the deep end till after that fire."

"What about Sylvia? Did she ever find out how her rabbit died?"

"I doubt it. I think that's one reason Connie made Sergio leave Zapata and go to work on our father's ranch. She felt it was so isolated, nothing could ever happen to 'contaminate' Sylvia. Or Rita. Connie insisted on home-schooling them, which I personally think was a big mistake."

He shook his head again. "Nothing wrong with the little school in Coyote. It's not like it had those big-city problems—gangs and drugs and all that."

"Did Rita seem well-adjusted up till Connie moved in?"

Kiko's expression lightened. "Yes. Yes, she did. Cute little kid."

"So you lost touch with *everyone* after that?" Tía Dippy asked.

Kiko pressed his lips together in a grim line. "Not quite, even though we were pretty scattered. The big fallout came when my mother got too sick to stay home anymore. Rita had been taking care of her for a couple of years, and thought she could do it all. But of course she couldn't."

Our sacks filled, we started back toward the kitchen.

"We all came back to Coyote to decide what to do," Kiko continued. "It was the first time we'd all been together in years."

"So you saw Rita then?"

"No. I was the last one to get there. By then, Rita wasn't speaking to anyone, and she'd locked herself in her room. Stayed there till we left. Seemed childish to me, and I wasn't in the mood to deal with it. It wasn't one of those happy reunions you see in the movies. No one could agree on anything. Connie wanted to take over, but our mother got agitated whenever she was around."

Tía Dippy nodded. "People with Alzheimer's can get violent."

This time she was the one who got the owlish look from Kiko over his half-rims.

"You knew about that?"

"Rita told us that much—not that your mother got belligerent, but that she had Alzheimer's."

"Rita said she stayed home with your mother the whole time," I added.

Kiko stopped still, and his eyes narrowed. "I don't know why she'd say that. Maybe Rita has a mental problem herself." He shook his head. "I don't know. I suppose stress could do that. Anyway, our mother spent the last two-and-a-half years in a nursing home and didn't even know who we were."

"Was Rita the only one who objected to the nursing home?" I asked. "Is that what caused the fallout?"

"We just couldn't deal with any of it, with her not knowing us, or what we should do. Everyone was angry, wanting someone to blame." Kiko sighed. "Instead of coming together, we pushed each other away. When I came down for the funeral, José—pardon me, Neville—started in on me, and I turned around and left five minutes after I got there."

Tía Dippy looked distressed. "I'm sorry we brought up sad memories."

Kiko patted her shoulder. "I've moved on—in more ways than one. I moved here after my wife left. And Rafael and I keep track of each other." He paused. "You should talk to him if you want to know more about Rita."

"Where does he live?" I asked, feeling a ray of hope.

"Right now he's in Gallina."

That was a surprise—didn't jibe with Jimmy Romero's info. Not that it mattered. Maybe I could go down there after all and talk with Rafael. Gallina was only a few miles past Coyote.

"I'm confused. I thought your brothers were either in Colorado or Texas." *Or in prison somewhere.*

"I guess it is a little confusing. Rafael was in Texas, but he went back to Coyote to help out after my father died. He and Connie locked horns, of course. But he saw to it that Rita got to go to public high school. I guess he gave up on Sylvia. Connie's husband finally got fed up and went to Montana. Told her she could come or she could stay. Maybe my mother was fed up too. She managed to show a little gumption and tell Connie to go with Sergio."

"So Rafael stayed in Coyote?"

"Up until Rita went off to be a nurse. Ma decided it was time to sell—she kept the half-acre the house was on and sold everything else. Rafael—I think he was glad to get out from under the ranch too. He went back to Dallas. Still lives there. He models or something. Makes a lot of money doing TV commercials."

"But you say he's in Gallina right now."

"Came down a few days ago. Business, he said. I don't know what business he'd have there. Maybe he just needed a break from the city."

We went back inside, where Kiko fixed us a chef salad that included vegetables from his garden. After lunch, he gave Rafael a call, paving the way for Tía and me to visit.

Chapter 28

"Well, what do you think, mijita?" Tía Dippy asked me on the way back.

I flexed my fingers on the steering wheel. "I have mixed feelings. I guess I'd thought we could ask some routine questions and get all the answers we needed. It's different when you're talking to someone face to face. Especially someone as nice as Kiko. I didn't expect to stir up such painful memories."

"Yo sé. Neither did I. But sometimes it helps to get those memories out in the open. Especially with a friend. With friends. People who care. People who won't judge."

"I hope you're right."

"Do you think you learned anything helpful?"

"A little. The 'real' Rita's personality certainly sounds different from Bernice's—when they were children anyway. Kiko liked Rita when she was little. I don't think Bernice was ever likable."

"No, I don't think so either," Tía Dippy agreed.

"And I learned that Rita probably never knew about the fire. I'm not sure if that has any bearing on anything."

"At least Connie didn't try to turn the little girls against Bernice."

"As far as we know."

"Well, she wouldn't need to, mijita. They probably never saw each other again."

"I'm beginning to think mental illness must run in the family. I can understand Connie being deeply upset, but it seems she was totally shattered."

"Sí. That makes me sad too. I don't remember Connie the way Kiko says she is now."

"Well, unfortunately, that's the way Rita remembers her. If she really was that unhinged, it could explain why Rita's a little off-center herself. I wonder how it affected Sylvia."

"I bet something in Sylvia's brain went—*cómo se dice?*—a little haywire too."

"I wouldn't be surprised."

"Maybe Sylvia looks like Rita and Bernice también. Maybe she's the one pretending to be Rita."

"Oh, god, that's all we need."

When we neared Hopewell Lake between Tres Piedras and Tierra Amarilla, I pulled into an overlook area. We got out of the car and breathed deeply. I felt I was inhaling the beauty as well as the fragrance of the towering pines. I hoped the absolute stillness of our surroundings would quiet the turmoil in my mind.

Tía Dippy slipped her arm around my waist. I turned to see tears in her eyes, and noticed again the age lines in her face. I hugged her tightly, as if I could stop her from being sad, or from growing older.

"We'd better go home," she whispered after a few moments. "If we're not back soon, they might start to wonder what your silly old tía has gotten you into."

"Or maybe they'll wonder what your windmill-tiltin' niece got her funny sweet tía into," I said as we got back inside the car.

"Why do you say that? About the windmills?"

"I don't know," I started the ignition and pulled back onto the highway. "I guess I assumed that Kiko was on good terms with his family, and I had this idealistic notion that he'd jump at the chance to come up to Chama and identify whoever-she-is. It sounds so foolish when I say it out loud."

"So you were wrong. But you could have been right."

I smiled. "Thanks."

She pulled a Kleenex out of her purse and blew her nose. "I have mixed emotions too. I was really glad to see Kiko. But I never realized...."

We rode in silence for a few miles.

"Tía, I'm not sure. Do you think it's a good idea for us to look up Rafael?"

"Qué sí. Maybe next time you'll be lucky!"

"We. Maybe *we'll* be lucky. I couldn't do this without you."

She sighed. "It's good to feel helpful, mijita. I know I'm a scatter-brain sometimes. You know they call me 'dippy'?"

The car lurched forward. "I know." I wished I could keep my face from turning red, but I could feel the flush creeping up. "But always with affection," I said truthfully, then paused. "Does it bother you?"

She laughed. "Not really. What do they say? If the shoe fits. Besides, I never liked my real name—too stuffy. I'd rather be dippy than stuffy."

I smiled and touched her hand. "Don't ever change!"

* * *

As I passed the B&B on the way to the RV park, I saw Vanessa's green Aztek parked on the side street. I began turning over ideas of ways to avoid her. When I brought Tía Dippy home, I could just stay there till—hmm, how long? Tomorrow morning? Next week? Next winter? Or I could leave the car at the RV park, circle a few blocks on foot, and sneak in the front door from the opposite direction. I might need to borrow one of Tía's wigs—the red one would do nicely....

I drew into the parking area at the RV park; then we walked over to the Salazars' Winnebago, where we found the grownups sitting in camp chairs under the cottonwoods. After we'd exchanged hugs all around, Tía Dippy and I pulled up chairs and joined the circle.

"Feeling better?" I asked.

Amá nodded. "It's amazing what a little aspirina and arnica gel will do. We're almost back to normal."

"Where are the kids?"

"They played croquet all morning. Right now they're taking the pets for a walk," Alana answered. "Rather, Digger is taking Omar for a gallop, and Spot is climbing a tree close to their tent while Carlos holds on to the leash."

Beto's gray eyes twinkled. "Alana was afraid they'd run out of things to do, but we can hardly keep up with them."

"Ever since they discovered that green area near the office, they've played croquet just about every day. That or basketball. And wait till they tell you about their woodcarving."

Ryan grinned. "Haven't even had time for r-e-a-d-i-n-g."

"How was your visit with Kiko?" Amá asked. "I'm curious to hear all about it!"

"He's still handsome, just like all the Méndez boys," Tía Dippy said with a wave of her jangly bracelets.

Amá blushed slightly, and I suspected she wouldn't ask directly about her old flame, Neto.

Tía Marta folded her arms across her chest. "Boys! Humph! Old men now."

Tía Dippy remained unperturbed. "And like I said, still muy guapo. Kiko's quite the gardener—and chef. Unmarried too, hermana."

"And the rest of the family?" Tía Marta asked, quick to ward off any matchmaking ideas her sister might have.

"Did you learn anything about Rita?" Alana wanted to know.

"Not really," I said. "He hasn't seen her in years."

"Well, that's disappointing!"

"In a way. But he did verify some things we already knew. Connie and Sergio are in Montana...."

Tía Dippy and I exchanged glances, and it seemed by unspoken agreement we wouldn't rehash the subject of the fire. Instead she gave a breezy account of the rest of the family.

"Neville!" Amá sputtered when she'd finished. "José Méndez is Neville Wentworth now?"

Even Tía Marta couldn't contain herself, holding her sides as she joined Amá and Apá in the laughter. "Pretentious little twit. Always was."

Beto looked up at the gathering clouds. "Well, it looks like you got home just in time. I guess we'd better be on our way before the rain starts."

Ryan stood and rested his hand on my shoulder. "Ready, sweetheart?"

Not really.

Alana rose and stretched. "I'll go track down the boys and tell them we're leaving."

Ryan looked at me quizzically. "Sharon?"

I got up slowly, and we said our goodbyes. I slipped my hand into Ryan's as we walked toward the car. When Alana and Beto caught up with us, she put her arm around me.

"Are you okay, Sharon? You haven't said much."

"Well, today was a little more trying than Tía let on. I'll tell you about it when we get back. But something else is on my mind right now."

"Oh?"

"Vanessa was parked by our place a little while ago. With any luck, she's left by now. If not...."

Alana's eyes blazed. "If not, she'll have the four of us to deal with."

Chapter 29

Ryan parked next to the passenger side of Vanessa's Aztek. Over my objections, he got out and knocked on her passenger door.

Vanessa, her hair more scraggly than usual and her tanktop even skimpier, got out on the driver's side and walked around the front of the Aztek till she was facing Ryan. "What's the matter with your wimpy wife? Does she have to hide behind you?"

I couldn't tell which was clenched tighter—Ryan's jaw or his fists. By then, the rest of us had joined him, and Vanessa looked a shade less aggressive. Since her surly boyfriend didn't appear on the scene, I felt a shade less repulsed.

"Were you looking for me, Vanessa?" I asked sweetly.

"Does Ranger Rick here have another wife?"

"Not that I know of. How may I help you?"

Vanessa sneered at my entourage. "You can't talk to me without your bodyguards?"

I turned to my bodyguards, who all had scowls to match hers. "Why don't you all go on inside, and I'll be there in a few minutes."

The others ambled off, and I continued standing by our cars. I had no intention of suggesting a more comfortable place for whatever "chat" Vanessa had in mind, and only hoped it would start raining on us soon, cutting our meeting short.

"My boyfriend told me about all your lies!" she began ranting as soon as the others were out of earshot.

I couldn't resist baiting her, even as my heartbeat started clattering against my chest. "Really? I didn't think there were so many."

This, naturally, set off a rash of obscenities.

"Look, Vanessa, why don't you tell me specifically what's bothering you, and we can deal with it. And you don't have to yell. I'm right here next to you." *Where I can smell that god-awful cologne you're wearing.*

"My mother says you're a liar too," she said triumphantly. "You don't fool her one bit."

Ouch. It hadn't occurred to me they'd check out my conversation with Creepy. And I didn't want to lose Alicia's confidence. Of course Vanessa might have been exaggerating, if not downright lying.

"Okay, here's the thing, I was telling the truth about looking for your mother's house."

"But she wasn't going to give you nothing."

I felt a couple of raindrops splat on my shoulders. A few more minutes, and the downpour should begin in earnest.

"You're right. I shouldn't have added that part. I apologize."

But Vanessa wasn't going to let me off the hook so easily. "Then why were you there?"

"I was curious, that's all. She said her house was behind your grandfather's, and I wondered where it was."

"*Mentira!*" she shouted. "Just another lie!"

"Sorry to disappoint you, but that's the truth." *Maybe not the whole truth.*

"You were following me!"

"I'll be darned. Here I thought you and your boyfriend were following me." Suddenly I was too angry for this banter. "Look at you. Parked here for god-knows-how-long—just waiting for me to show up. Don't accuse *me* of something you're doing yourself!"

Lightning flared, followed by a loud crack of thunder and a torrent of rain. I began shivering and wrapped my arms around myself as Vanessa and I kept glaring at each other. My rain-drenched hair must have looked as stringy as hers by now. I saw goosebumps pop out on her bare bulgy midriff, so hoped she'd be ready to call off this power match. But her parting shot caught me completely off guard.

"You and Rita have something cooked up," she said in a menacing tone—the first time I'd ever heard her speak in a low voice. "And I'll keep on watching you till I find out what it is."

With that, she got back into the Aztek, slammed the door, and drove off.

* * *

"I need a warm h-hug, a hot sh-shower, and a hot c-cup of tea," I called out through chattering teeth as I stood dripping just inside the door.

Ryan was already halfway down the stairs, towels and my favorite terry bathrobe in hand.

"Warm hug coming up," he said, enfolding me in his arms for a few moments.

I had left my shoes outside, but still left damp footprints in the hall. "I need to clean this up."

"Don't worry about it. I'll get some paper towels. Take care of yourself first."

Fortunately there was a small half-bathroom just off the foyer. I shed my wet clothes, dried off, and put on my comfy bathrobe. The shower could wait. I was hardly glamorous, but at least I wasn't freezing anymore.

When I came out, Wendy was standing in the foyer waiting for me, a worried look on her face.

"I thought I heard something about hot tea, and I have some ready in the dining room."

We all gathered around the table and drank the soothing tea. Some of my edginess drained away as I related my encounter with Vanessa. But even though I wasn't afraid of her, the thought of having her shadow me was disconcerting.

"Oh, Sharon, there might be an easy way around that," Wendy said. "Why don't you talk to Luis Tovar. He's one of the sheriff's deputies who lives here in town."

"I really don't want to make a big to-do over it."

"You wouldn't have to. That's why I think it might help. You see, he knows everyone in town, and we all know him. He's good as they come, but also big and scary-looking—has kind of a gruff voice. So if someone's kid gets out of line, Luis gives him a talking to, and that's usually all it takes."

I felt a little skeptical. Alicia's "kid" was way past the age limit. Still, the idea gave me a glimmer of hope. "You think that might work with Vanessa?"

"It couldn't hurt to try. If she keeps hanging around here—or follows you someplace else—you could give Luis a call, and he could come scare her off. I don't think she wants any more trouble with the cops."

"You're right. I'll talk to Luis first thing tomorrow."

Chapter 30

"First thing" was not at all what we'd expected. Our cell phone jerked us awake about six the next morning.

Ryan fumbled for the phone, listened for a moment or two, then sat bolt upright, got out of bed, and began dressing.

"What's wrong?" I asked, even as I left the cozy warmth of our bed and started looking for jeans and a heavy sweatshirt to ward off the early morning chill.

"The kids spotted a bear."

"A bear! Did it get in their tent? Are they okay?"

"They're fine. Amá's the one in a dither."

"Is it still around?"

"No, someone chased it back into the woods. Are you ready?"

"Sure." What I wasn't sure of was why we were needed so urgently, but Ryan's gruff manner seemed to discourage any more questions.

I popped a breath mint, then combed my hair on the way downstairs. Alana and Beto emerged from their room at the same time—all of us looking a little frazzled. We saved five whole minutes by going to the RV park in the van instead of walking.

We'd barely parked by the entrance when the boys came running to meet us, shouting and talking at once. Oblivious to the cold, they were wearing Levi cutoffs, t-shirts, no socks, and those clunky athletic shoes that make their feet look enormous, with untied shoelaces flopping as they ran. They must have dressed as hurriedly as we had.

Apá wasn't far behind them, wearing gray sweats and tennies.

"A bear! A bear!" Carlos said, his eyes wide with excitement, as he opened Alana's door.

"Right by our tent!" Omar added, taking my hand as he helped me out of the van and began to hurry us toward the campsite.

Apá held up one hand. "Hold on a minute."

"We need to talk," Beto said.

The men exchanged knowing looks that seemed to exclude Alana and me. I pretended not to notice. No way was I going to be relegated to join "the womenfolk" before finding out what was happening here.

I put my arm around Omar and held him close for warmth. "Aren't you cold?"

Alana had already rummaged in the van for a couple of extra blankets, which she handed the boys, who were standing on first one foot and then the other. They quickly wrapped the blankets around themselves, poncho-fashion.

Unsmiling, Beto cleared his throat. "Did you boys have any food in your tent? Anything that would have attracted the bear?"

"No, Dad. We followed all the rules."

Rules? Suddenly it clicked. "You knew there might be bears around here?"

"You knew?" Alana echoed, her temper rising.

"Now, Corazón," Beto soothed, putting his arm around her. "Listen a minute. This is northern New Mexico. It's bear country."

Alana looked at Ryan and me accusingly. "You never said anything about bears when you told us about this—this utopia."

I saw the boys' faces fall, their earlier enthusiasm ebbing away.

"Alana," I said gently, indicating the boys with a nod of my head. "Let's hear what they have to say."

When she saw their crestfallen expressions, she took a deep breath and mumbled, "I'm listening."

Ryan stepped in. "It's rare for bears to come into town, but it does happen once in a while. So people are warned when they camp here, just to be on the safe side. After all, we're right at the edge of the woods."

"You should have told us."

"And what would you have done? Kept the boys from camping out?"

"You could have given us the benefit of the doubt."

"You're right. We were just afraid you'd worry."

Alana smiled wryly. "You're right too."

"Lots of people sleep in tents here, Mom," Carlos ventured to say. "They wouldn't let people do that if it wasn't safe. They explain all the rules."

We were still standing near the van, and I was beginning to wish for a cup of coffee. But no one made a move to head for the campsite. Then I realized that Apá had probably wanted a chance to talk this over with Ryan, Beto, and the boys before facing Amá again. I could only imagine her reaction.

"So tell me what happened," Alana addressed the boys.

"Don't worry, Mom, it didn't even come in our tent. Digger started growling, and me 'n' Omar heard somethin' outside."

"We heard this crashing noise," Omar put in. "And we got kinda scared."

"So we were gonna get out and run real fast to the motorhome."

"But when we looked out, we saw this big black bear pushing some stuff around in somebody's fire-ring. So we just stayed where we were."

"By then," Apá said, "there was enough commotion that everyone in our end of the park was awake."

"Dr. Johnson said bears don't really like people, and it ran away," Omar said.

Ryan nodded thoughtfully. "It sounds like someone else might have been careless. Left food at their campfire."

"Dr. Johnson told us people think bears are cute and they try to treat them like little teddy bears," Omar said somberly. "But that's dangerous for people and bears both."

Carlos looked close to tears. "If it keeps coming back, the Game people might have to kill it."

"Dr. Johnson said 'a fed bear is a dead bear.'"

Alana looked teary-eyed herself as she hugged the blanket-clad kids. "I'm proud of you both. You listened, and you did everything right. And won't you have an adventure to tell your friends back home!"

Carlos and Omar brightened immediately.

Beto's eyes twinkled. "Now let's go down and explain to Amá."

* * *

While the others were reassuring Amá that everything was under control, I looked around the boys' tent, curious to see just what might have lured the bears in the first place. With a stick, I poked through remains of the ashes in their fire-ring and that of their closest neighbors.

The neighbors, two bikers dressed in cut-offs and t-shirts, came outside their tent to give me their version of what had happened. At the campsite next to theirs, a family was cooking breakfast over a Coleman stove. Beyond that, a few other tents were set up, some with motorcycles parked outside, but no one paid any attention to us—the bear episode apparently over and forgotten. Maybe Ryan was right. Bears in New Mexico? Ho hum.

Fortunately, the "next-door" bikers were in a talkative mood. "I'm probably the one who scared the bear off," one of them said. "When I realized it was out there, I started making a racket myself, yelling and banging on our cast-iron skillet."

"It was our fire-ring the bear was rifling through," the second one said. "We couldn't figure out why. We knew we hadn't left any food around. But come over here." He led me to the edge of the woods, just a few yards beyond their tent-sites. "Part of a chewed-up donut. Now where did that come from?"

"Did you find any scraps...anyplace else?" I asked.

"Yeah. In our fire-ring. There was another crumb or two between that and the woods. Not really enough to call a trail." He scratched his head. "We don't know what to make of it. We thought it was the kids. The fire-ring is between our two tents."

I must have bristled, because he touched my arm gently. "I don't mean anything personal by it. Kids are kids."

I unbristled. "I know. And that would be a logical conclusion, except that these boys know the bears could be put down for being a nuisance. And believe me, they love animals too much to let that happen."

The biker grinned. "I do believe you. I've seen these kids with their pets." He shrugged. "We'll just have to clean up

all the crumbs, I guess, and hope the goblin or whoever
doesn't come around anymore."

Or whoever. I shivered. Who, and when, would someone
go the trouble to leave bait by the boys' tent? In a fire-ring
that could easily have been mistaken for theirs?

Chapter 31

Before leaving the RV park, we reminded the kids once again to be extra careful, and Alana gave them her cell phone to keep with them at all times. To their chagrin, and my relief, they were told they'd have to sleep in the RV for the few remaining days of their vacation.

Ryan, Alana, Beto, and I went back to the Parlor Car just in time for Wendy's tasty eggs Benedict and fruit salad. Over breakfast, we told the Johnsons about the boys' bear encounter and thanked Bonsall for whatever he'd said that had made such an impression on them.

After breakfast, I turned my attention to Luis Tovar. I began having second thoughts about seeing him. What exactly would I say? Everything I went over in my mind sounded petty and "tattle-tale-ish."

"Vanessa's annoying. Make her stop."

But Wendy's advice rang in my ears: "It couldn't hurt to try."

There was no municipal police force in Chama, so either the state police or the sheriff down in Tierra Amarilla, fifteen miles away, handled whatever problems arose. Although "T.A." was the county seat of one of the largest counties in New Mexico, the town itself was quite small. Moreover, it was practically deserted. Down a narrow two-lane road about a mile from the main highway, the courthouse, sheriff's office, elementary school, and a couple of other civic buildings stood in stark contrast to their dismal surroundings. Most of the houses along the way were either boarded up or in shambles.

I called Deputy Tovar, glad that he lived in Chama. He wasn't home, and I was told he didn't have office hours—or even an office in town—but I could probably find him at The Village Bean.

I walked over to the café, but didn't see anyone who matched the description Wendy had given me. Next, I looked on the patio, which was shaded and somewhat secluded. I would have recognized Deputy Tovar even if he hadn't been in uniform. Besides being the tallest and heftiest person there, he had salt-and-pepper hair, thick eyebrows, and piercing blue eyes. He was somewhat older than I'd pictured—probably somewhere in his fifties.

Looking sharp in his neatly pressed brown and tan uniform, he was having coffee with a paunchy man dressed in cowboy attire.

"Excuse me," I said, then introduced myself. I decided against handing him my card, since I wanted to keep this conversation informal. I was afraid seeing "Attorney at Law" printed beside my name might put him off—especially if he didn't cotton to "big-city" lawyers.

"Could I have a few minutes of your time whenever it's convenient?"

"Interesting you should show up," he said as he studied my face. "I was going to give you a call."

"Really?" *Whatever for*, I wondered.

Deputy Tovar rose and pulled out a chair for me. After I sat down, he gave a brief nod to the other man at his table.

The man got up slowly and hitched his jeans over his potbelly. "Well, Luis, I better be on my way," he drawled. He tipped his hat to me and sauntered off.

"Coffee?" Deputy Tovar asked me.

"No thanks."

"Well, now, Ms. Salazar. Why don't you tell me what's on your mind?"

"Well, um, something's come up, and I'm hoping you can help me out."

He took a sip of coffee and waited for me to quit beating around the bush.

The only other people on the patio were a family of five, sitting far enough away that I supposed this was as private a place as any.

I took a deep breath and plunged in. "I was told that sometimes if you see people about to get in trouble, you can give them a 'Dutch-Uncle' talk and get them turned around."

He smiled. "Sometimes."

"I'm sure you know Vanessa Mondragón."

He raised bushy eyebrows and appraised me disapprovingly. "I do."

His stare made me uncomfortable—as if I'd said the wrong thing. And I hadn't even begun my spiel.

"I know this sounds odd," I said, "but Vanessa has been following me around. On top of that, she told me she intends to keep following me. I thought maybe you could—you know—ask her to quit."

"Is that all?"

"Well...yes. I think she'd listen to you, and that would be the end of it."

He continued staring at me, making circles on the table with his coffee cup. I decided I'd said all I meant to say—which sounded a little feeble now that it was out in the open. I also figured it was *his* turn, so I smiled politely and stared back.

When he had no comment, I decided to end the staring contest and break the silence. "You said you were going to call me about something?"

"That's right. Alicia Mondragón phoned me last night. She said you were harassing Vanessa, and she thought maybe I could—'you know—ask you to quit.'"

My mouth dropped open, and I felt my face grow hot.

"Well, I can promise you," I said tartly, "I'll stay as far away from Vanessa as possible. I just hope she'll do the same for me."

I picked up my purse and started to leave.

"Just a minute, Ms. Salazar. Please sit down."

I understood then how this man could intimidate would-be delinquents. His voice demanded obedience. I sat.

"There's more," he said.

"Yes?"

"Can you tell me how you come to know Rita Méndez?"

Here we go again. "There's not much to tell. I ran into her at the beauty shop and discovered she was related to someone I knew back home. I've seen her a couple of times since then. That's about it."

"That's not the way I heard it."

"I see. What have you heard?" I asked as pleasantly as I could.

"Among other things, that you and Ms. Méndez are thick as thieves, and together you've been hounding Vanessa."

This was too much. "That's the silliest thing I ever heard. I hardly know Ms. Méndez. And I certainly have more entertaining things to do with my life than spend time with Vanessa."

He nailed me with those steely eyes of his. "Now there's no need to get sarcastic."

And no need to get Deputy Tovar's back up, Sharon. Remember, you're the stranger here, while Vanessa's the fine upstanding citizen. So swallow it.

"I'm sorry. I'm just baffled."

He leaned back, and his stare seemed a trifle less hostile. The family who'd shared the patio with us had left; the only sounds that reached us now were the low murmur and occasional laughter of people passing by.

Finally Deputy Tovar said, "Pretty coincidental you showed up when you did."

"In what way?"

"Ms. Méndez didn't hire you?"

"To do what?"

He shifted in his chair and looked away from me for a change. "You tell me."

Be nice, Sharon, be nice. "I don't know what to say. I don't work for Rita Méndez. I'm here on vacation."

Why did this conversation sound familiar? I suddenly remembered it was Vanessa who had first accused me of working for Rita, Vanessa who seemed to think I was "hounding" her.

"Are you sure it was Alicia who called you, and not Vanessa?" I asked.

He glared at me again. "I think I know who I'm talking to, Ms. Salazar."

Ooops.

"She told me you'd have an answer for everything," he continued. "Seems that way."

"If that were true, I wouldn't be here." I smiled to soften my remark and got ready to leave again. "Anyway, thanks for your time."

He didn't smile back. "Just keep in mind, I keep a close watch on what goes on around here. Not much gets by me."

I deliberately misinterpreted his remark and thanked him again. "That's all I wanted to hear!"

Chapter 32

I'd barely begun walking away from the table when I saw Vanessa's green Aztek crawl down the street. I turned and raised an eyebrow at Deputy Tovar. He shrugged, then looked away.

I carried on an imaginary conversation with him:

"Did you see that?" I'd say.

"See what?" he'd say.

"I told you she was following me!"

"You've got to be kidding. This is the main drag. Are *all* these people following you?"

Back to reality. And of course, what with tourist-traffic, everyone drove slowly along this short stretch of Terrace Avenue.

When I reached the sidewalk, I watched the Aztek inch as far as Sixth Street, then make a U-turn.

I went back and seated myself across from Deputy Tovar. "Let's count the number of times Vanessa drives by here."

"You think this has something to do with you?"

No need to get sarcastic, Deputy Tovar.

"I'm just going by what she said," I answered sweetly. "Either she's seen me here, or she thinks I'm at the B&B, two blocks down. That's where my car's parked."

He gave me a look that said he thought I was certifiable. Then I saw a flicker in his eyes that told me he'd noticed Vanessa on her return trip.

"Well, I can't sit here all day and read people's minds," he said as he donned his dark glasses and got up to leave. "I suggest you find something else to occupy your time."

I was embarrassed and a little angry. But maybe he had a point. Maybe I'd occupy my time scarfing down sweets. I decided to exit though the café and buy some macadamia nut cookies to soothe my injured feelings.

Looking out the window, I saw Vanessa's Aztek creep past Deputy Tovar, who had crossed the street and was talking to the man I'd seen him with earlier. He didn't appear to notice her—apparently didn't see anything odd about the way Vanessa was occupying *her* time.

I paid for my cookies, waited till Vanessa had driven in the opposite direction once again, and headed home.

* * *

"How'd it go?" Ryan asked when I got back. He was relaxing on the patio, enjoying another cup of coffee.

"It didn't go. Probably my own fault."

"Tell me."

"Oh, people don't like outsiders waltzing in and telling them how to run things, so I tried to minimize the situation with Vanessa, and it probably sounded to him like a little-girl cat-fight or something."

I sat down next to Ryan and told him about my conversation with Deputy Tovar.

"Well, look at it this way—you succeeded in the minimizing thing," Ryan said, giving my hand an affectionate squeeze. "C'mon, honey, don't look so dejected. You did the best you could."

I smiled at him. "I do have another idea."

"Uh-oh. That didn't take long."

"I just needed you to remind me I was successful at something."

I reached in my purse for my cell phone. "Vanessa's phone number should still be listed in the log."

"Which means she probably has our phone number too."

"Too late to worry about that. Anyway, I'm giving her a call."

"I thought she was busy patrolling the B&B."

"She's got to go home sometime—if only to go to the bathroom." I scrolled through the "Dialed Calls" menu. "Here's it is. Twice. Hmm. Not a Chama prefix, so I hope that means it's a cell phone."

"Let's hope she has it with her."

I highlighted the number, then hit the "SEND" button. After several rings, she finally answered.

"What!" she barked.

"Vanessa, it's Sharon. I thought I'd let you in on my plans for the day. That way you won't have to waste so much gas driving in circles."

"I don't know what you're talking about."

"Whatever. Here's the thing. I'm going down to T.A. this afternoon. I'm going straight to the sheriff's office. I'll drive slowly so we can get there at the same time. I'll call ahead so they'll be expecting us, okay?"

"Bitch!" she yelled, then clicked off.

* * *

Ryan and I walked over to the RV park, where we found the grownups at a picnic table playing a lively game of Mexican Train. Spot was lying at one end of the table, keeping an eye on the dominoes and occasionally rearranging them.

Digger was watching Carlos and Omar, who were sitting in camp chairs and whittling industriously on two long narrow aspen branches.

"What are you making?" Ryan asked as he sat down next to them.

Carlos looked up, his eyes sparkling. "Mr. Marvin showed us how to make hiking sticks. We've already cut off the small branches, and when these are smooth, we'll go over there and he'll help us paint them."

"Who's Mr. Marvin?"

"He's parked a little ways from here. That's who Abuelo plays music with. Him and a bunch of other people."

"You should see all the stuff Mr. Marvin makes," Omar added, a note of awe in his voice. "He's carved little trains that look real, and he even makes some kind of a musical instrument."

Apá nodded. "Dulcimers. Beautiful craftsmanship!"

Carlos grinned. "He thought we weren't quite ready for that yet, so we're starting with sticks."

Alana laughed. "I can't believe I was worried you kids might not have enough to keep you busy."

When it was time for lunch, the games and hiking sticks were put aside; Alana and I spread out the tablecloths; and Amá brought out bread, sandwich fixin's, and lemonade. I added my cookies to the pool.

"Eating outside like this really gives me an appetite," Amá remarked.

"I always have an appetite," Tía Marta said ruefully. "I hate to step on the scales when we get back."

"Speaking of getting back," Apá said, "it's almost that time."

"I know." Alana poured another round of lemonade. "I wish we could stay longer. At the same time, I'll be glad to get home again."

"*Yo también*. That's exactly how I feel," Beto said.

What did I feel? A wave of homesickness swept over me. I wondered how much it had to do with the thought of greener grass—the crazy notion that life was problem-free somewhere else.

I was disappointed that the main problem I'd faced here was unresolved. I didn't seem any closer to finding out Mr. Álvarez's fate than when I'd arrived. Part of me said it wasn't my responsibility anyway. Another part reminded me that I genuinely liked him and cared what happened to him. Seeing Rafael this afternoon would be my last-ditch effort at getting to the bottom of the "Rita-Bernice" mystery.

Chapter 33

With so much going on, it was easy for Tía Dippy and me to slip away shortly after lunch. Alana had suggested we take her van so that Vanessa could sit and stare at our immobile Honda all day if she wanted to. Ryan offered to go with us, but Omar and Carlos had begged him to do some woodcarving with them after lunch. I could tell he thought spending time with them would be more fun than hobnobbing with relatives of Rita and Bernice.

"Don't worry about us," I told him. "If my phone call didn't discourage Vanessa, I really will drive straight to the sheriff's office."

"What can they do?"

"I don't know, but I doubt if she'd hang around to find out. The more I think about it, I'm sure she conned Deputy Tovar into thinking he was talking to Alicia. Alicia's a nice person, and he might have wanted to do her a favor by 'warning' me. Vanessa herself probably doesn't have much clout."

"Maybe I'll follow you as far as the turnoff to T.A. If we haven't seen Vanessa or her boyfriend by then, there shouldn't be any trouble the rest of the way."

"Good idea!"

Talking tough with Vanessa over the phone was one thing; the thought of driving down that desolate road from the main highway into T.A. gave me chills.

* * *

"I think we're in the Painted Desert," Tía Dippy said in wonder.

"It sure looks that way!"

After an uneventful drive as far as the T.A. turnoff, Ryan had gone back to Chama, leaving Tía and me to continue on to Gallina. We had turned onto Highway 96 at the Abiquiú Dam, and discovered a panorama of rugged colorful cliffs north of us that stretched for miles. There was hardly any traffic, so I could drive at a leisurely pace and enjoy the surroundings.

Tía Dippy craned her neck to get a better view of the landscape. "Even if we weren't going to see Rafael, this trip would be worth it just for the scenery."

I was glad for her good spirits and optimism. It helped dispel the anxiety that was building in me. I hoped the visit with Rafael wouldn't dredge up the same painful memories as our visit with Kiko. At the same time, wasn't that exactly what would happen if I wanted to learn anything about Rita and her connection to Bernice?

* * *

Rafael Méndez greeted us with a warm smile and led us into the living room, where Tía and I sat on a couch while he sat in an overstuffed armchair facing us. The couch must have been designed for very tall people, and we had to sit near the edge so our feet would reach the floor. I pretended I was sitting on a picnic bench so it wouldn't bother me not to be able to lean back.

Rafael was one of the handsomest men I'd ever seen. His facial features were perfectly proportioned, his clear brown eyes framed by thick lashes. Like Kiko, he was well-built, and I suspected he spent many hours at the gym. The only hint that he was fifty-something were the small lines that appeared around his mouth and eyes. His hair showed very little gray.

Tía Dippy readjusted her red wig and smoothed her purple flowered skirt over her lilac stockings. I caught myself combing my fingers through my short curls and wishing I could touch up my lipstick.

"I'd offer you a more comfortable place to sit," Rafael apologized, speaking in a languid Texas drawl. "But this is as good as it gets. I drove up here day before yesterday, and I'm just renting for a couple of weeks. So it's pretty spartan."

One thing he and Rita had in common: They didn't believe in sprucing up a place they were merely renting. Of course, since Rafael already knew he'd stay only a short time, that made sense.

I had noticed that most of the houses in the little villages we'd passed—as well as here in Gallina—were modest homes built on large lots, with plenty of land between themselves and their neighbors. When we'd gone through Coyote, I'd wondered which road led to the Méndez ranch.

"Something to drink?" Rafael asked. "Cranberry juice? Mango? Carrot? I'm afraid that's all I have."

Tía Dippy opted for cranberry, so I went for the mango.

"Kiko said you had some questions about Rita," he said after he'd handed us our drinks and sat down again. "So do I. Maybe we can help each other."

Suddenly I felt uncomfortable bringing up my doubts about Rita's identity. The imaginary conversation I'd practiced with an imaginary Rafael seemed to evaporate. He might not appreciate my linking his sister to Bernice. He'd surely be offended by my considering her a golddigger.

175

When all else fails, procrastinate. I took a long sip of my fruit juice, then studied the liquid in the glass as if I were holding a crystal ball.

I finally quit stalling. "I don't know how to put this, but I think the person who calls herself Rita might be someone else."

To my surprise, he nodded. "I've wondered about that myself. I got a phone call from Kent Vigil. He used to be principal at the high school here in Gallina. Someone phoned him asking questions about Rita. He got to thinking about it and thought I ought to know."

Someone: Dan Oliver. Checking for Alicia. She had told me the principal sent her a photocopy of Rita's yearbook picture.

"How did Mr. Vigil know to call you?"

"We go back a long way. Where to start. Let's see.... My sister Connie was reluctant to let Rita go to public school. You know about the home-schooling?"

"Yes, both Rita and Kiko mentioned it."

"Kent Vigil was very diplomatic, and between the two of us, we managed to get Connie to come around. Working together, Kent and I got to be friends, and we've kept in touch off and on over the years."

"Was it hard for Rita to fit in? I mean, I imagine most of the kids already knew each other."

"Yes and no. I think it took some 'getting acquainted' for everyone in a way. You see, the high school in Gallina serves a number of little nearby towns, and another thing Kent did was encourage the kids to mingle. Rita had a different kind of problem...."

"Oh?"

"She didn't know how to mingle. She and Sylvia didn't have many social skills. In fact, I'm not sure poor little

Sylvia could have made it at all, even if Connie had let her. She was rather unattractive—seemed very repressed."

"And Rita?"

"She was shy. She finally managed to adjust, but it took awhile. Again, I think Kent had a lot to do with smoothing the way."

"She said she earned a scholarship to St. Victoria's."

"More of an honorary thing. Not much money in it. But I think it gave her some much-needed confidence."

"Kiko told us about all the changes that took place after Rita graduated."

Rafael raised an eyebrow. "All the changes?"

I felt flustered. As if Rafael had seen some obscure meaning in a simple remark. I took another sip of juice and set my glass on the end table beside me.

"All the people moving." Tía Dippy, who had listened intently but quietly up till now, stepped in. "You, Rita, Connie and her familia. Your mother selling the ranch."

Rafael closed his eyes a moment, then opened them and smiled. "Our family is pretty far-flung, as they say. Somehow I came to be sort of a go-between—the one who tries to keep everyone connected."

"Do you and Rita stay in touch?"

"For a long time we did. We'd call each other every few weeks. And whenever we'd come back home to see Ma, we'd try to come at the same time." He took a deep breath. "Things changed after Ma got sick. Rita had been doing private-duty nursing, but she quit in order to come take care of her. When I look back on it, I realize the rest of us felt Ma was in good hands—which she was—but we didn't see what a toll it was taking on Rita."

Tía Dippy nodded. "It can be exhausting."

Rafael looked out the window, his gaze fixed on something in the distance. "Poor Rita. Somehow she got it into her head that she was going to get Alzheimer's too. I think it was just the added stress that made her get so irrational. She got almost compulsive about Ma's medication—afraid she'd either give her something twice, or forget to give it to her at all."

"That must have been scary," I said. "Is that when Rita realized she needed help too?"

"That's the scary part. Rita wouldn't admit she needed help."

"How long did this go on?"

Rafael rolled his shoulders, as if trying to roll off a heavy burden. "Rita'd been taking care of Ma for a couple of years, and I'd go out to visit as often as I could. But I didn't see things getting really bad till the last month or two. That's when I called the others and said we needed to make some other arrangements. This was about five years ago."

"What did Rita do then?"

"Moved down to Española so she could be near Ma. That's where the nursing home was. A really nice one too. We'd thought we had unburdened Rita, but she was resentful instead. I guess Kiko told you how the family all split apart?"

"Yes."

"Rita was the only one Ma'd respond to, so— unfortunately—after a while, everyone quit coming to see her. I know that sounds cold, but Ma would scream at us to get out, and we felt we were upsetting them both rather than helping."

"So when was the last time you saw Rita?"

Rafael was quiet several moments. "At Ma's funeral."

Chapter 34

Tía Dippy and I were quiet too.

"It's okay to talk about," Rafael said softly, seeing our distress.

"I have to ask, did Bernice come to the funeral?" I said.

"Bernice? Why would she be there? God, that would really have put Connie in a tailspin!"

"You must think I'm rude asking so many questions."

"Not at all. I think we're both trying to get some answers. But Bernice...that came out of left field."

"I'm afraid I've been asking more than my share."

A glint of humor showed in Rafael's eyes. "Maybe we're both afraid to come right out and say what's bothering us."

I smiled. "I think you've nailed it. Okay, if you'll bear with me for a few more questions, I'll try to explain."

"I'm all ears."

"Was Sylvia there?"

"Yes."

"Had she gotten any prettier? Was she married?"

Rafael laughed. "I didn't think about it at the time—about the way she looked. But I'd say yes, she's improved. She's married, has three kids. They go to a public school. So I'd say she's broken the leash."

Tía Dippy and I exchanged glances. *There goes our look-alike theory.*

"When was the last time you saw Bernice?" I asked in a small voice.

"Easter."

The grim look on his face told me he didn't have to explain which Easter.

"So she was just a little girl," I said.

"Yeah."

"Did you think she looked like Rita?"

He looked at me intently. "On the surface, yes. Very much."

"Did you ever get them mixed up?"

"Once." He grimaced. "They were together only a couple of times while I was still at home. Poor sweet Perlita. She and Hector tried so hard to make it work. They came up to visit now and then. Came up for my high-school graduation. Bernice and Rita were about three years old. Both pretty little girls." He paused, seeming to gather his thoughts. "My grandmother thought it was cute they looked so much alike, so she bought them matching pink dresses. Then she fixed their hair the same—with those long curly curls—corkscrew curls I think they're called. Kinda old-fashioned now."

"Was that when you got them confused?"

"Yeah. I felt bad about it too. I scolded Rita for something Bernice had done. Some kid thing. Playing with the scissors when she'd been told not to—something like that. Rita started crying, and I figured it out."

"Do you think you could still mistake them now that they're adults?"

"No. Absolutely not. Maybe for a minute or two, but not if I was around them any length of time."

"One last thing. Do you know where Bernice is now?"

That intent look again. "Monterrey, Mexico, last I heard. Same as Flavio."

My eyes widened. *Wasn't this the brother who spent so much time in prison?* "I thought Flavio—I thought nobody knew exactly where he was."

"Rita knew. I don't know how. But she thought he should know when Ma died. When she contacted him, Bernice was there. Now you know as much as I do."

"That's all Rita told you?"

"That's all. She didn't even tell Perlita."

"I wonder why. Wouldn't it ease Perlita's mind to know her daughter is safe?"

Rafael shrugged. "Not especially. I don't think it would give her any comfort to know Bernice was hanging out with Flavio. Don't get me wrong. I used to look up to him when we were kids—maybe because he was a few years older. Even after we grew up, I had this kinda unrealistic hope that he'd turn his life around. But, well, anyway, he and Bernice are a bad mix. God only knows what schemes they've cooked up."

I heartily agreed with him, but Tía Dippy frowned at me, so I cleared my throat and answered noncommittally, "I see."

"Rafaelito," she said, patting her red wig demurely. "Are you planning to come see Rita?"

"Yes, I've just been trying to decide how to go about it. We didn't part on very good terms. But Kent seems to feel she's in some kind of trouble. *Causing* some kind of trouble, to be exact."

"But that's not like her, verdad?"

"No. It's not. But maybe she really did have some kind of mental problem that I didn't take seriously."

"Your family has gone through so much," I said. "I feel bad stirring up unhappy memories for you and Kiko."

"Don't apologize. We need to find answers. And you're very understanding about the rift in our family."

"Well, my own family is pretty—disconnected. My birth family, that is. So it's easy to sympathize."

"You're adopted?"

"No, but I might as well have been. My parents were divorced—a few times—and my best friend's family more-or-less took me in and made me one of their own. Then when I got married, I became part of another wonderful family."

Tía Dippy put her hand in mine. "Wonderful, sí. And sometimes a little loca."

I smiled, glad she'd said something to keep me from babbling on and on or getting weepy.

Rafael chuckled. "I can see that. The wonderful part anyway."

Tía Dippy blushed and smoothed her skirt again.

Rafael hid a grin, and I wondered if he was used to women—and men—finding him attractive. He had a magnetism that went beyond his good looks, but I didn't see any trace of conceit.

"You were going to explain? About your questions?" he asked me.

How could I phrase this without insulting his family? "Well, we both—you and I—thought someone might be impersonating Rita."

"It occurred to me. I just can't figure out why—or who. If it's true, it must be someone she met at the nursing home. Maybe someone who thinks she inherited some money."

"I hadn't even thought of that! I'm afraid my thoughts were closer to home. The thing is, I used to know Bernice, even though I haven't seen her in years. When I met Rita, the resemblance struck me, so...."

He stood up abruptly. "Hold on." He took a few moments to process what I was saying. "Okay. Now I follow you. I didn't see what you were getting at before. But there's more to it, isn't there."

I spread out my hands. "It's hard to explain. Even to myself. Whoever she is, she's taken up with an elderly man, a good friend of a good friend. If it's Rita, it could be innocent. If it's Bernice, I have my doubts."

I had some doubts about Rita too, though not as strong.

"I was hoping maybe if I knew more about Rita—or Bernice—I'd have a better idea one way or another," I said.

Rafael lowered himself slowly to the chair again. "You're very tactful. I have a feeling it's more serious than that. To tell you the truth, what you've told me is very disturbing. There are some things I should probably explain too."

I hoped my curiosity wasn't sprawled across my face like a flashing light. But I found that Rafael was just as good a procrastinator as I was.

His restlessness returned. He stood and gestured toward our glasses. "Something else to drink?"

Tía Dippy nodded and handed him her empty glass. "Just a little."

I smiled and declined.

He puttered around the kitchen for a few minutes and came out with refills.

"I've decided to go up to Chama early tomorrow morning," he said as he handed Tía Dippy another glass of cranberry juice. "I need to see Rita for myself before I know what to do next. I'd like to surprise her. Do you have any ideas?"

"Let's see. She spends most of her time with Mr. Álvarez." I paused. "She drives a silver Jaguar. You could see whether it's parked in front of her house or his—or somewhere else—and catch her there. You have her address?"

"Kent gave it to me."

"Why don't you call us after you've met her. If she's really Rita, maybe we can all get together for lunch—if that seems like a good idea."

"I'd like that."

We exchanged cell-phone numbers, and I gave him Mr. Álvarez's address as well. Then Tía Dippy and I got ready to leave. Evidently Rafael wasn't ready yet to share the things he "should probably explain." Maybe after tomorrow they wouldn't need explaining. Or maybe they would.

Chapter 35

I dropped Tía Dippy off at the RV park, telling her I'd join the family later. I returned to the B&B, glad to find no one else there. I parked myself in the library and set up my laptop. Too many bits of information were swirling around in my head, and I wanted to set them down on paper—or at least see them on the laptop screen.

Using dates Jimmy Romero had given me, plus things I'd gathered from the Méndez brothers and Andy Estrada, I pieced together a timeline of sorts to see if I could connect any dots.

Méndez Chronology

7 years ago	Juana Méndez became ill.
	Rita returned to Coyote to care for her.
5 years ago	Juana entered a nursing home.
	Rita moved to Española to be near her.
	(Rita began having mental problems?)
	Family became alienated.
3-1/2 years ago	Bernice escaped to Mexico.
3-1/4 years ago	Bernice might have been in Laredo (?)
3 years ago	Bernice might have been in Arizona (?)

2-1/2 years ago   Juana died.
                           Rafael saw Rita at Juana's funeral
                           and hasn't seen her since.
                           Bernice was back in Mexico (?)

3 months ago   Rita came to Chama.

I read what I'd typed and mulled it over. I had only approximate times for most of these happenings. I wasn't even sure how reliable the "Bernice-sightings" were. If Bernice did take a chance on coming back to the States, she must have realized it wasn't such a good idea to resurface in Laredo—so close to home. Arizona would certainly be safer.

I began typing again:

One thing stands out—no one in the Méndez family has seen Rita for the past two-and-a-half years. Bernice hasn't been seen by the family in several years either—except supposedly by Flavio, the wild card. Where does he fit in? If at all.

I backed up my notes and turned off the computer. But my mind was still at work. Could Rita and Bernice have gotten together during the time no one else had seen either of them? The thought opened all kinds of unsettling possibilities.

* * *

Whatever else went on in our lives, we could be counted on to enjoy three squares a day—plus in-between snacks as deemed "necessary." By the time I returned to the RV park, someone had picked up pizza from Paisano's, and everyone had gathered at the picnic tables by the Winnebago.

Ryan and I had gotten in the habit of taking a short stroll either before or after supper; but this evening, he suggested I find out what was going on with my godson instead.

"We spent most of the afternoon whittling away at various things—even tried carving out some replicas of the chipmunks," Ryan told me. "Then the kids went into town for ice cream. When they came back—I don't know—they seemed kinda subdued."

"I noticed they were quieter than usual. But this day started pretty early. We woke up with the bears, remember? Maybe they're just tired."

"Could be. But you know Alana's antenna. She pried a little bit, but then she backed off."

"She thinks I have better prying skills?"

He laughed. "She just thought you might have a different approach."

* * *

After supper, Carlos and Omar went down to the riverbank to skip rocks across the stream. I caught up with them and tried my hand at rock-skipping.

"Can I talk to you a minute?" I asked after sinking a few pebbles.

The boys gave each other an "uh-oh" look, which I pretended not to see.

"Is something bothering you guys?"

"Tell her," Omar whispered.

"Let's sit down," I suggested and started walking upstream till I found a grassy place to sit. The boys followed and sat cross-legged, facing me.

We were quiet awhile, Carlos weaving a piece of grass between his fingers. Finally he said, "You know that lady that no one but me thinks is La Fea?"

I nodded, somewhat dismayed to realize he'd held on to that notion.

"I saw her again."

"Where was this?"

"Down at the fudge place. Me 'n' Omar went there to get some ice cream." He stared at the ground. "Are you gonna tell me it wasn't really her?" His tone was polite, but I sensed his frustration.

"No. The truth is, I don't know. I change my mind about her on a daily basis."

Carlos looked up at me, hope and relief in his expression. "My mom says it's some other lady."

"Did you tell her about today?

"No. I knew what she'd say."

"Carlitos, you have to understand, your mom has lots of reasons for thinking it's someone else. There are some personality traits we'd expect to see in Bernice that just aren't there. And some traits that do fit Rita from what we've learned."

"You mean there really are two people?"

"Oh, yes, honey. I feel bad if you thought we were just inventing Bernice's aunt. She really exists, and they really do look alike, and...Rita really is kinda strange."

"Is she mean too?"

"I'm not sure about that part."

"The lady we saw had mean eyes," Omar put in. "And Ted didn't like her either."

Ted Rembetsy, who owned the little fudge factory/ice-cream shop, always had a friendly greeting for everyone. It was hard to imagine him disliking someone.

"What made you think that?" I asked.

"You could just tell."

"He wasn't rude to her or anything," Carlos elaborated. "But when she started talking to us, it was like he could tell we didn't want her to."

"He goes, 'can I help you,' and she gives him a dirty look and goes, 'no'—"

"And then he starts talking to us while he was getting our cones—"

"He was talking about trains and stuff, and she couldn't talk because he was talking," Omar explained.

"After we got our ice cream, he came outside with us and kept talking."

"I guess she got tired of waiting for him to quit, so she left."

"Did Ted say anything about it afterwards?" I asked.

Carlos shook his head. "No. He just smiled at us and told us to be careful."

"Let me backtrack. You say she started talking to you? What about?"

"She asked if me 'n' Omar were twins."

"Hmm. Now that's something La Fea would know. But not Rita. Do you think she was just making conversation?"

"I think it was La Fea acting like she was that other lady."

"Did she say anything upsetting?"

"Nah," Carlos admitted grudgingly. "She was just kinda nosy."

"She asked if we lived in Chama," Omar said. "So we said yes. We told her we're twins and we live here."

I laughed. "I hope she didn't ask for directions anywhere."

Carlos gave a small grin. "Yeah. I guess."

"My mom said you should always tell the truth," Omar said. "Except when you don't trust people."

The lawyer in me could think of exceptions to the exception, but I was glad the boys had applied it here. If this person was Bernice—and even if she wasn't—prying information from the boys was way out of line. Not that she'd had much chance to pry, thanks to Ted's concern.

"You know something? If it really was Bernice pretending to be someone else, she wouldn't want to blow her act. She might have been just as uncomfortable about seeing you, so she was only asking the kinds of questions she thought would make you believe she was a stranger."

Carlos's grin widened. "I didn't think of that."

Something else I hoped he didn't think of: If it really was Bernice, she'd know he was lying. If she suspected he'd seen through her charade, she'd retaliate.

My stomach turned upside-down, as images of her viciousness invaded my mind. I stood up and brushed the grass off my jeans. "It's starting to get dark. And chilly. We need to get back." I was glad for the cool and the dusk. I knew my face would give me away again, and I also needed an excuse for shivering.

Chapter 36

The next day began calmly enough. No early phone calls.
No bears. The morning excitement was a lively game of
croquet at the RV park between the boys on one team and
Beto and Ryan on the other. Alana and I cheered them on
for a while, then joined the rest of the family for a second
cup of coffee.

By mid-morning, I began listening for Rafael's call. By
mid-afternoon, I began to worry. We'd finished lunch long
ago; the boys had walked their pets a couple of times and
were now caught up in their carving projects. The grownups
were chatting and/or playing Mexican Train. Outwardly, we
were a picture of serenity. Inwardly, my nervous system
must have resembled an electrical cord knotted beyond
recognition.

I tried to recall the exact words we'd exchanged with
Rafael before Tía Dippy and I started back home. I thought
we'd agreed to get together for lunch if Rita turned out to be
Rita. Since I hadn't heard, did that mean she was really
someone else? Bernice?

Or it could mean that they were so glad to see each
other, time got away from them—lunch with us forgotten.
Or it could mean—what?

By late afternoon, I was visibly jittery, willing the silent
cell phone to ring. Ryan took me aside and suggested I do
the calling, something I should have thought of myself.

Rafael's voicemail picked up after several rings. "Sorry I
missed your call. Please leave a message."

I clicked off, my mind racing.

"No answer?" Ryan asked.

I shook my head. "He probably turned it off—might have forgotten to turn it back on again."

Our number would show up on the caller ID, so I might as well have left a message, but for some obscure reason I didn't want to record my name or voice. And I didn't know how to express my fears to Ryan.

He wasn't fooled, of course. "Let's drive by Rita's, or Mr. Álvarez's, and see if Rafael's car is there. Do you know what he's driving?"

"A blue Neon, I think. One was parked in the driveway."

"A rental car maybe?"

"No. He said he'd driven up. Dallas is a long way, but he didn't seem to be in a hurry. I mean, he hadn't even made up his mind how he was going to approach Rita, and he planned to stay in Gallina a couple of weeks."

We cruised past Rita's place, but didn't see either Rita's car or Rafael's. We did notice Vanessa's green Aztek parked across the street. I suppose she'd abandoned spying on me and had gone back to tracking Rita. However, seeing our Honda, she apparently decided to tail us again. Fine with me. Right now, Vanessa was the least of my worries.

Next, we drove down Mr. Álvarez's street, where we saw Rita's car but not the Neon.

Ryan slowed down in front of his house. "Do you want to ask Rita if she's seen her brother?"

"No. I'd rather she didn't know there was any connection between us."

I had to hope that, wherever he was, Rafael had his cell phone with him and there was no way Rita could see our caller ID on it. I gave him another call; still no response.

"Shall I go around the block? Go by Alicia's?"

"I doubt that we'd see him there—unless he's found out something...."

Ryan turned onto the side street, then stopped at the corner of Alicia's street, Vanessa right behind us. "Do you see his car anywhere?"

I rolled down my window, then looked up and down both sides of the street. "I can't tell. Someone else's cars are blocking my view."

"Well, we'll just have to risk stirring up the hornet's nest."

We puttered down the street, noting that the maroon van was parked in the driveway of the home I thought to be Alicia's. On the porch was a black-and-white cat sunning himself. Max, apparently content in his new surroundings.

Vanessa's boyfriend was standing in front of his house, two doors down. She must have alerted him on her cell phone. He was wearing the same undershirt as best I could tell. Of course, one grease stain pretty much resembles another, so maybe this was a different dirty shirt.

He staggered to the middle of the street, forcing Ryan to swerve and slam on the brakes. Vanessa, of course, closed in behind us. Déjà vu.

Creep banged his fist down on the hood of the car, and to my dismay, Ryan got out.

"Are we supposed to pay you a toll for driving down your street?" Ryan asked.

"Who's you callin' a troll, *ese*?"

"Where'd you learn about trolls, *ese*?"

Creep scratched his greasy head.

"Look, we're not trying to make trouble," Ryan told him in Spanish. "Just let us by, and we'll get out of your way."

Nice touch. Acting as if we were the ones in the way.

Creep spat on the ground, missing Ryan's shoe by half an inch. "What, *pendejo*? I don't talk good enough for you? You chood talk English."

By now, Vanessa had shut off her engine, leaving the Aztek practically on our rear bumper, and joined Creep. I began to wonder if they really did own the street. They certainly didn't seem to expect anyone else to be using it.

Suddenly it occurred to me that Vanessa might have noticed Rafael's coming and going. I got out of the car and approached her, attempting to smile.

"Vanessa, did you happen to see a visitor at Rita's? Someone in a blue Neon?"

She glared at me. "What's it to you?"

Creep seemed to forget about his grudge-war with Ryan and took a few unsteady steps toward Vanessa and me. Surprisingly, his attitude seemed more curious than belligerent. "That blue *carro*? I seen it there."

"Really? When?"

"This mornin'. Early." A cunning look crossed his face. "I knew che'd be gettin' it on with someone else."

"That was her brother."

Vanessa rolled her eyes. "Yeah. Right."

"Look, Vanessa," I said. "We really are on the same side here, believe it or not. Her brother came up here to see— um—what she was up to. Now we can't find him, and we're worried."

About then another car ventured to borrow their street and made a timid beep as it pulled up behind the Aztek. Vanessa shouted a curse, Creep flipped it off, and Ryan suggested that we move out of the way and continue our talk somewhere else.

Creep lurched to the sidewalk while Vanessa and Ryan moved our respective cars out of the way. Then we gathered in front of Creep's house, Ryan and I positioning ourselves upwind of the other two.

"Tell me, ah—what is your name?" I asked Vanessa's boyfriend, making an effort to overcome my aversion.

"You don' need to know," he said in a conversational tone.

"Ho-kay." *Moving right along.* "I'd really appreciate your help with this. Can you tell me what time the man in the blue car came to Rita's and what time he left?"

He shrugged. "Maybe nine o'clock, he come there. I wait."

"You were waiting in front of Rita's?"

He shrugged again.

"It's a free country!" Vanessa shouted, her chin jutting out as if ready for combat.

"You're absolutely right," I said, although I hadn't any idea what she was talking about. It appeared that she and Creep must take turns in their espionage campaign. Once again, illogical as it seemed under the circumstances, I felt a wave of sympathy for Rita.

I addressed Vanessa's boyfriend again. "Did you happen to notice how long he was there?"

"Maybe twenty minutos, he leave. Maybe thirty. It don't take long," he added with a leer.

Disgust radiated from Ryan.

"Had enough?" he asked me, placing his hand on my shoulder.

I reached up and squeezed his hand. "Almost," I said softly. "One more minute."

"You're very observant," I flattered Creep. "Do you think something else could have happened? Maybe they had an argument. Maybe she told him not to come back again. Maybe he left mad instead of happy." *Leading the witness, Sharon.*

Creep's forehead contorted into a wrinkled frown—
something that could have passed for a thoughtful
expression in someone else.

"Maybe. He walk away fast, slam the door of the *carro*,
drive off."

"Was he driving fast too?"

"Jess. I follow him. Then I quit."

Vanessa's defenses were up again. "I don't see how this
can help. We don't know why he was there." She glowered
at her boyfriend, letting him know what she thought of his
original theory. "The guy came. He went. He left in a hurry
because he was going back to Texas. So *El Toro* here
couldn't chase him all over the country."

My eyes widened. "You knew he was from Texas?"

"Well, duh. The car had Texas license plates."

"I see. Well, thanks for your time. If I find out anything
myself, I'll let you know," I lied.

I didn't know what to think. Actually, Vanessa had
summed it up pretty neatly:

He came. He went.

But why didn't he call?

Chapter 37

"Ryan, did you notice something strange about Vanessa and her boyfriend?" I asked as we drove away.

"No, not at all," Ryan said, giving me an amused look. "Was there something strange about them?"

I poked him in the ribs. "Well—you know—they didn't seem very lovey-dovey."

"Nothing a little soap and water couldn't cure."

"Maybe that's all there is to it."

"You're right, though. I would have expected them to be a little more—what?—compatible, I guess."

I sighed. "I think El Creepo was telling the truth about seeing Rafael. But I still don't trust them. I think they have some agenda of their own."

Ryan pulled up at the B&B. "Now what, honey?"

"I'm at a loss. Could be Rafael simply thought his visit with Rita wasn't any of our business. But that wasn't the impression he gave."

"What about calling Kiko? Rafael might have gotten in touch with him."

"That's a thought. Before I call him though, I think I'll call his friend in Gallina. No point worrying Kiko if Rafael is simply sitting at home with his phone turned off."

I located Kent Vigil's number through Directory Assistance. He answered on the second ring. I figured I'd better get right to the point so he wouldn't think it was a sales call.

"Hello, Mr. Vigil. This is Sharon Salazar. I'm calling about a mutual friend—Rafael Méndez."

"Yes?"

I cleared my throat, hoping my voice didn't sound as nervous as I felt. "He was supposed to call me this morning, and I still haven't heard. I've left a couple of messages. I'm beginning to worry. It isn't like him not to return calls."

I crossed my fingers since I had no idea whether it was like him or not.

"Where are you?" Mr. Vigil sounded polite but cautious.

"I'm in Chama. My aunt and I visited Rafael yesterday. We knew their family back in Texas." *I'm not a stalker.*

"Well, I'm sure there's some logical explanation."

"I hope so. I'm sorry to bother you. I couldn't decide whether to call you first, or his brother. I guess it seemed more likely that Rafael came back to Gallina, and I hoped it wouldn't be too much trouble for you to check."

"Came back? From his brother's? I'm confused."

"I apologize. I'm feeling a little 'out of it' myself. He was coming up to Chama this morning to see Rita, and—"

"Rita!" A note of alarm crept into his voice.

"That's why I'm worried."

There were a few moments of silence, then, "Let me call you back."

"Please." I gave him both my cell-phone number and the number of the B&B. "I know I'm a stranger to you, but you can double-check the Parlor Car number, and the Johnsons will vouch for me."

"I'm glad you called, Ms. Salazar. I'll be in touch with you shortly."

* * *

Instead of feeling relieved after talking to Kent Vigil, I felt more on edge than ever. While he was checking on Rafael's whereabouts, I thought of an excuse to call Rita. I rummaged through a drawer in the end table where I'd stashed the paper napkin with her address and phone number. I called her from our cell phone, leaving the B&B line free.

"Hi, Rita," I said breezily. "How's everything?"

"Fine," she answered in clipped tones.

"We're leaving town in a couple of days, and I was hoping we could get together one more time before then."

"Sorry. Joaquín and I are leaving for Colorado Springs tomorrow, so it looks like we won't see you again."

She didn't sound sorry. Agitated was more like it.

"Oh, dear. Just my luck. What's in Colorado Springs?"

"Does something have to be someplace to take a little vacation?"

"Of course not. I've heard there are lots of interesting things to see there. The Olympic Training Center—"

"Yes, yes. If you must know, I've about had it with Vanessa and Toto. We just want to get away."

"I understand."

"Was there something else?"

"No. I'll tell Perlita 'hi' for you when we get back to Texas."

Silence. Then, "Don't bother. We talk all the time. I really have to go now."

She clicked off without further ado.

So now I was back to the wait-and-worry game. I'd hoped to hear from Kent Vigil on the Parlor Car phone, but it remained soundless. Listened-for calls must have something in common with watched pots.

"I don't know what to think of my 'chat' with Rita," I said after telling Ryan about it.

"Maybe she *should* get a restraining order against Vanessa and Tonto, or whatever his name is."

I couldn't help smiling. "I think we each have our own version of his name."

Ryan grinned. "Right. Anyway, if they're parked by Rita's apartment day and night, the way it sounds, it should be easy to prove they're stalking her."

"Well, I can certainly sympathize with Rita's frustration."

But was that the only problem that made her so testy? Was it really Vanessa's surveillance or was it Rafael's visit that triggered this sudden "vacation"? I wished there was some way I could keep her from leaving, but short of disabling her Jaguar, there didn't seem much I could do.

Out of desperation, I called Alicia to ask if she knew Rita and her father were leaving town. I should have remembered that I'd bombed out the last time I'd "tattled." Also, maybe it really was Alicia—not Vanessa—who'd sicked Deputy Tovar on me.

"Sharon, it's a little late for you to start reporting to me."

"Sorry. I forgot you have your own reporters."

I was the one who clicked off this time, feeling more than a little irritated that I'd been cast in the role of "enemy."

Ryan was right though. I couldn't solve the world's problems, let alone those of a family that stonewalled me at every turn.

Besides that, I could hardly throw rocks at Cici for dramatizing events out of proportion. Here I was interrupting Kent Vigil's peaceful evening so I could send him traipsing after Rafael, who'd more than likely not only forgotten to turn on his cell phone, but had forgotten Tía and me as well.

Ryan put his arm around my waist and tilted my face toward his. "Sweetheart, don't be so down on yourself."

"How did you know I'm planning my pity party?"

"I know you."

"You're invited."

"I have a better idea. Amá's reclaimed her kitchen, and she's expecting us for supper."

"That beats my pity party any day."

Still, I couldn't completely let go. I asked Wendy to call me if she heard from Kent, or Rafael, or anyone else on my worry list.

I wished I could keep Mr. Álvarez's gentle face from intruding on my thoughts.

Chapter 38

I spent a restless night, my sleep invaded by dreams of the Méndez family. In the latest, I dreamed that Rita, dressed in a filmy black dress that billowed around her ankles, and armed with a pearl-handled Lady Derringer, lured Rafael into an abandoned building on the eerie road to T.A. As he stepped inside, the roof caved in on them, completely burying them. Only smoke and dust rose from the rubble. Then Kiko showed up, and the two of us began digging through the ruins, shouting for Rafael. I moved some rocks aside, and Bernice emerged, unscathed. Her dress was like Rita's, except that it was blood-red. When I asked her what happened to Rita, her eyes turned opaque.

"Don't you know?" she whispered. "Rita never existed."

Ryan shook me awake. I thought I was screaming, but in reality I was barely whimpering.

I sat up and looked out the window at the dawn-lit sky, trying to get my bearings. Ryan cradled me in his arms until I stopped shaking.

"Tell me," he said when I calmed down.

Once I described the dream to him, it seemed to lose some of its grip on me. Still, the images lingered.

"Do you think it could be true? That there's no such person as Rita? There's just Bernice?"

"Not unless Bernice can bi-locate."

I thought about that a minute, then brightened. "Not unless Bernice flew up to Gallina in a private jet to have her yearbook picture made, then flew back to Zapata to graduate with you and Leo."

"There you go."

"Ryan, I owe you a *real* vacation."

"You know something? You can't say this vacation has been boring!"

"Parts of it were even fun."

"Most of it was fun—water-skiing, recovering from water-skiing, doing laundry, getting rained on...."

"I do know how to plan 'em, don't I."

He laughed softly. "Did I forget to mention Wendy's breakfasts, the campfires, Apá's concerts, our hikes, the train ride, doing stuff with the kids."

"Speaking of breakfast...."

He kissed me gently. "I have a pre-breakfast idea."

I snuggled closer to him. "Me too."

* * *

"Looks like tomorrow will be our last morning here," Alana said wistfully.

We were gathered around the dining table once more, finishing a breakfast of fresh peaches and Wendy's avocado and bacon omelets.

I looked across the table at Alana, glad that Ryan had reminded me of all the pluses in this holiday. "It went by too fast, even with our extra week."

"I'm afraid we stretched our budget to add that extra week, but it was worth it. I think the kids even discovered they could live without Nintendo."

The telephone rang, jarring me out of happy thoughts. Why should it be for me, I asked myself. After all, people are always calling to make reservations with Wendy, or to schedule appointments with Bonsall—or just to make social calls. Yet somehow I knew it was for me, and I knew the news wasn't good.

* * *

"That was Kiko."

No one spoke, but the apprehensive look on their faces must have mirrored my own.

Wendy and Bonsall had cleared away the dishes, and we moved into the living room, but none of us sat down.

I clasped my hands together and began explaining.

"After I called Kent Vigil, he and his wife went over to Rafael's. His car was there, but he didn't answer the door. They finally let themselves in and found him on the floor in the bathroom, unconscious. He'd vomited, but they didn't know if it was food-poisoning or—or something else. They rushed him to the nearest clinic and had his stomach pumped and all that. He didn't seem to respond, so sometime after midnight, the doctors sent him by ambulance to St. Victoria's Hospital in Santa Fe, where they could do more tests.

"Is Kiko with him?" Ryan asked.

"Yes. The Vigils called him last night. I was right about Rafael getting in touch with him after his visit with Rita. In fact, Rafael didn't call, but *drove* to Tres Piedras. Kiko wasn't home—didn't get home till late. Rafael had left a note saying he'd call. But the next call Kiko got was from the Vigils. Kiko said he'd been up all night, and wanted to wait till he felt a little more coherent to phone me. He wants me to call Tía Dippy. He said she felt more like family to him than anyone else. I think Rafael was the only one he was close to, and now...."

And now—what?

* * *

204

Tía Dippy grabbed her purse and was ready to head for
Santa Fe, almost before I got the words out. For a change—
except for her bright red wig—she was dressed more
conservatively today, clad in white slacks and a turquoise
tunic, with only five or six charm bracelets clinking together
in harmony.

The two-hour drive seemed to take much longer, and the
scenery we usually enjoyed dragged by unnoticed. Ryan
drove, with Tía sitting in front with him. They made a few
attempts at conversation, which dwindled away. I sat in the
back, wrapped in guilt. Had our visit with Rafael triggered a
showdown with Rita/Bernice? I told myself he'd planned to
see her with or without my meddling. But I couldn't help
wondering if he'd have approached her more cautiously if I
hadn't made it seem so urgent.

I phoned Kiko to tell him we were on the way and to get
directions. Winding our way through Santa Fe's narrow zig-
zaggy streets, we finally arrived at St. Victoria's.

I have an aversion to hospitals in the best of
circumstances, and felt my anxiety level rising as we
stepped through the doors. Tía Dippy gripped my arm and
gave me a little shake.

"We have to be strong, mijita. Take a deep breath."

Suddenly aware of my shallow breathing, I inhaled
deeply.

When we arrived at the waiting room in the ICU wing,
Kiko's eyes filled with tears the minute he saw Tía Dippy. He
stood and gave us both hugs.

Kiko clasped Ryan's hand warmly when I introduced
them. Then Kiko introduced us to Kent Vigil and his wife,
who were standing near him. They were a handsome couple,
both tall with silver-gray hair. She wore hers in a single long

braid down her back. His was cut short. Both had black eyes and high cheekbones that spoke of Indian ancestry.

"Sit, sit," Kiko said, taking Tía by the arm and leading her to a long couch by a water cooler. The rest of us found chairs nearby.

"How is Rafael?" Tía asked.

Kiko seemed to wilt. "The same. I don't understand it. The doctors don't understand it. Especially since it came on so suddenly. Tests show something wrong with the liver, but that doesn't make sense. Rafael's a health nut—doesn't drink or smoke."

Kiko stood again, held his hand out to Tía Dippy, and raised her beside him. "I'm going to look in on him. Come with me?"

She nodded, and they left the waiting room.

"Mrs. Salazar," Kent Vigil said softly, leaning toward me.

"Sharon, please."

He smiled, though there was a bleak look in his eyes. "You're right. This isn't a time for formality. What I wanted to say, I apologize for seeming so remote when you called yesterday. I thought...." He paused, obviously groping for a tactful way to say he thought I was a groupie.

"It's all right. I suppose Rafael has a lot of admirers."

"But only one partner. Tom is due in Albuquerque sometime tonight."

"What a jolt this must be for him. For me too, and I hardly know Rafael."

"Oh? I got the impression you were good friends."

I frowned, then blushed as I remembered the line I'd given Kent about Rafael always returning my calls. "I owe you an apology too. I misled you. I was afraid you'd think—probably what you thought."

"I'm glad you got through my thick head. I just wish Rafael had called me himself when he realized how sick he was."

"I'm surprised he didn't call too. I wonder. Does the house he's renting have a landline?"

"No, but there's his cell phone."

I hesitated. "Do you suppose it could be...lost?"

Kent shrugged. "He probably left it in his car."

Maybe. Maybe not. The ideas that were forming in my mind were disconnected, and I didn't want to jump to conclusions till I knew more about Rafael's condition and what the doctors determined. Still, a few facts remained:

Rafael went to see Rita—or Bernice—yesterday morning, but didn't stay long.

He went to Kiko's afterwards, but missed seeing him.

He became unexplainably ill sometime after he got home.

He didn't call anyone for help.

Chapter 39

Kent Vigil broke into my thoughts. "I'm not sure you misled me. Kiko told me your families had been friends for many years."

"Families.... Yes."

"My parents' generation—and Kiko's," Ryan added. "They all grew up together in Zapata, but they lost track of each other after the Méndezes moved away."

"How did they happen to reconnect?"

"I guess we can thank Rita for that," I said.

Kent frowned.

"I don't mean to sound facetious," I amended, then gave Kent a brief rundown of how I'd run into Rita and the events following that.

He listened intently, stopping me from time to time only to clarify one point or another.

"Kent, right before Tía and I left Rafael's the other day...."

Was it only two days ago? It seemed so much longer.

"Yes?" Kent prompted.

"Something I said seemed to disturb him. Right after that, he made this sudden decision to go see Rita. I can't help feeling responsible for whatever happened to him."

"Don't beat yourself up over that. He would have gone there sooner or later anyway. He just hadn't decided when."

"He told us there were some things he wanted to explain—about Rita, I think. Do you know what he might have meant?"

"Possibly."

I hoped Kent would elaborate, but he looked away, then changed the subject.

The wait for news about Rafael seemed endless, and after a while, we gave up trying to make conversation.

* * *

Two hours later, Rafael took a turn for the worse. Kiko and Tía Dippy were asked to wait outside while the medical team took over.

When the doctor finally appeared in the waiting room, his face looked grim. Kiko stood to face him, then slumped back onto the couch, his face turning a dull gray. Tía, who'd told me we had to be strong, began crying softly.

My legs felt as if they were encased in concrete, but somehow I was able to move toward them, along with Ryan and the Vigils.

The doctor turned to us, his kind gaze sharing our sadness. "I'm sorry."

Kent's shoulders shook as he embraced his wife, and I realized he must have felt the loss of their friend as much as Kiko mourned the loss of his brother.

A chaplain materialized and ushered us to a conference-type room where we could be together in privacy. Tía Dippy had composed herself, and Kiko seemed grateful for her support. More and more I came to appreciate a depth to her that she'd hidden under a bushel basket—or maybe under one of her cockeyed wigs.

Holding back an uncontrollable urge to laugh, I excused myself and went to the restroom, where I could be alone. I leaned against the wall and laughed and cried till I ran out of Kleenex.

Ryan was waiting in the hall when I came out.

"I feel kind of out of place," he confided.

"I do too, a little. I mean, I like—liked—Rafael and Kiko both, but I'd barely met them. I'm glad we could bring Tía though."

"Do you think we could get away from here for a little while, and offer to come back for her later?"

I agreed with Ryan, and we suggested the idea to Kiko and Tía when we rejoined them.

"You can take my cell phone," Ryan told her. "We have Sharon's, and you can call when you're ready."

"Where will you be?"

"I thought we'd visit the nursing school," I said off the top of my head. "It's right next door."

"Wait up a minute." Kent Vigil caught up with us as we started down the hall. "This might not be the best time for this. But I don't know when a better time would be."

"We really don't have any special plans. We just wanted to give Kiko—and you—some breathing room."

"I thought as much. And appreciate it."

"What did you have in mind?"

He took a torn piece of notebook paper out of his shirt pocket, unfolded it, and handed it to me. "This was in Rafael's jacket." Kent closed his eyes for a brief moment. "We thought he might need the jacket later, so we brought it with us."

Printed neatly on the paper were the name "Barbara" and a telephone number.

"Do you know who this is?" I asked Kent.

"It's an Española exchange, and I think it's probably the number for one of the nurses who looked after their mother—Barbara Abernathy."

"I wonder if Rafael already called her," I mused aloud, staring at the number as if it could provide an answer.

"Hard to say. We found his jacket dumped on the bedroom floor. Maybe he'd taken it to Chama—it's cool that early in the morning—then hadn't even felt like hanging it up when he got back. My guess is, he was planning to call Barbara after he'd seen Rita. But he didn't have the chance."

Kent wasn't filling in the blanks, but the wheels in my head began a slow squeaky grind. "You'd like us to look up Barbara?"

"If you don't mind. Española's only twenty miles from here. I'd talk to her myself, but I don't feel I can leave right now. It might be a long shot, but if it sheds any light on what happened...."

"I don't mind. I'm just not sure where to start."

"Start by telling her you're Rafael's friend. It's true," Kent added kindly.

Chapter 40

Ryan and I drove down a winding dusty road on the outskirts of Española to find Barbara Abernathy's home, a faded pink adobe that resembled a small lopsided box. I'd called to ask if we could come by, and she'd assured us in a raspy voice that we'd be welcome. She added that she had emphysema, however, and didn't have the energy for long drawn-out visits.

Barbara was sitting on her front porch when we arrived, breathing through an oxygen tube, the tank at her side. She was thin to the point of emaciation, with wispy shoulder-length gray hair and watery gray eyes. Her skin had the sallow hue that smokers sometimes acquire.

We introduced ourselves, and she offered us some folding chairs that were propped against the house.

"Hope you don't mind putting them up yourself," she croaked. "I don't have the strength."

"No trouble." Ryan smiled at her and unfolded the chairs.

She eyed him with a trace of impishness after we'd seated ourselves. "I don't have many good-looking young men come to see me nowadays."

"Their loss," he replied gallantly.

She cackled, then turned to me. "You say you're a friend of Rafael Méndez?"

"Yes. Our families knew each other in Texas." I took a deep breath. "I have some bad news.... Rafael died this morning."

"Rafael? Dead? That can't be!"

"I wish it weren't true."

"What happened?"

"We're not sure."

She regarded me suspiciously. She was a nurse, after all, and not side-tracked by my evasiveness.

"I don't know the medical terms," I said. "Whatever it was came on suddenly, and he didn't come out of it."

She nodded. "Heart disease. Runs in the family." Tears began rolling down her wrinkled cheeks. "So sad. So much grief in that family."

"Had you talked to him recently?"

"Me? No, not in years. Well, not that many years. It just seems like a long time."

I showed her the slip of paper Kent had given me. "Evidently he was planning to call you. I'm not sure, but I think it might have been in connection with Rita."

"Rita? I haven't seen her since her mother died."

"What was she like?"

"Rita? Or her mother?"

"Both, I guess. I've heard that Rita was the only one her mother had anything to do with after she got sick."

"That's true. But Rafael kept coming out to see her anyway. The others quit."

I wished I knew what it was Rafael needed to talk to Barbara about. So far I hadn't found out anything I didn't already know, except that the Méndez family had a history of heart disease. Something Rita would probably know and could use to her advantage. A chilling thought.

"It seems odd that Rita was the only one Juana wanted to see," I said, returning to the subject of Rita's relationship with her mother.

"Not that odd. People get strange ideas. Funny thing though. Right toward the end, she got upset with Rita too.

One day Juana'd be glad to see her. The next day she'd act like all the demons in hell were after her if Rita showed up."

Ryan and I exchanged glances, and I felt the back of my neck start to prickle.

"Rita had a relative who looked a lot like her. Do you suppose that's who was upsetting Juana?"

Barbara looked skeptical. "She signed in as Rita. Don't know why she'd say that if she was somebody else—especially if she was already related."

"I know it seems unlikely. And it's been a long time ago, but it really is important. Can you think back and try to picture anything different about Rita on the days Juana seemed so terrified?"

Barbara's voice became a dry whisper. "You think that's what Rafael wanted to ask me?"

"Yes, I do."

She closed her eyes. "Then it *is* important."

Several minutes went by, and I wondered if she'd fallen asleep, but apparently she was only concentrating intently.

"Well now." She opened her eyes. "I was paying more attention to Juana than to Rita back then. And Rita never stayed long when Juana got that way. But it did seem like Rita was in more of a hurry to leave than I would've thought. You'd think maybe she'd go down to the lounge or something and wait a while to see if there was a change in the way her mother was acting."

"So you're saying it wasn't like Rita to leave in such a hurry?" I repeated.

"No, it wasn't. At the time, I guess I was just concerned about getting Juana calmed down. And then there were other patients to take care of, and I really didn't have time to worry about it. It must've slipped to the back of my mind, though, or I wouldn't've remembered it just now."

"Was there any difference in Rita's appearance on those off-days?"

"Come to think of it, I remember at least one time she was wearing dark glasses. I told her maybe that's what set her mother off. She said she'd take off the glasses, but she didn't. By then, Juana was screaming, and Rita left. And to tell you the truth, I was just as glad. I had my hands full with Juana as it was."

"Did this happen very often?"

"Let me see. Maybe two or three times. It might've seemed like more because it made such an uproar." Barbara thought that over, then seemed to debate with herself, mumbling aloud. "But no—not that many...unless she came on my day off. But no—someone would've said something."

She looked up at me. "When did Rafael get the idea it was two different people? Why didn't he say anything?"

"I don't think he suspected anything until recently."

"You say there was a relative looked like Rita?"

"Yes. A granddaughter named Bernice. Did you ever meet her?"

Barbara shook her head. "No. I met some of Juana's children, but I don't recollect any grandchildren."

She seemed to shrink, though I didn't see how she could possibly get any tinier. "This is terrible. Poor Juana. She had a stroke not long after those clashes. Killed her. The stress killed her, I'm sure. It just never dawned on me someone would've upset her on purpose."

"I don't think that was her intention. I think she was just trying to see if the switch would work. Evidently it didn't fool Juana."

"Well, I'm glad she didn't mean any harm, but it was still kinda mean. Nothing to be done about it now, I guess. It's a shame though. I was fond of Juana. The Juana I knew—which wasn't the same one the family knew."

Barbara's wheezing became more pronounced as she reminisced. "Sometimes Alzheimer's patients think they're a whole 'nother person, and they don't even remember their old selves. But every now and then, they get a flash of memory. I guess that's what happened when she saw the person who said she was Rita."

"Juana must have felt comfortable with you, since you didn't expect her to be someone else."

Barbara smiled and coughed. "Well, that's the truth now."

"We should probably go. We promised we wouldn't stay too long."

"It's nice to have company. That's a fact. But I am getting a little tired. My sister'll be here soon. I took care of people all my life, and now someone takes care of me. I guess that's the way of it."

* * *

After leaving Barbara's, we headed back toward Santa Fe. "Are you hungry?" Ryan asked.

"A little. It's nearly 5:00. Breakfast was a long time ago."

We stopped to eat at a Dairy Queen in Pojoaque.

"I thought Tía Dippy might have called by now," Ryan said between bites of cheeseburger.

"I know. But Kiko latched on to her like she was a life raft."

"Yeah. they seem pretty tight. Do you suppose she's forgotten that guy she met at the RV park?"

I gave an airy wave of my French fry. "Just a summer fling."

Ryan chuckled. "Glad your sense of humor's back."

"I'm latching on to that like my own personal life preserver."

Chapter 41

Just as we reached Santa Fe, Tía Dippy rang me on my cell phone to tell me they had left the hospital and to meet them in the lobby of La Quinta Inn. Once there, we found that everyone planned to stay in town overnight. They were exhausted, and tomorrow would be another grueling day.

They planned to get up early and go to Albuquerque, where the autopsy would be performed. My head began to ache, just thinking about the headaches Kiko was facing. Or maybe Rafael's partner, Tom, would be the one to make funeral arrangements and contact the estranged family members. I supposed the burial would take place in Dallas. That would require another set of logistics.

At least the hotel was cheerful and inviting, a welcome respite from the hospital scene. After greeting Tía and Kiko, who were seated on a leather couch in an unoccupied corner of the lobby, Ryan and I joined the Vigils at the coffee bar. I poured myself a cup of decaf, then poured French vanilla creamer into it from a slew of teeny tiny containers.

"I'm curious to know if you learned anything from your visit with Barbara Abernathy," Kent said in a low voice while stirring his own coffee.

"She certainly gave us something to think about." I said, then related the details of our visit. "Did Rafael know his mother began rejecting Rita—or who everyone assumed was Rita—toward the end?"

"I doubt it. Even if they told him, he might not have attached any significance to it—just chalked it up to the progression of the disease. His mother had shut out all her other children. Why not Rita too?"

"There had to be something else bothering Rafael. I feel like I didn't ask the right questions."

"No, I think you did. I just don't know what to do with the answers."

Kent patted my shoulder, then he and his wife excused themselves to find chairs near Kiko.

"I wish he wouldn't be so oblique," I muttered to Ryan.

"I have some ideas of my own."

Before Ryan could explain, Tía came over to tell us she was staying overnight too.

"We have separate rooms," she whispered as she blushed and fiddled with her wig.

I gave her a big hug. "I never doubted it."

"I'd like to go to the H-E-B and get a toothbrush and some extra makeup and things, if it's not a problema for you to take me."

"Of course not."

"I don't know," Ryan said, giving Tía another hug. "We'd have to go all the way back to Texas to find an H-E-B. What about Home Depot?"

"Oh, you!" She tweaked his ear, then went to get her purse and tell Kiko we were leaving for a short while.

"I've heard there's a real 'five-and-dime' near the plaza," I said as we started out. "Why don't we go there, then take a little walkaround and get some fresh air."

Tía hesitated, then nodded. "Bueno."

* * *

After she made her purchases, we cut through the plaza to reach the opposite sidewalk, which ran the length of the historic governor's palace. Here Native Americans—some in colorful tribal attire and others in t-shirts, Levi's, and Nikes—placed jewelry and pottery on velvet cloths they'd spread out on the walk in hopes of enticing tourists.

We stopped to admire several lovely designs, and Tía Dippy bought me a dainty cross inlaid with coral and mother-of-pearl. From there we went to the Cathedral of St. Francis, where we found the surrounding courtyard as calming as the cathedral itself.

As we strolled among the evergreens, Tía told us that Kiko was especially upset because he'd missed Rafael yesterday. "Now Kiko blames himself, pobrecito. Thinks he could have done something, but I don't see how."

"Neither do I. But I know the feeling."

We began walking back toward the Plaza. On the way, Tía asked about the "mysterious errand" Kent sent us on this morning.

"Kent found a note in Rafael's jacket with the name of a nurse who'd helped care for Juana Méndez. Kent thought if we talked to her, we might find something that would—" I stopped short. "He didn't say it in so many words, but I think he was looking for something that would link Rita to Rafael's death."

"Ay, dios mío." Tía crossed herself. "And did you find it?"

"Not directly." I told her what we'd learned about "the two Ritas," then remembered that Ryan was about to tell me something back at the hotel, right before we left.

"What are your thoughts?" I asked him.

"I'm thinking that when Rafael went to Chama, something happened to make him suspect that Rita—or her double— had something to do with their mother's death. Personally, I think the double is Bernice, and I'm beginning to wonder if maybe both of them—Rita and Bernice—were in on it together."

"Good lord. That never even occurred to me!"

Tía's eyes widened as she crossed herself again.

"Didn't you tell me," Ryan continued, "that both Kiko and Rafael hinted that Rita—the real Rita—seemed to have developed some kind of mental disorder in recent years?"

"You're right," I said slowly. "But that's still a stretch."

Tía shivered. "What if the policia—um—dig up Juana's body?"

"I'd hate to see that happen," I said. "Say there was evidence of an overdose of some drug she was supposed to be taking. Something like that. There's no way to prove who gave it to her. So it would fall back on the nursing home. Possibly on Barbara."

Tía blinked away tears and laid her hand on my arm. "Let's go back now."

* * *

As soon as we returned to the hotel, Tía Dippy hurried to Kiko's side. His haggard face softened when he saw her coming toward him.

"Do you feel we should stay too?" Ryan asked me.

I shook my head. "I don't think we're needed here. Just Tía. And who knows how long she'll want to stay with Kiko."

"In their separate rooms."

I jabbed him lightly in the ribs. "I've been thinking, since the rest of the family is going home tomorrow, maybe we can move Tía's things from your folks' RV into the extra room at the B&B, and she can ride home with us when she's ready."

"Believe it or not, I was thinking along those same lines."

My thoughts turned to Rafael again. He was the one link to everyone else in the family. I wondered if they'd come together now for his funeral. I wondered if Rita and/or Bernice would show up.

221

Chapter 42

I was glad we returned to Chama to be with our own family for the last evening of our vacation. Beto, Apá, and the boys had taken one last fishing trip at Mundo Lake, and we were treated to rainbow trout for dinner. Afterwards, we sat around the campfire while Apá serenaded us on his accordion.

As if they knew we were winding down, Digger laid his head on my knee and looked at me with soulful eyes, while Spot settled himself on Ryan's lap.

Carlos moved his camp chair closer to mine. "I'm going to miss you, *Nina*. I wish you'd move back to Zapata."

I put my arm around him. "I'll miss you too, Carlitos. Tell you what. If I don't get back home soon, I'm not going to have any clients left. No job anymore. So," I continued in a stage whisper, "maybe I'll just move in with you all. But don't tell your mom. We'll let it be a surprise."

He giggled. "What about Uncle Ryan?"

"Oh, I'll bring him along too. The more the crazier, right?"

I was only half-joking about my clients. With our trip in mind, I'd cut back on appointments; Dave, the associate I worked with most, handled the cases that were still pending. I always managed to find some time each day—if only for an hour—to touch base with him. And, I reminded myself, I was lucky the paralegal I depended on was bright and capable. But I missed being in the middle of it all.

It felt good to focus on work for a change. When we were in Santa Fe, I worried about what had happened to Rafael, and how Kiko would manage. Here in Chama, I worried about Mr. Álvarez. Maybe I shouldn't have been so snippy with Alicia. I probably should have stayed on the line long enough to find out what they intended to *do* about her father leaving town with Rita, if anything. Could anything be done? Maybe, depending on what the police found out about Rafael's death. Even if Rita wasn't a suspect—yet—she was supposedly one of the last people to see him alive. Reason enough to bring her in for questioning.

Funny, even though "Rita" was probably Bernice, after calling her Rita every day for the past two weeks, that name seemed more natural. And there was one major difference between them that bothered me: Bernice had had a serious drinking problem. I didn't think she could fake being sober. Not consistently, anyway. Maybe Ryan was right. Maybe Rita and Bernice had some scam going together....

Digger pawed my knee, reminding me that right now I should concentrate on right now.

I stroked his soft fur with my free hand, which he gave a happy lick. "I'll miss you too, silly dog."

"We'll be back," Alana promised.

* * *

After breakfast the next morning, Ryan and I walked to the RV park. Beto and Alana packed their suitcases, then drove over in their van to pick up the kids, their pets, and all their camping gear. Then away they went amid a swarm of hugs, kisses, tears, and waves.

Although Amá, Apá, and Tía Marta had originally planned to leave today too, they changed their minds and extended their stay.

"We really don't have any reason to hurry home," Amá explained. "And now that we've been here two weeks, we get a break on the campground fee."

Tía Marta nodded, settling herself in a campchair to enjoy another cup of coffee. "Back to the hot weather, when it's so cool here? No thanks."

"Besides," Apá added, "I'm enjoying the jam sessions with my new compadres."

Amá motioned me to follow her back into her kitchen on the pretext of getting more coffee. "I worry about my sister," she said, once we were alone. "It was very generous of her to console Kiko, but she's too impulsiva sometimes."

"Would you feel better if you called her? She has Ryan's cell phone."

Amá looked visibly relieved as she picked up her own cell phone from the counter and keyed in the number. After a few exchanges with Tía Dippy, Amá handed the phone to me, her lips a grim line.

"What's going on?" I asked Tía.

"Nada yet. We're in Albuquerque. Just waiting for them to release, um, release...."

The body. So straightforward. So hard to say.

"Did Tom get in okay?"

"Yes, he's here. Nice boy."

This was followed by silence.

"Are you there, Tía? Did we get cut off?"

"Sí. No. I'm here. In the courtyard outside the lobby. With everyone else. We're at Tom's hotel. I was finding a quiet place to talk."

"I see. You were telling me about Tom?"

"Pobrecito. Still in shock. He did tell us that Rafael always said he wanted to be cremated, then buried back in Coyote. With his padres. Not in Texas."

"That should make it easier for Kiko. Not having to go to Dallas."

"Mm. It's still difficult—muy difícil. Tom, he's not able to deal with anything right now. So Kent Vigil very kindly offered to make the funeral arrangements and get in touch with the rest of the familia. Pues, you remember the way Kiko told us they are. He dreaded calling them."

"That is nice of Kent. He doesn't have any ties with them, so he can handle it without getting involved in their feuds."

"I'm glad you called, mijita. I'll call you back when there's more news. Tell Ysela not to worry about me."

"Tell the sun to stop shining?"

She gave a small laugh. "Give her my love."

Amá was handling her restlessness by bustling around her small kitchen, rearranging the salt and pepper shakers, the sugar bowl, tidying things that didn't need tidying.

I set the phone on the counter, then put my arm around her. "Tell me."

"What is she thinking? Here she goes traipsing off to Santa Fe—to Albuquerque—to who knows where? Does she plan to stay with Kiko till his family arrives? All those people who don't get along...."

"Maybe after all this time, they'll let bygones be—"

"Ha. They cherish their grudges."

"Maybe they won't all show up."

Amá burst into tears. "That would be sad too. Poor Kiko. All alone."

I didn't say anything.

She took a Kleenex out of her apron pocket and wiped her eyes, then smiled sheepishly. "Not exactly alone. My sister's with him."

"And other friends."

"I shouldn't criticize Kiko's family. After all, we're not perfect."

"We're not?"

She laughed. "We are who we are."

"Amá...what did you mean about the Méndezes holding on to their grudges? It sounds like something that goes back a long way."

Chapter 43

"A long way, yes. I'm not sure grudge is the word I meant."

Amá began studying items in the pantry. Then she brought a large container of dry pinto beans to the table.

"Come sit down, mijita, and we can talk about it while we sort the beans."

We sat across from each other at the dinette, and Amá poured several cups of beans on the table.

"I'd thought maybe you'd want to take a vacation from cooking," I said lightly.

"I enjoy cooking. Like your friend Wendy. And why get a motorhome with all these fancy up-to-date appliances if I can't use them, no?"

We spread the beans around and began picking through them one by one to weed out the tiny rocks that always managed to infiltrate.

"*A ver*. We were friendly with the Méndez family when we were children—up until they moved away. Neto even escorted me at my quinceañera." Amá looked up from her sorting and smiled. "I guess we all have little crushes when we're growing up, no?"

I grinned. "True."

"I liked Connie, and we were friendly, but not as close as my sister and Perlita. Connie was very...intense. I don't know if you remember Eppie telling you that Connie and Perlita went to live with their great-grandparents when the rest of the family moved to New Mexico. Perlita was about seventeen at the time, and Connie fifteen. I remember because Connie made her quinceañera when I did, and they left right afterwards."

"What's going on?" Tía Marta called through the screen door.

"We're getting the frijoles ready to soak," Amá answered. She shook her head at me and put her fingers to her lips.

Tía Marta came inside, her sturdy oxfords clumping across the room, and sat next to me. "I can help. Why didn't you call me?"

"We're just about finished." Amá scooped the beans we'd separated into a colander and rinsed them in the sink. Then she put them in a large kettle, covered them with water, and put them on the stove.

"They won't be ready in time," Tía Marta declared, adjusting her thick glasses as she watched Amá go through her well-practiced routine.

Amá ignored her, turned on the heat, and set the timer.

"Do you know when Eppie will be back?" Tía Marta asked.

"Quién sabe?" Amá brushed the remaining debris into a wastebasket, then wiped the table with a clean dishcloth. "Maybe she'll come running once Kiko's family shows up." She sighed. "You might as well know. I was getting ready to tell Sharon about their great-grandmother."

Tía Marta folded her arms across her chest. "Why?"

Amá looked at me and spoke as if her sister wasn't there. "Marta doesn't like gossip. And she'd consider this gossip."

"Is it true? Is it kind? Is it necessary?" Tía Marta quoted.

"It's true. Maybe not kind. But it's necessary because Sharon wants to understand."

Amá sat down again, facing us. "Their great-grandmother was hateful. Period. All Connie's friends were scared of her. We called her '*Huela Bruja*'—'Grandma Witch.'"

"That's necessary?"

"Wait and see. And don't interrupt."

"I admit she wasn't nice," Tía Marta surprised us by saying. "We always thought grandmas were supposed to be sweet like ours, till we met her."

I thought Huela Bruja must have been pretty terrible for Tía Marta to say something even mildly negative about her.

"Anyway," Amá went on, "there was some family superstition that someone gave one of their ancestors the *mal ojo* centuries ago, and every generation had at least one 'bad seed' ever since."

"If you believe such nonsense," Tía Marta retorted. "Evil eyes, bad seeds—"

"Pues, their family believed it. And Huela Bruja seemed to prove it. Then there was Flavio—maybe others I don't know about. Even when he was a baby, Flavio wasn't like other kids. I used to think there was something wrong with *me* for not liking him. How could I feel that way about a baby? Connie's little brother? But after a while, I realized it wasn't just me." Amá shuddered. "He was a sneaky kid—couldn't get along with anyone, and it got worse when he started school."

"I think that's why they moved," Tía Marta said. "They said they wanted to go work on their uncle's ranch, but I always suspected that was just an excuse."

"I guess moving away didn't change anything," I said. "Flavio still got in trouble."

"Poor Connie," Amá said, a look of sadness in her eyes. "She wouldn't give up on him, even though they were far apart. She kept in touch with the whole family and always encouraged her brothers to do well in school. She went to the university herself and studied psychology. She thought it would help her understand what made Flavio tick. I don't think she gave up till that incident with Bernice. Something in her snapped."

Tía Marta gave a heavy sigh. "And the whole family snapped with her."

"From what you say, mijita, Rafael tried to keep the family together the way Connie had done, but I think they were all too afraid. I think it was seeing the same things in Bernice they'd seen in Flavio. Though Flavio probably wasn't as bad. But it made them wonder if the curse might be real."

"Waste of time, worrying about curses," Tía Marta declared. "It could have been a mental disease they just didn't know the name for."

"Sí. But some people are just plain evil, and no one has an explanation."

"Speaking of Bernice and Flavio," I said, "the last Rafael heard of them, they were in Mexico together."

"If anyone could help her get back in the States, he'd be the one," Amá said.

"I wish I could go to the police with all my guesswork about Bernice and Rita—and Flavio—but it's all so flimsy."

Amá smiled. "You'll think of something."

* * *

Following our conversation, I made a few phone calls. First, to Rita herself. No answer, which didn't surprise me.

Next I called Kent Vigil. He promised to get back with me after he'd checked Rafael's address book for family information. Right now, he and his wife were still in Albuquerque.

Rather than wait on Kent, I decided to call Alicia. She was polite, but distant. At least she didn't hang up on me.

"I apologize for being so abrupt when I called the other day, Alicia. I was under a lot of stress."

"Aren't we all."

"I know. And I hate to bother you with this, but I really need to find Rita.... Her brother died suddenly, and I'm sure she'd want to know."

The unintentional irony of my words sliced through the telephone wire and back. I could hear the sharp intake of Alicia's breath.

"I wish I knew where they went," she said. "Vanessa wanted to follow them, but, um, I didn't want her on the highway. Neither she nor—her friend—has a valid license, and I was afraid they'd be stopped."

Alicia nearly choked on the word "friend," as if she couldn't quite acknowledge his relationship to her daughter. I could also understand why their driving would make her nervous—with or without licenses.

"You didn't happen to talk with your father before they left?" I prodded.

"I did, and I was worried about him. He seemed rather tired, and I was afraid the trip might be too strenuous for him."

"Rita wasn't worried?"

"Ha. What do you think. She agreed that he wasn't 'perky' as usual, and she thought getting away for a 'quiet little retreat' was just what he needed. I asked her if she didn't think it would be a good idea to check with his doctor first. She said that was silly, all his prescriptions were up to date, and besides, they wouldn't be gone long."

"Did she say where this little retreat would be?"

"Not exactly. I asked her, and she said she wasn't sure but she'd always wanted to see Mesa Verde."

"Mesa Verde! She didn't mention Colorado Springs?"

There was a long pause. "Is that what she told you?"

"Yes. They're in opposite directions, aren't they?"

231

"More or less."

"Have you tried calling her on her cell phone?"

"Yes. A few times. She didn't answer. Not that I expected her to."

"Do you know her license-plate number?"

"That, I do." Alicia sounded hopeful. "Do you know someone who could find them?"

"The State Police in Colorado and Arizona would be the best bet—they have a network in place to notify people about a death in the family. They can send out an 'ATL'—Attempt to Locate—and zero in on Colorado Springs or Mesa Verde.... The problem is, I doubt if Rita and your father are in either place."

"Yes, I think she went to a lot of trouble to mislead us."

"Unfortunately, 'somewhere out there' isn't going to get a lot of attention."

"Seems rather pointless to call the police then."

"Not necessarily." Alicia sounded so downhearted, I tried to muster a little optimism. "There's always the off-chance they're in one of the places she mentioned."

"I guess it's a start. We don't have anything else to go on," Alicia said without much conviction. "I owe you an apology too. You've tried to help us, and we've been too stubborn to listen. You might want to talk to Vanessa and—Trog. I don't even know his real name, but that's what I call him."

How appropriate, I thought, then covered the mouthpiece so I wouldn't say it out loud. "Oh? Do they know something about finding your father and Rita?"

"No, but Trog says he's noticed some curious things happening at her place. I don't know how reliable it is, but I guess it wouldn't hurt to ask."

Chapter 44

We met in a small conference room in Dan Oliver's office half an hour later. Although the office was normally closed on Saturdays, Dan was willing to accommodate us. I hoped meeting there would keep the atmosphere businesslike.

One wall of the room was lined with bookcases; on the opposite side was a sliding glass door that led to a small courtyard. Along the far wall were an oak desk and two dark-green armchairs. We were seated at a larger oak table in straight-back chairs cushioned in the same shade of green, with Vanessa and her boyfriend across from Ryan and me, and Alicia at one end.

Alicia must have persuaded Vanessa and Trog, formerly thought of as Creepy, that a little propriety was in order. Trog arrived sober, in clean jeans and undershirt, and with his hair slicked back. Vanessa was wearing a blouse that actually covered her pudgy midriff.

I smiled at Vanessa and was met with her usual surly stare. Trog, on the other hand, seemed too filled with an air of self-importance to be belligerent.

"Alicia tells me you've observed some strange goings-on at Rita's. Maybe they'd shed some light on what she's up to."

"There's some guy stayin' at her house," Trog announced smugly.

"You don't know that," Vanessa contradicted.

"I seen him!" Trog came close to yelling.

"Just you?" I asked. "Vanessa didn't see him too?"

"Oh, yeah," Vanessa said. "We both saw him go in her house. But we don't know that he stayed there."

"You don' know. I do," Trog said.

I jumped in, hoping to find something they agreed on. "Tell me about the time you both noticed him. It must not have been a secret if Rita knew that, uh, someone—the neighbors maybe—would be sure to see him."

Trog and Vanessa looked at each other. She scowled and shrugged. Then they took turns explaining.

"Che knows our carros, my troca. So we don' drive there no more."

"We wait till after dark to go over there."

"To go to Rita's?" I asked.

Vanessa rolled her eyes. "Of course not. What do you think we are? Stupid? The person who lives across the street is a friend of mine. She doesn't like Rita either."

I nodded. "So she lets you watch Rita from her house. Rita's not worried about the neighbors watching her?"

"The neighbors don't pay attention. They're old. They go to bed early. All the lights are out."

"Che don' see us. We sit outside."

But not behind the tree, I hope.

As if she'd heard my thought out loud, Vanessa said, "We sit on a blanket on the lawn. We're very quiet."

That's a first.

"That's very smart," I said. "Tell me what you saw."

Trog, his ego puffed up, puffed his chest out accordingly. "We seen this ol' man go in her house."

"When was this?"

"Night before last," Vanessa said. "About 11:00. I remember, because it was getting pretty cold and I kept looking at my watch. She turned out her lights, so we were about to leave. Then this dude shows up."

234

"What kind of car was he driving?"

"He wasn' drivin' no carro. He was walkin'—very sneaky."

"Well, that's interesting! I wonder how he got there! Never mind. Tell me what he looked like. Or could you tell in the dark?"

"Jess—"

"No!" Vanessa yelled. "Not in the dark. Jeez, you don't tell it right. He was only inside about twenty minutes, and then he came out again."

"I tol' you it don' take long." Trog winked at Ryan, who ignored him.

"Let's stick to the subject and keep our voices down," Alicia said, her tone icy.

"We didn't see 'the subject' right away," Vanessa said sullenly, "When he came out, he got in Rita's car, and the overhead light came on. He was very old. With a wrinkly face. Not much hair. White hair."

"He was wearin' one of those chirts without arms," Trog added.

"Sleeveless shirts, you mean? Muscle shirts?"

"Jess. Big tattoos all over," Trog said with a touch of envy.

If "the subject" was Flavio, which I suspected, he would have been in his late fifties. Not that old. But his hard-bitten life might have aged him. And I was impressed with the details Vanessa and Trog had given.

"Where did he go from Rita's?"

"I don't know," Vanessa said. "We went home."

"I go back early the nex' mornin'. Still dark. The carro was back." Trog looked triumphantly at Vanessa. "I tol' you he stay the night."

"Have you seen him since then?" I asked.

"No. Even though El Toro here thinks he's still there."

235

"Tell me, um, Toro, why do you think that?"

"Rita, che leave that mornin'."

"The same morning?"

"Jess. Friday. Jesterday. I seen the blinds closed. Today I seen 'em open."

"Well, this is very enlightening."

"Sharon, have you called the police yet?" Alicia asked.

"Don't bother," Vanessa cut in. "I already called a friend of ours. He knows all about law enforcement. He said you can't just go around arresting people."

"What are you talking about?" Alicia asked.

"I talked to Luis yesterday. I told him I was you. I hope you don't mind."

"Well, that depends," Alicia said indignantly.

Vanessa sighed. "It wasn't nothing. I just thought he'd listen more if he thought it was you instead of me. If you must know, he sounded very grumpy."

Maybe Deputy Luis Tovar clicked to the fact that this wasn't the first time Vanessa had impersonated her mother. Maybe he'd be less grumpy with me if I needed to call him again.

"You're right," I said. "Rita can't be arrested just for leaving town."

Vanessa began sulking. "Jeezus, if we can't do nothing, this whole thing was a waste of time."

"Not really. I think it helps to pool our ideas."

I stood, signaling an end to the meeting. "I'm glad we could get together."

Trog looked a little deflated now that his moment in the limelight was over, and I found myself smiling at him. "Not many people are as observant as you. You've been more helpful than you realize."

His swagger returned as he and Vanessa left the room, still bickering with each other.

"I'm sorry about Rita's brother, but if that's the only way we can find her...do you mind calling the police?" Alicia asked when Vanessa and Trog were gone.

"Not at all."

She walked over to the bookcase, where Dan kept an assortment of phone directories for New Mexico and surrounding states, and selected the ones I'd need, which she set on the desk by the phone.

"I'll need the license number of Rita's Jaguar before I call."

Alicia recited the number, which I jotted down along with some other notes to identify Rita and the car.

Still standing, I lifted the handset and said a silent prayer that Rita could be found before anything happened to Mr. Álvarez.

Chapter 45

"I should follow the stock market more closely and invest in one of those gazillion telephone companies," I told Ryan as I redialed Rita's number. We had returned to the B&B and were once again in the upstairs library. Ryan was sitting in a roomy beige armchair, but I was too wound up to sit.

I had told Alicia that I had a number of calls to make—which was true. It was also true that I preferred to make those calls in private. It felt good to do something constructive. I had faith in the police; what I didn't have faith in was the likelihood of Rita being where she'd told us. I was too impatient to wait for the police to track her down—if that was even possible. An idea had been forming in my mind, and now I was giving it a try.

As soon as we got back, I'd telephoned Kiko and Tía so they could go along with the plan. Now, as I listened to the constant ringing on the other end of Rita's line, I paced the room, muttering at an invisible Rita to "answer the damn phone." When the automatic message kicked in after five rings, I hung up.

"Maybe it's just as well she doesn't answer," Ryan said. "I don't think this is such a good idea."

"Well, I'm running out of ideas. You talked me out of having Luis arrest Flavio."

"Honey, we don't know for sure it's Flavio. But whoever it is, apparently Rita invited him, so he's not trespassing."

"You're right." And, as Ryan had reminded me earlier, Rita's "visitor" might be dangerous. In any event, he would probably let her know that someone had spotted him, and they might put another plan in place. Not that we knew what the original one was.

I decided to keep trying Rita's number every five minutes. In the meantime, I pushed the lace curtains aside and stared out the side window at the top branches of the blue spruce to our left. Below, in the garden across the street, I could see cheerful rows of Shasta daisies, rose-colored coneflowers, and lighter pink cosmos.

Two minutes later, I redialed. I was so surprised when Rita answered, it took me a few seconds to get focused again.

"Oh, Rita, I'm glad I finally caught you."

"What do you want? Why do you keep calling?"

Keep calling? Either she'd heard the phone ring all along or had just now turned it on and seen my number repeated on her caller ID.

"Believe me, I wouldn't call if it wasn't important. And I'm sorry the news is bad. It's about your brother Rafael."

"What about Rafael?"

"He's—well—there was an accident."

"An accident? What kind of accident?"

"Reading between the lines, it sounded like a drug overdose. I'm sorry, but I'm not very clear on details."

"I'm sorry too."

I was struck by the complete lack of emotion in her voice. There was a brief silence before she asked, "How did you find out about it?"

"That's the strange thing. He was visiting a friend here in New Mexico. Evidently he planned to come see you too." I crossed my fingers. "He had your address in his jacket pocket. He didn't have your phone number, but he had mine."

"Yours! Why would he have yours?"

"I have no idea. I thought maybe you'd know."

There was a longer silence.

"I suppose I could contact your sister Perlita, but since you say she's angry with me, I'd rather not. I thought it would be better to tell you first, since I know you, and you can contact the rest of the family."

"I suppose."

"There's another reason I called you. Rafael keeps asking for you. And for Bernice."

"Bernice!" Alarm sounded in her voice. "*Keeps* asking? He's still alive?"

"Last I heard. He's at University Hospital in Albuquerque. But—I hate to say this—it doesn't sound good."

"What, um, what does he ask about?"

"I really don't know. That's just what I was told. They were very stingy with information. You know the privacy policy these days. But I'm sure Rafael would like to hear from you," I said, then gave her Kiko's cell-phone number. I hoped she wouldn't question the prefix. At least it was a New Mexico area code. Kiko would want to change his number later, but he told me it was worth it if it would smoke Rita out.

"How is Mr. Álvarez?" I asked. "I hope you don't have to cut your vacation short." I wondered if I'd ever get my fingers uncrossed. Omar's mom would be proud of me.

"He's a little under the weather," she answered in a monotone.

"Oh, Rita, You must be so worried! Looks like you have a lot to deal with right now, and I've just burdened you with more. Two people you love...well, it's a good thing for Mr. Álvarez you're a nurse and know just what to do...."

For all my babbling in this one-sided conversation, I hoped it came across to Rita that she'd have a lot of explaining to do if "the good nurse" slipped up. Especially if she wound up with a lot of explaining to do about her brother too.

"Oh, it's not that serious," she said impatiently. "Not for my Sweetikins anyway. I'll bring him home, then go on down to Albuquerque to see Rafael."

"Where are you right now? Will it be a long drive?"

"Don't worry about it, Sharon. I'll be there when I get there."

* * *

"What if Rita decides to call the hospital directly for information about Rafael," Ryan asked me after I'd hung up. "I think we should have talked this out a little more."

"We just have to chance it. Worst case, when they tell her he's not a patient there, she knows I've lied."

I sat in the matching armchair, then stood and began pacing again. "OR she might think I simply got the name of the hospital wrong. There are lots of hospitals and urgent-care places in Albuquerque—I looked them up in the directory at Dan's office. She probably wouldn't call them all when it would be easier just to call 'Rafael' himself."

"And what happens when she reaches 'Rafael'?"

"Kiko promised not to sound too coherent, except for giving her a room number that doesn't exist. I'm hoping she's watched enough TV to think she can waltz into his room and fiddle with the IV or unplug something."

"You're hoping her imagination is as vivid as yours?"

"At the very least! If it's Bernice, hers is way beyond mine. In fact, I'd almost forgotten—she used to act in school plays back in grade school, didn't she? I think she's been honing her acting skills for a long long time."

"So what happens when she gets to the hospital?"

"I really don't care. I just hope she gets Mr. Álvarez home safely. I mean, it would be nice if they discovered exactly what caused Rafael's death and we could point the finger at Rita-Bernice, but tox reports take forever. So right now we're stuck. Unless...."

Ryan stood and put his hands on my shoulders. "Unless we take time out for lunch, you're going to wear a hole in the carpet."

Chapter 46

We ate at Cookin' Books, where we ordered Reubens and garden salads.

"This lunch is too good to miss, honey," Ryan said, savoring a thick bite of his sandwich. "So try not to think about anything else."

"I promise, love. Phone turned off. Mind turned off—más o menos."

But Ryan was the one who was still thinking about the strange turn of events and all the people involved. He waited till our meal was finished to bring it up again.

"I wonder if Jimmy Romero has dug up any more information about the Méndez family. Something a little more grounded than 'the family curse.'"

"You're saying you want me to get on the phone again?"

He grinned. "That, or try ESP." His grin faded. "If the person we've been calling Rita is really Bernice, then where is Rita?"

I shuddered. "If Bernice had no qualms about getting rid of Rafael, why would she let Rita get in her way? I'd almost rather think they were in some money-grubbing scheme together."

We left the deli, stopping to admire the red poppies in the side yard, then gazing across the street at the green and blue mountains. I felt tempted to forget all the problems that pushed their way into our lives, and simply drift in our surroundings.

When we got back to the B&B, I drifted a while longer under the spell of the tall pink hollyhocks on the patio, till I finally roused myself to call Jimmy Romero.

"Sorry to be a pest," I said, "but have you found out anything about the Méndez family since the last time I called?"

"Well, maybe what I *didn't* find is significant. It's strange and frustrating both."

I wondered briefly if the state of frustration had given Jimmy's hair the "electrocuted" look.

"What didn't you find out?"

"I can't find birth records for either Rita or Bernice. Not in Texas. Not in New Mexico. Not in Colorado."

I was momentarily speechless. When I recovered, my voice came out in a squeaky croak. "That's weird. There must be some mistake."

"A very coincidental mistake."

"Right." I cleared my throat. "But I still don't know what to make of it. Even if they'd been adopted, wouldn't there be some kind of documentation?"

"Well, maybe that's the operative word. I know I just kinda dumped this on you, but I've had some time to think about it. Here's a possibility. Maybe the uncle who owned the ranch hired undocumented workers. Illegals. Maybe they wanted their children to be citizens, so they let the Méndezes 'adopt' them."

"If they were born in this country, they'd be citizens anyway."

"You know that, and I know that. But maybe the workers didn't."

"Wouldn't the girls need birth certificates to start school?"

"Supposedly." I pictured Jimmy shrugging and further raking his hair. "They could have used baptismal certificates, forged documents, or—someone could have looked the other way."

Kent Vigil. That could explain the "secret" Rafael hadn't shared; could explain how Kent helped Rita get into public school. It wouldn't explain how she and Bernice got social security numbers or driver's licenses.

"Remember, Sharon, the 'information highway' wasn't as sophisticated twenty, thirty years ago. Anyway, there've always been ways around the system."

"It's just hard to understand how records in two different states slipped through the cracks—Rita's in New Mexico, and Bernice's in Texas."

"I hear ya. Well, you have my theory, for what it's worth. I'm at a loss to understand why I could run down Vital Statistics on everyone else in that family, and not those two."

It was a theory that made sense; still it was a little "hole-y." Jimmy promised to keep in touch if anything else turned up—or didn't turn up—the way it should.

I was curious to talk to Tía Dippy and Kiko about Perlita's supposed pregnancy, but felt they had enough to worry about right now. Instead, Ryan and I went back to the RV park, where we found Apá, Amá, and Tía Marta playing Mexican Train at the picnic table. I waited till they finished, then told them I needed to ask questions—again.

Ryan and Apá wandered down to talk to the musicians, leaving the rest of us to talk about "female stuff," as Ryan put it.

We moved to camp chairs under the cottonwoods, where Tía Marta remarked that the weather was much too lovely, the air too fresh, to be inside. However, Amá's frijoles flavored with mysterious spices were simmering on the stove, and the aroma wafted outside, making me hungry, even after our big lunch.

Before telling Tía Marta and Amá about the missing birth records, I was curious to hear what they had to say.

"I know it's a long time ago, but do you all remember when Perlita was pregnant with Bernice?"

"As a matter of fact, I do," Amá said. "Several of us were expecting at the same time, so we'd get together and compare notes." She gave me a sidelong glance. "We used to joke that it must be something in the cerveza."

Tía Marta guffawed. "Never did figure it out, did they."

I laughed with them, then asked, "About Perlita—she really was pregnant?"

Tía Marta gave me an odd look. "Well, of course. It was a big event. She and Hector had been married for—what? Do you remember, Ysela? Had to be eight or nine years."

"That sounds right. And they were so excited." Amá chuckled. "Perlita wasn't sure till she was about four months along, and she must have started wearing maternity clothes on the way out of the doctor's office."

"Kiko told us she had a difficult pregnancy," I said.

"Really? Hmm. I didn't know about that. Maybe she had trouble in the later months. Now her mother—Juana—she was the one. She was pregnant at the same time. With Rita. Perlita worried about her mother because of her age. So Perlita went out to New Mexico to help. A cousin or somebody was there too."

"How far along was Perlita when she left?"

"Five months? Six? She'd just started showing."

"Okay. Let me get the birthdates straight. Who was born when?"

"They were all about a month apart, I think—except the twins of course. But you know what I mean. It seems that

Bernice came in March, Rita came a couple of months later, and Ryan and Leo were born in between."

"Did Hector go to New Mexico with Perlita?"

"Not right away. But sometime before Bernice was born. He and his brother had a locksmith business. I guess his brother figured he could do it alone for a while. And maybe Hector picked up some work in New Mexico."

"So when did they come home again?"

"Not long after Rita was born, I think. Once they knew Juana was okay. It's been so long. No me acuerdo. What about you, Marta? Do you remember?"

"No, we were pretty wrapped up in your household—two new babies and little Alana to take care of. She was just a few years older herself and already trying to be a little mother."

Amá reached over and gave Tía Marta's hand an affectionate squeeze. "I don't know what I'd have done without my sisters. The three of us each took turns taking care of my three—one on one whenever we could."

"And Ricardo was a good father," Tía added. "But being a building contractor kept him pretty busy—six days a week sometimes."

They reminisced for a while, and I'd about decided to postpone asking any more questions about Rita and Bernice. Hearing tales of Ryan and his family, the bonds of warmth and affection that held them together, was much more appealing to me. Eventually, however, Tía Marta brought us back to the subject I'd brought up.

"Why all these questions about Perlita and Bernice, mijita?"

I told them about Jimmy Romero's fruitless search for original birth records and his subsequent theory about illegal adoption.

Tía Marta shook her head. "I can't believe that. I'm sure Perlita was pregnant. She wasn't a devious person. Maybe the babies were born at home instead of a hospital."

Amá agreed. "The paperwork never got sent, or got lost. Some clerical goof. That makes more sense, no?"

I sighed. *No. No sense at all.*

Chapter 47

I excused myself and made quick calls to Alicia and Kiko. Although Alicia hadn't heard from her, Rita-Bernice had called Kiko shortly after my conversation with her.

"I mumbled a lot," Kiko told me. "Told her two or three different room numbers—didn't want her to think I was groggy about everything else and sharp about that. She asked why I asked for her, and I told her I was tired and had to hang up. That part wasn't a lie. I don't know if she believed any of it."

"She might be skeptical, but that's okay. As long as she doesn't have any heavy-duty doubts till she's brings Mr. Álvarez back home."

"Kent's going to wait till then to call the rest of the relatives. I doubt if Rita would call anyone else in the family anyway, but I don't want to take the chance of someone telling her a different story."

"You don't know how much I appreciate your going along with this."

"I can't help Rafael. The least I can do is try to help your friend. Besides, we're not exactly in a hurry. They haven't even done the autopsy yet."

"Any idea when it'll be?"

"Scheduled for Monday morning. Busy place. They handle autopsies for the whole state of New Mexico. Guess we weren't first in line."

"I'm sorry for the complications, Kiko." I wished I could offer something more comforting.

"Can't be helped."

"Well, I won't keep you any longer. But I'd like to talk to Tía before hanging up."

"You bet. Here she is."

"Are you all holding up okay?" I asked as soon as she got on the line.

"Sí. No te preocupes. Don't worry, mijita."

I could hear the strain in her voice. "I do worry. I hope this doesn't sound—frivolous—but maybe it would help to take a break." *To put on a Band-Aid.* "Maybe you could visit the Indian Pueblo Cultural Center...or the Botanical Gardens...."

Tía Dippy seemed to cheer up a little. "You're right. It will be good to get our minds on something else. If only for a little while."

"Good." I paused. "I have another reason for calling you. *You* know I've had Jimmy Romero checking on the Méndezes, but I don't know how Kiko would feel about it."

"Yo comprendo."

"Okay. Jimmy can't find birth records for either Rita or Bernice. I don't know if it's important, but it's certainly strange. Can you find out—directly or indirectly—what the story is?"

"Sí. Now I'm curious too."

"Where are you right now?"

"At the mortuary. Kiko and Tom just finished making arrangements when you called."

"Oh. Bad timing on my part. I should have asked right away."

"No, mijita. It was good timing. We were on our way out. Just trying to decide what to do next. You've given us some good ideas."

* * *

We had just finished dinner when Alicia called with "good news/bad news."

"Rita dumped my father off, then left in a hurry."

Alicia went on to say that her father's blood pressure was very high and he seemed to be hallucinating. She rushed him to the clinic, where they were met by his doctor. The medical staff discovered that Mr. Álvarez was also dehydrated, and they began treating him immediately. "Right now it's 'wait and see.' I'll keep you posted."

Her call left me feeling depressed. Maybe it was because Rafael's emergency trip to the hospital had ended in death. And Rita was somehow involved both times.

"I suppose I should call Rita and let her know Rafael died, so we can end the charade. And so Kent Vigil can notify the rest of the family," I told Ryan.

"If you call too soon after she brought Mr. Álvarez home, she'll know you gave her the runaround."

"She'll figure it out soon enough, once she gets to Albuquerque. If she tries to pin me down, I'll just act confused. As Kiko would say, 'That part won't be a lie.'"

"Well, why don't you wait till she gets a little farther away from Chama."

I followed Ryan's advice and waited a couple of hours to call. As it turned out, I didn't have to worry about what to say. She'd saved me the trouble by having her phone service terminated.

Even though it was late, I called Kiko right away so he could get his own phone service changed. Kent might as well wait till tomorrow morning to do his part.

* * *

The next morning Ryan and I walked to St. Patrick's, about half a mile from the B&B. As always, the air was chilly

251

and crisp under a bright blue sky. We wore coats on the way there, which we'd carry home on the way back. The rest of our family rode in the Salazar's little tow-Beetle and met us at church.

After Mass, Alicia waved Ryan and me down. The three of us began walking down Pine Street together, while the others stayed behind to chat with some parishioners they'd met on our train ride.

"I was so upset last night," Alicia apologized when we'd gotten past the crowd, "I never even thanked you for whatever you did to get Rita to return."

I put my hand on her arm. "Don't give it another thought. I was worried too. How is your father doing today?"

She shook her head and smiled wryly. "He's remarkably resilient. Not only is his condition stable, but he's demanding to go home. I think he should stay awhile longer, but maybe he really would do better in his own surroundings."

"What about Rita?" Ryan asked.

"Haven't heard a word. I'll stay with my father, and if she shows up, I'll close the door in her face. I'm tired of dancing to her tune."

If Rita returned, which I found more and more doubtful, I hoped a confrontation with Alicia wouldn't cause Mr. Álvarez's blood pressure to go up again. At the same time, I was glad to see Alicia's spunk.

"And guess what else?" she continued. "My uncle's will was finally settled, and he was very generous to my father and me both."

"That's good news," Ryan said. "When did you find out?"

"Last Thursday. And yes, I'm assuming my father was notified at the same time. And yes, I think that has something to do with Rita's sudden need for a vacation."

She pressed her lips together briefly before speaking again. "Please don't mention this to Vanessa, about the will. I'll keep working—for a while anyway—simply because I like my job. But...." She swallowed. "I think she needs to buckle down, and she won't do it if things are too easy."

"It's hard to be tough with your own kids," I said gently, then crossed my fingers before adding, "but I'm sure she'll come around."

We reached Third Street, where we parted company, Ryan and I turning east toward the B&B a couple of blocks away, and Alicia turning west toward her own street.

"What do you think?" Ryan asked when we were back in our room. "Problems solved?"

"Problems just beginning. I've had tunnel vision, worrying about getting Mr. Álvarez home safely. Now what? Rita disappears into the Bermuda Triangle? I think my little scheme backfired. All it did was alert her that we've connected her to Rafael. I don't want her to get away with this!"

"Sweetheart." Ryan turned me toward him and put his arms around me. "That's not all it did. Mr. Álvarez is home, and he's recovering. You can't do everything. And I think you did the most important thing."

I wrapped my arms around Ryan's neck, nestled my face on his comforting shoulder, and released a small measure of my anxiety in a flood of pent-up tears.

Chapter 48

Rita surprised us all by returning to Chama Monday morning. Alicia came by the B&B mid-morning, clearly distraught. Ryan and I were sitting on the patio drinking coffee when she rushed into the back yard. Ryan stood to pull out a chair for her. She sat down and clenched her hands together on the table, her body rigid. She spoke rapidly, as if the words tumbled out of their own accord.

"They kept my father at the clinic an extra day, but he was doing so well, they released him this morning. I picked him up, and when we got back to his house, there was Rita, pretty as you please. Just sitting in an easy chair in the living room, as if it was a throne and she was Lady of the Manor."

"Oh, no! I can't believe she'd have the nerve—"

Alicia began crying, her usual cool manner completely crumbling. "I made the mistake of asking what she was doing there. My father said—oh, god—he said she was his wife now, and this was her home...." The tears began streaking down her cheeks in earnest. "I couldn't stand to hear any more. I just left."

I felt like a sledgehammer had slammed into my stomach. What Alicia felt must be a hundred times worse. I tried to sort out my thoughts, and finally came up with some ideas I hoped would help.

"Alicia, I think you need to talk to the doctor and tell him outright that you believe his blood-pressure medicine was either tampered with or withheld."

"Without any proof?"

"I think he'll believe you. What I hope is that he'll be willing to put some home-health care in place. Rita might object, saying she's a nurse, blah, blah, blah. But he can say it's 'standard procedure,' or some ambiguous term. If the lady doth protest too much, she's bound to know how suspicious that would look."

"Dr. Dunn would not only be willing, I think he'd be glad. He was quite puzzled at my father's relapse."

"Okay. One stumbling block out of the way. Next, you need to go out and buy a nice wedding present—"

"You can't be serious!"

"Think about it, Alicia. I know it's not in your nature to be phony. But you need to stay in their good graces, now more than ever."

Alicia was quiet a few moments, then nodded.

What I didn't say—what seemed cruel to say—was if Rita-Bernice assumed Mr. Álvarez's days were numbered anyway, she might be willing to let Nature take its course without giving Nature a nudge. Ironically, it was our best hope.

"I'll take them some flowers," Alicia said. "But I'll call Dr. Dunn first."

* * *

Following Alicia's visit, we took a long overdue trip to the Laundromat. By that afternoon, several plans had fallen into place. Before Alicia even called him, Dr. Dunn had arranged for a visiting nurse to check on Mr. Alvarez every day. The doctor was used to overriding Mr. Álvarez's arguments, and Rita-Bernice exercised the good sense not to interfere.

Rafael's autopsy was completed and cremation scheduled. The Vigils had gone back to Coyote the day before and spent the afternoon calling Rafael's relatives. Tom had returned to Dallas, where he would call friends and arrange for a memorial service there.

Wednesday, Kiko and Tía Dippy came up to Coyote, bringing Rafael's ashes with them. Tía Dippy called to ask if Ryan and I would meet them at the Vigils; Kiko had something important to tell us, and he wanted the Vigils to be present.

* * *

"Here I thought we would just come up to Chama and sit still and look at scenery," I told Ryan on the trip from Abiquiú to Coyote.

"Oh, I doubt if we could sit still that long."

"Right. We're *driving* and looking at scenery."

"It's worth looking at. Tía Dippy told me about this highway."

"That seems so long ago."

The sheer immensity of the landscape both humbled and reassured me. As if to remind me that there was some order in the universe in spite of whatever chaotic events took place in our own small part of the planet.

* * *

The Vigils lived in a spacious ranch-style house on two acres. Their house was separated from the one Rafael had rented by a dense row of junipers. I realized the Vigils wouldn't have known when Rafael came and went without going out of their way.

They greeted us at the door and led us into their living room, which was furnished in a Western motif. We were seated on caramel-colored leather cushions on chairs and couches framed by thick knotty pine. Several large Navajo rugs adorned the walls, and a variety of smaller scatter rugs covered hardwood floors.

After plying us with iced tea and lemonade, they gradually turned the conversation over to Kiko, who was sitting on a loveseat with Tía Dippy.

"At first, it was hard for me to believe that Rafael's death was anything but an accident," he began. "I still found it hard to believe Rita might have caused it, even though she'd gotten a little strange. Then when Eppie told me you thought Bernice might be masquerading as Rita...." Kiko closed his eyes as if squeezing back tears.

Tía Dippy slipped her hand into Kiko's, and he closed his fingers around hers.

"It doesn't make it any easier to lose Rafael," she said. "But quizás it makes more sense."

Kiko opened his eyes, but stared at the floor. "And if it really is Bernice...."

Then what has happened to Rita? My earlier conversation with Ryan echoed in my head.

"Maybe they just traded places," I offered, thinking out loud, but not really believing it. "The way twins do sometimes."

Kiko looked at me in surprise. "You already knew?"

"Knew what?"

"That Rita and Bernice are identical twins."

My turn to be surprised. More accurately, stunned. "Twins?"

"Sharon just used that as an example—about twins trading places," Tía Dippy explained to Kiko. "None of us knew. Or even guessed. Not until you told me."

"I see," Kiko said. "Well, after Eppie told me all about your visit with Rafael, I thought that was what he intended to explain. But only if 'Rita' turned out to be Bernice. He probably didn't see any reason to mention it otherwise. Neither did I up till now. Now I think you need to know."

I shook my head in bewilderment. "But Amá and Tía Marta remember when Bernice was born."

Tía Dippy smiled sadly. "I thought so too, mijita. But we were wrong. Kiko can tell you better than I can."

"It's something I hadn't even thought about in years. What happened, my mother already had seven kids and thought her family was complete. Then fifteen years after Rafael was born, she found out twins were on the way. She wasn't in good health as it was, and she'd always had difficult pregnancies. She didn't know if she'd be strong enough to take care of a newborn—let alone two babies. And here were Perlita and Hector, who'd wanted children for so long and didn't have any. Go figure."

I nodded. "So it seemed like a good idea for Perlita and Hector to raise one of the twins. But why the secrecy?"

"It seemed like a good idea at the time. Maybe if they'd thought it through, they'd have done it differently. But Perlita desperately wanted to treat the baby as her own. And she especially didn't want Connie to know for some reason. Maybe because Connie can be kind of preachy."

"So Perlita pretended to be pregnant herself, then went up to help your mother through her own pregnancy. Were the babies born at home?"

"Yes. With the help of a midwife. Probably not the best decision. My mother nearly died, and Perlita thought it would be best if she kept both twins. She stayed a couple of months longer to help my mother regain her strength. By then, my mother couldn't bear to part with both of them."

"How was it decided who'd keep which twin?"

"Oh, what's the term they use nowadays? Bernice didn't seem to 'bond' with my mother. Probably not with Perlita either. But I think she was so thrilled at having a baby, she was sure she could overcome all obstacles. She and Hector really loved Bernice."

I recalled Rafael's saying that Perlita and Hector had tried so hard "to make it work." It had struck me as a rather odd choice of words, but I hadn't had time to give it any thought back then. Now I understood.

"Did all of you—except Connie—know about this arrangement?"

"No. I probably wouldn't have known if I hadn't lived nearby. Flavio and Rafael were still at home, so they knew of course."

"Rafael confided to me when Rita started high school," Kent said. "To explain why there wasn't a birth certificate. Seems they'd gone to great lengths to protect the secret."

"And none of you ever told anyone?"

Kent shook his head. "No need to."

"I can't prove it," Kiko said, "but I think when Bernice went to Mexico, our dear brother Flavio told her. I always wondered how Rita knew he was down there. I think he called her, rather than the other way around. And I think he called some time *before* our mother died. Rita's had her problems, but—from what Rafael said—she's very soft-hearted. That snake Flavio probably played on her sympathy. 'Poor Bernice'—Rita's very own sister—had gotten a bad rap. She needed a chance to start over."

And what had Bernice done for her very own sister in return?

Chapter 49

We returned from Coyote to find Vanessa parked at the side of the B&B.

"Oh, no. What now?" I muttered.

She didn't waste time letting me know. As soon as she saw us pull in, she stormed out of her Aztek. She was wearing black short shorts and an orange tube top, neither of which did anything for her figure. She'd pulled her hair into a pony tail that was already coming apart.

I'd barely opened my car door when she began yelling, "You're a lawyer. I want you to annul my grandfather's marriage—if you want to call it a marriage!"

Ryan came to stand beside me. As before, I preferred to deal with Vanessa outside rather than inviting her into the comfort of the parlor. I looked up at the vivid blue sky. Where were thunder and lightening when you needed them? Oh, well, with any luck, my answer should cut this meeting short.

"In the first place, Vanessa, I don't practice law in New Mexico. Second, I'm not in the annulment business."

My words fell on deaf ears. "You gotta do *something*!" she shouted. "Now that they're married, she gets everything."

"When he dies, you mean?"

She rolled her eyes. "Well, duh!" Evidently my coldness hadn't fazed her.

"I'd be more worried about your grandfather's health than his finances, if I were you."

Her eyes narrowed to slits. "What's that supposed to mean?"

I sighed. "Just what I said. Look, Vanessa. I wish they hadn't gotten married either. But there's nothing we can do about it."

Apparently I got through. She turned, slammed back into her Aztek, and peeled off.

Before Ryan and I had time to catch our breath, Deputy Tovar drove up in his sleek metallic brown patrol car with "Sheriff" emblazoned in big letters on the side. He pulled into the spot Vanessa had just vacated, rolled down the window, and put his forearm on the frame. "Everything okay?"

"Yes and no. Do you have a minute?"

He cut the engine. "Sure."

I introduced him to Ryan, who asked him to come inside with us. Detective Tovar seemed even taller than I remembered, towering over both Ryan and me as we entered the house. Wendy poked her head out of the kitchen, then came into the parlor to greet us. It was the first time I'd seen a real smile on Deputy Tovar's face.

I asked her to stay, knowing she'd be interested in the update on Mr. Álvarez. After we were all seated, I began by telling Deputy Tovar that Vanessa wasn't the problem.

His bushy eyebrows shot up at that remark, but he waited patiently to hear whatever else I had to say. I realized that the truth—the whole truth—would probably sound too outlandish to be believable. So I targeted what I thought would be helpful.

"Have you heard that Alicia Mondragón's father had to be hospitalized a few days ago?"

He nodded. Of course he'd heard. Other patients at the clinic would have spread the word.

"And that he was married?"

Wendy gasped.

Deputy Tovar straightened suddenly, as if jolted by a hotwire. "No sh—no lie!"

"I'm sure it'll hit the grapevine soon enough, but—well, for now, the only people who know aren't exactly eager to share the news."

"Right. That's not good news at all. I hate to see Joaquín get taken in like that."

"So do we. What's worse, Alicia and I think his medicine was tampered with, and that's what caused his illness." I raised my hand to ward off an objection. "We have no proof. So it's not a police matter. But maybe—just as a concerned friend—you could drop by to see him."

"I might want to do that anyway."

"I'm hoping to kill two birds with one stone.... Oh, dear."

My bad choice of clichés left me flustered, and Ryan stepped in. "If Bernice knows you're likely to come see Mr. Álvarez from time to time, that might be enough to scare her off. I'm sure she knows who you are. So you might even go in plainclothes rather than your uniform. Might seem less obvious that way, but still get the point across."

"Bernice?"

"I forgot. Rita. That's a story for another time. It'll keep."

Deputy Tovar looked at his watch and stood to leave. "Guess it'll have to. I need to get going. But I like your idea. I'll show up at Joaquín's in my 'friend-clothes.' At least till I get a feel for what's going on over there."

"Whew!" Wendy said after he left. "This is very disturbing! What else has been going on?"

We had told the Johnsons earlier about Rafael's death, but hadn't had much chance to talk since then.

"If you have time, I'll fill you in."

"I have time."
I filled her in.

* * *

Kiko brought Tía Dippy back to Chama and planned to have dinner with all of us before driving on to Tres Piedras. The memorial service wouldn't take place for another week, and they felt they needed breathing space before then.

As Ryan and I walked over to the RV park, I was caught up once again in the stark contrast between the tranquil picture-postcard scenery and the discord boiling below the surface. Discord was putting it mildly. I was sure Rita-Bernice had poisoned Rafael in a way that couldn't be detected and was simply biding her time till she could do the same to Mr. Álvarez.

"It's a good thing Max went to live with Alicia," I said.

"Max?"

"Oh. I must have forgotten to tell you. Mr. Álvarez's cat. Alicia told me about him on our first visit. Some instinct warned her that Max might not be safe, so she brought him home. If only it had been that easy to protect her father."

"I'm still wondering about what Vanessa asked you. Will Rita-Bernice automatically get everything when Mr. Alvarez dies? Even though they've been married—what?—only five or six days now?"

"Depends on whether or not he left a will. If he did, that's the key. If he didn't, it could get sticky. Of course, for all we know, they already have a joint bank account. Or he could have added her name to any number of assets. The headache goes on."

"If he did any of those things, he must have done them pretty recently."

"I'd sure like to look at that marriage certificate, and any other legal documents, and see whose name is on them."

Ryan looked puzzled a few seconds before the light dawned. "Bernice or Rita?"

"If she didn't use her own name, the whole thing goes up in smoke. If someone catches it."

"Wait and see, huh?"

"Yep. Wait, wait, wait. Tell you what, though. Let's plan to leave Saturday, no matter what. For now, we've done all we can do. We can always come back later if we're needed."

"You don't want to stay for Rafael's funeral?"

I shook my head. "Now that your folks have extended their vacation, Tía Dippy will be staying with them again. Unless she and Kiko have other plans. And—I don't want to see any of Kiko's family. Bernice's mom might be there, and I'd feel so awkward. Besides, I'm ready to go home."

"Me too, sweetheart. Saturday's not that far away."

We reached the Winnebago in time to help Amá and the tías set the picnic table for a light supper of cold cuts and potato salad. Meanwhile, Apá and Kiko were talking about the Zapata they used to know—the "Old Zapata" Tía Dippy had told me about earlier.

Even though I knew Amá and her sisters were friends of the Méndez sisters—Perlita and Connie—and even though I knew Amá had had a crush, as she put it, on one of the Méndez brothers, I hadn't given any thought to the possibility that Apá might have known the Méndez family too. I suddenly realized how memories had intertwined them all.

After supper, Tía Dippy and Kiko wandered a short distance away from the group, and he kissed her tenderly before leaving. The rest of us cleared the table; then Apá built a campfire, and we pulled up chairs around it.

"Why the frown?" Ryan, his brown eyes teasing, linked his fingers in mine.

"Oh, I'm just wondering where this relationship is going."

"Ours? I thought we were going off into the sunset together."

I smiled. "We are. It's Tía and Kiko I'm thinking about."

"Oh. Does their relationship have to go somewhere?"

"No. I think it's nice they're happy."

I didn't want to tell Ryan my selfish—silly—reasons for not wanting them to get married. In the first place, I was the one imagining the leap from friendship to wedding bells. For all I knew, that was the furthest thing from their minds right now. But if they did decide to marry, both sets of families would be united as well, by something more concrete than memories. And the thought of being related to Bernice—however distantly—made me ill.

Oh, Sharon. There you go. Borrowing trouble again.

I leaned closer to Ryan and kissed him, embracing the here and now instead.

Chapter 50

"On the phone again," I sang to Willie Nelson's tune as I placed a call to Ryan's brother in San Antonio the next morning. I'd had another disturbing dream about Rita. In this one, she claimed she'd poisoned Bernice, which left me feeling both confused and alarmed when I woke up. It also made me determined to spend our remaining days in Chama doing something useful.

After Leo and I caught up on the lighter side of family news, I related highlights—or lowlights, depending on how you looked at it—of the Bernice/Rita saga.

"I need your medical expertise, Leo." I described the events preceding Rafael's death. "I suspect she didn't use poison as such, if you know what I mean. Not something obvious like strychnine or cyanide. Besides, those work too fast. Maybe some prescription meds that would counteract each other or cause an allergic reaction. Or maybe just some herb I don't know the name of. Do you know of anything like that? Something that would fit Rafael's pattern?"

"Whoa! Sharon honey, I'm an RN, not a forensics expert."

"Is that a yes?"

He laughed.

"Well, I guess that is asking a lot," I said, feeling some belated guilt. "And I don't want to put you to a lot of trouble. I can probably track this down some other way. Truth is, I'd rather talk to you."

"How can I say no when you sweet-talk me like that?"

266

"Thanks, bro. But don't spend too much time on it, okay?"

"Hey, it's my day off. What else do I have to do but find out all there is to know about poisoning people?"

We sent each other virtual hugs and ended our call.

* * *

Leo surprised me by calling back a couple of hours later. "Got a little help from a friend who's into toxicology. From everything you told me, it sounds like the culprit was mushrooms."

"Mushrooms! How did you come up with that!"

"Okay, first of all, there are some very specific varieties, like the 'death cap' and its cousins. Just a tiny bit can be lethal. But—here's the kicker—large dose or small, the symptoms don't even begin to show up for at least six hours. Could be longer."

"Hmm. Let me sort this out. Say Rita-Bernice fixed breakfast for Rafael—"

"Omelet with a little this, a little that, some bacon, some mushroom...."

"He leaves her house, drives to Tres Piedras, waits around for Kiko a while, drives home. I suppose that could take six hours, but—I don't know—"

"Well, you'll probably never find out what else he did in that time. Maybe he went to the library, took a walk, took a nap. Who knows. And besides, you've gotta add some time before his friends found him."

"You're right. Next question. What are the symptoms, and what happens once they start?"

"Different strokes for different folks. Stomach pain to begin with. Nausea. Vomiting. Diarrhea. He might not have even connected the symptoms to breakfast, especially if

267

he'd had something to eat since then. This is all guesswork anyway, isn't it?"

"Yeah. But your guesses sound logical."

"Okay, let's suppose he doesn't take the pain seriously, maybe thinks it's due to stress. Most people don't call the doctor the minute their stomach starts hurting—though they should. A little free advice thrown in here."

"I'll remember that."

"Good. Where were we?"

"Stomachache."

"Right. So he takes some Pepto Bismol or something. More time goes by. Maybe it gets so bad he can't even get to the phone."

"I think his phone is lost. His cell phone. It was the only one he had."

"Doesn't even have the energy to walk over to his neighbor's house."

"Gosh, Leo. That sounds awful. He must have been in excruciating pain."

Leo didn't answer.

"I guess losing consciousness was a blessing," I murmured. "Except that he couldn't describe his symptoms to anyone."

Leo took a deep breath. "By then.... Look, honey, if too much time had gone by, it probably wouldn't have mattered anyway. The damage starts long before the symptoms do. Kidney and liver failure...."

My throat hurt from trying not to cry out loud.

"Sharon? I'm sorry, Sharon. I shouldn't have told you this way."

"I don't think there's an easy way," I said, stifling a sob. "It's not your fault."

"It's not yours either. There's nothing you could have done. Hear me?"

I nodded.

"Are you there?"

"Y-yes."

Leo talked a while longer. I'm not sure what he said. Words meant to comfort. His kindness soothed me, and I was able to pull myself together. Still, I wondered what I would do with this information now that I had it. Information: A best guess at that.

* * *

Ryan and Apá decided to spend the rest of the day fishing at Mundo Lake. Amá, Tía Dippy, and Tía Marta wanted to enjoy a leisurely day reading or letter-writing. With everyone else busy, I figured this would be a good time to catch up on things at work and was soon involved in a lengthy conference call.

Afterwards, the need to be alone set in. I took a short brisk walk to the Y where Terrace Avenue branched off the highway. Then I turned back till I reached The Village Bean, where I stopped for a cup of coffee and a cinnamon roll. To my surprise, Rita was there, staring out the window and drumming her coral-polished nails on a small corner table. It was hard not to notice the huge teardrop-shaped diamond sparkling on her ring finger.

I hesitated before approaching her. She probably needed some alone-time too. Instead, she looked up and motioned me to her table.

I sat next to her, touched her hand lightly, and forced a smile. "I see congratulations are in order." *And where is the happy bridegroom?*

"Thanks."

"How is Mr. Álvarez?" I broke off part of my roll and took a small bite.

She rolled her eyes. "Fine. Just fine. Alicia doesn't believe it. She spends her lunch hour hovering. That's why I'm here. He's asleep, and I didn't feel like conversing with daughter-hen."

I started to say something about married couples needing separate interests when it occurred to me that Rita hadn't displayed any interest outside of smothering Mr. Álvarez. *Ouch.* Another bad choice of words.

"Well, I'm glad to hear he's doing so well. You must have had quite a scare."

She looked startled for a moment, but recovered quickly. "It was a little alarming. You wouldn't think missing one pill would have such an effect."

I raised an eyebrow. "Well, you know more about those things than I do."

I hadn't intended a double meaning to my words, but maybe they fit, because Rita stiffened. I took a sip of coffee and backpedaled. "I guess people don't always have the same reaction, so it's hard to tell." *How's that for blah, blah, blah.*

Rita wasn't impressed, judging by her stone-faced glare. Then she shifted gears and smiled. "I confess I've been under a strain. It's nice to run into a friendly face."

I supposed it was my face she meant. Her insincerity matched my fake smile. So who was I to throw rocks?

"Joaquín asks about you," she offered.

"Really? I'm surprised he remembers me."

"You made quite an impression. Why don't you drop over and see him?"

"I'd like to."

Rita looked at her watch. I noticed that she'd worn a long-sleeved blouse again, a coral silk today, and needed to push the cuff up a tad to see the time. Not pushed back far enough for me to determine if her wrist was tattooed or tattooless.

"Alicia should be going back to work. Let me see if he's awake yet." Rita pulled her cell phone out of her purse, punched in a number, and exchanged a few words with Alicia. "He's up and about, so why don't you come over now? Before the visiting nurse comes. She's something straight out of the Gestapo, I think."

I laughed. "Okay, I'll finish my roll and coffee and come by shortly."

Although I had looked forward to seeing Mr. Álvarez again, something about Rita's invitation felt off-kilter. After my first meeting with him, she'd made excuses NOT to have me return. Why the change? Maybe I was being overly suspicious. Maybe after dealing with Alicia, the Gestapo person, and Deputy Tovar, she found mine a friendly face after all. I'd soon know.

Chapter 51

Alicia was leaving just as I walked up to the front door of Mr. Álvarez's house. This time, instead of distrusting my presence, she seemed relieved that I was there.

If Mr. Álvarez had been asking about me, there wasn't any sign of it today. However, he seemed pleased to have company when I re-introduced myself. Rita was buzzing around the kitchen—making sweet tea again? My stomach churned at the thought of consuming anything she prepared.

She brought out a pot of coffee along with sturdy earthenware mugs.

"I'm sorry I'll have to pass it up," I lied, glad to have an excuse. "I just had two cups at The Bean, and I already feel like I'm floating."

She shrugged and poured coffee for herself and Mr. Álvarez. I noticed she added two heaping teaspoons of sugar to his and drank hers black.

Sugar? Maybe. Mr. Álvarez leaned back in his recliner and was soon snoring softly. Rita and I were sitting in armchairs across from each other, with the recliner completing our triangle.

"Looks like I picked the wrong day after all," I said lightly as I stood to leave.

"No, you didn't. Sit down. We have some things to talk about."

I continued standing. "We do?"

Her voice was sharp. "Don't act so dense. Sit down."

I felt a childish urge to say, "You're not the boss of me." Instead, I sat down.

"You lied to me about Rafael," she said.

"Not intentionally." I folded my hands on my lap, the next-best thing to crossing my fingers.

"Intentionally. He was already dead when you called me."

"Well, it took me a while to reach you, so he must have died between the time I found out and the time I told you."

"Sharon, quit lying. He wasn't alive and he wasn't asking for anyone."

"Then you tell me. Obviously, you know more than I do."

"I called my—sister. Perlita. I called Sunday night, and some friend of Rafael's had told her that he died Friday. You called me on Saturday. What's your game?"

"What's yours?"

She slid her hand between the cushion and the armrest and pulled out a small handgun, which she pointed at me. "I asked first."

I closed my eyes and said a silent prayer. My skin suddenly felt cold and clammy, and I began shivering. My mouth went dry, filled with nothing but an odd metallic taste. When I recovered enough to speak, my voice was barely audible. "If you wanted to scare me, it worked. I'll try to answer your questions, but it's hard for me to think like this."

It occurred to me that no one had a clue where I was. Not my family. Not the Johnsons. I wondered when the visiting nurse was due. The Gestapo seemed rather appealing to me about now.

Rita-Bernice didn't release her grip on the gun, but she did rest it on the arm of the chair. I hoped this meant she was more interested in getting information from me than in

273

harming me. I also hoped I could put together enough half-
truths or outright lies to spin a believable tale.

"I wasn't playing games, but maybe it seemed that way
to you," I said. "When I first met you at the beauty shop, I
wasn't sure I believed you. So I called someone to make a
background check. And of course, everything he told me
checked out."

She raised the gun and made little circular motions with
it. Like she was imitating someone out of a bad movie. Too
bad it wasn't a movie. No way, in real life, would I try to
wrestle a loaded gun away from someone.

"Your nose is growing, Sharon. You already knew who I
was. I spotted Alana's little brat at the grocery store when
you first got here. Watching me. Don't tell me he didn't say
anything about it."

My eyes widened. "He mentioned it, but we didn't believe
him."

We should have trusted Carlos's instincts. If I hadn't been
sure before, I knew for certain now. Rita would not have
recognized Carlos. But Bernice would.

"Come on. Meeting me at the beauty shop was no
accident."

"You're right. But it had nothing to do with Carlos. Alicia
showed me a Polaroid snapshot of 'Rita.'" *There goes my
nose again.* "I was struck by the resemblance to—to you. I
was curious to see Rita in person. This might come as a
surprise, but I've really come to think of you as Rita. You're
very different from the Bernice I used to know."

She smirked. "Better or worse?"

I hesitated. "Better. I think you take better care of
yourself."

She gave a short laugh. "Good ol' Sharon. Always
tactful—even with a gun in her face."

I didn't laugh with her.

She pretended to study the coral fingernails of the hand not holding the gun. "It's true. Rita was a good teacher. Of course I had a couple of years to learn."

"You learned well, Bernice. Even Alana was fooled."

Seeing Bernice's interest pick up at having her praises sung, I added, "Can't we talk about this without the gun?"

She eyed me shrewdly. "Not yet."

Her manner seemed more relaxed, although her fingers were still wrapped around the handle. I was still on edge, but at least my pulse had slowed down a bit.

"Well, I figured Alana would be a hard sell," Bernice said, picking up the thread of our conversation.

"That was brave of you to meet us at the station after our train ride. If Alana had recognized you, she'd have lit into you."

"She can be bitchy, but it was a risk I had to take."

I felt a flash of anger. Look who's calling someone "bitchy." But right now I had to focus on stroking Bernice's ego. Maybe the more we talked about how clever she was, the better my chances of getting out of this mess. *Besides, I promised Alana there wouldn't be any mushy skulls.* Now I felt like laughing and crying hysterically—mostly crying. *Pull yourself together, Sharon.*

"Alana noticed that you didn't even talk like us," I said, willing my voice to stay even. "Didn't have that Zapata dialect."

"Yes, I did that well, if I do say so myself. As long as I was speaking English. Never quite lost it in Spanish."

And that's why you pretended you hadn't learned it.

Mr. Álvarez stirred slightly, and I glanced over at him. Bernice kept a watchful eye on me, and Mr. Álvarez began dozing again.

"So if you believed I was Rita, why didn't you leave it at that?"

"I did. The investigator I told you about must have contacted some people in your family. Rafael, for one. I don't know about anyone else. I guess it got Rafael's curiosity up."

"I think you're the one who got his curiosity up. I think you're the one who called him."

"You have his cell phone, don't you. So you already know I called him."

She didn't bother to deny it.

I thought fast before continuing my partial fabrication. "He called me from Dallas first. The investigator had given him my number. Rafael told me he was going to see you. He said if the meeting went well, he was going to call me so we could all get together. I got worried when he didn't call."

"How did you find out what happened?"

"Well, I don't know exactly what happened." I could uncross my fingers briefly on that one before thinking up more tall tales. "All I know is, by the next morning, when I still hadn't heard, I began calling hospitals in Santa Fe and Albuquerque. By the time I found the right one, he'd gone into a coma."

"So why did you lie when you called me?"

I took a deep breath. "To see your reaction."

Bernice tightened her grip on the pistol. "You shouldn't be so nosy."

"You're right. Because—you know what?—I didn't find out anything. But you seem to think I did. At least, I guess that's why you got me here. Look, let's just say—and I'm thinking out loud here—they found out his coffee was spiked or something. How on earth would they connect it to you?"

"If someone told them."

"Someone. Meaning me? Bernice, I know better than to bother the police with speculation about something that can't be backed up. I'm no threat to you. You haven't confessed anything to me—not about Rita; not about Rafael. Congratulations. You're in the clear." *I didn't even mention mushrooms. Now put the gun away.*

"What haven't you confessed?" A man I had never seen before entered the living room from the kitchen and scowled at Bernice. From his tattooed arms to his thinning gray hair, I knew this had to be her brother Flavio, the man Vanessa and her boyfriend had described to me earlier. He looked so dissipated it was hard to believe he was only a few years older than the handsome Rafael.

How long had he been listening to our conversation? For that matter, how long had he been staying in this house?

Chapter 52

Flavio moved closer to Bernice so that he was standing between Mr. Álvarez and me. It didn't seem to bother Flavio that Bernice was armed. I myself was quite nervous. Maybe she'd just start shooting us all. Mr. Álvarez continued snoring blissfully in his recliner.

"Well?" Flavio demanded.

She gave a half-hearted shrug but looked at him warily. "Just like Sharon said. There's nothing to confess."

Like having one of those comic-book lightbulbs go off in my head, I knew what Bernice was trying to hide from Flavio. Before giving myself time to think twice, I blurted out, "Bernice, you can get by with poisoning people—Rita and Rafael, and I don't know who else—but for sure you'll get caught if there's any bloodshed."

Flavio gave a start, but kept his attention on Bernice. "Rafael? You poisoned Rafael?"

"Of course not." For once Bernice's arrogance seemed to slip.

I half-turned to face Flavio. "You didn't know he'd died?"

Bernice's face contorted. "Shut up! I haven't had a chance to tell him yet. I haven't had a chance to think about anything but getting my Sweetikins well."

I think both Flavio and I were struggling with our gag reflex.

"Cut the crap, Bernice," he said. "Quit playing with my head, and quit playing around with that gun."

To my utter surprise, she handed it over. Instead of pointing it at either of us, Flavio held it loosely at his side.

"Well, I'll leave you two to sort this out." I stood to leave once more, praying my knees wouldn't turn to slush and give way on me.

Flavio wheeled around toward me. "Where the hell do you think you're going?"

"Home?"

"Sit down," he ordered me, then said to Bernice: "What did you do to Rafael?"

"Nothing! Okay, he came by for about five minutes. He was convinced I was Rita, so he left."

I wondered if I should mention something about Bernice's nose growing, but thought better of it.

Flavio swore at Bernice to quit stalling and tell him how Rafael died.

"I don't know. Ask Sharon. It happened a long time after I saw him."

"That's true," I said. "He saw Bernice Thursday morning and died Friday afternoon. But it appears he was poisoned, and I think she had something to do with it."

Bernice started to lunge toward me, but Flavio blocked her by raising the gun between us.

"Why did you kill Rafael?"

"Why not? What do you care?" she screamed at him. "It was your idea to get rid of Rita. So what if I got rid of Rafael?"

"I hardly knew Rita," he yelled back. "Rafael was the only one who ever gave a damn about me. The only one who ever stuck up for me."

"Well, la-de-da. So when did you get a conscience? You're getting soft, Flavio. You couldn't even get rid of the brat and his nosy family."

"You wanted me to go around shooting everyone in sight? Including Ms. Busybody here?" he sneered. "No one to blame but me?"

"Who—what—who are you talking about?" I ventured to ask, with a sick feeling that I knew the answer.

"I only meant to scare them," Flavio said. "I thought luring the bear into camp would send everyone home."

My fists clenched involuntarily as my anger flared, but I decided against arguing with Flavio or his gun.

"Were you staying at the RV park?" I asked instead, remembering the number of tents I'd seen set up near Carlos and Omar's.

"Not that it's any of your business, but yeah, I came up on my bike when my sister here said she needed my help." He glared at Bernice and began yelling at her again. "Now I know what you really wanted. I know why you were so anxious for me to come 'housesit' at your place when you and 'Sweetikins' left town. If they got suspicious about Rafael dying and came to your house, they'd find me instead. You set me up!"

Mr. Álvarez continued to sleep and I tried to be invisible while Bernice and Flavio flung accusations at each other. Bernice kept stepping back away from Flavio, and he kept moving closer to her. After a few minutes, I realized they were totally focused on their own battle, and I took a chance that since I was almost out of sight—or at least not in their direct line of vision—I was also out of mind. I slipped unnoticed out the front door, and fairly flew down the walk. When I stopped for breath, I whipped out my cell phone. Before even calling Ryan, I placed a call to Deputy Tovar.

This time I didn't have to waste words or time.

"You'll need backup," I told him.

"I'm on my way."

Epilogue

When we got together after the confrontation with
Bernice and Flavio, Ryan went into hover mode. I was so
thankful to see him again that I didn't mind. Hover mode
gave way to honeymoon mode, and I didn't mind that
either.

I had told Deputy Tovar that Bernice's crimes extended
beyond the Village of Chama, and maybe that's what led
him to enlist the aid of the State Police. In any event, they
arrived together in time to ward off a shootout between
Bernice and Flavio. Even better, the two were still hurling
accusations—if not gunfire—at each other, and a number of
incriminating facts came to light.

We learned that Flavio had helped Bernice get off booze
and wangle her way back into the States with phony
documents and a rich widower. After relieving the hapless
gentleman of his life and his income without getting caught,
Bernice realized she'd found a rather lucrative way of
making a living, which Flavio expected her to share with
him.

"I guess Cici really did see Bernice in Arizona," Ryan
remarked.

"Probably so. The timing fits. And Kiko was right that
Flavio had started keeping tabs on Rita even before their
mother died."

Seeing an opportunity to cash in on whatever inheritance
was at stake, Flavio had revealed to Bernice and Rita that
they were twins. Rita, being the kind of person she was, felt

awful that "life had treated Bernice badly" and wanted to make it up to her. Bernice, being the kind of person she was, decided her share of the legacy would be larger if Rita wasn't around. Of course, Flavio was still expecting his cut for setting the scheme in place.

Bernice moved in with Rita not long after leaving Tucson. Apparently she persuaded Rita it would be "fun" to see if they could fool people by switching places and asked Rita to keep the move a secret. Their mother—even in her advanced stages of Alzheimer's—wasn't fooled, but Barbara Abernathy and the nursing staff chalked up her "confusion" to the disease.

After Juana died, Bernice continued living with Rita, studying her every move until she felt confident she could replace her without being detected. Bernice then poisoned Rita and buried her in a shallow grave near their old ranchhouse in Coyote. Isolated from view, the site went unnoticed till Flavio told all.

In claiming Rita's identity, Bernice had cleaned out Rita's bank account, moved to Santa Fe, and gotten intrigued with the idea of using the matchmaker ads to snare her next victim.

After marrying Mr. Álvarez, Rita/Bernice told him that— knowing how he valued *la familia*—he would be glad to know her brother Flavio had come to visit the newlyweds. Flavio knew that Bernice was substituting Nexium for Mr. Álvarez's blood-pressure medicine, and it was only a matter of time before he had another attack. In retrospect, I'm certain Flavio wanted to make sure Bernice didn't cut him out of what he considered his share of Mr. Álvarez's "fortune."

Bernice blamed me that the plan blew up in her face, and she's certainly an enemy to be reckoned with. However, Flavio had no qualms about offering to testify against her in exchange for a lesser sentence for his part in the conspiracy against Rita.

But Bernice's troubles had only begun: Two incidents led to her indictment in Rafael's murder as well. First, a legal search turned up a carefully concealed supply of dried mushrooms in her kitchen. Her fingerprints, and hers alone, were all over the plastic container. Then when the final tox report was released, it verified that the toxins specific to that variety of mushrooms were discovered in Rafael's system.

The only thing connecting these two facts was Bernice's arrogance. Against her lawyer's advice, she insisted on exercising her right to testify in her own defense. She claimed she had no idea the mushrooms were poisonous. "My brother gave them to me himself when I offered to fix breakfast," she said, wiping away crocodile tears.

The jury was unimpressed, and Bernice is now serving a life sentence at the women's prison in Grants, New Mexico. I can't help wondering how many other deaths can be laid at her doorstep, how many cold cases solved. Did I mention that her troubles are only beginning?

* * *

After everyone else in our family had gone back home, Tía Dippy stayed behind with Kiko. He insisted that Rita get a proper burial, and planned a joint memorial service for her and Rafael. Kiko told his siblings and their families they were welcome to attend if they'd leave their grudges behind; otherwise, to stay home. José/Neville and Connie declined the invitation, but the rest of the family joined Kiko, Tía Dippy, and the Vigils for a sad but sweet reunion.

Perlita and Tía Dippy renewed their friendship, and Tía told me later that Perlita was as kindhearted and forgiving as Bernice was mean and vindictive.

"Perlita understands that none of this was your fault, mijita. But she never thought of Bernice as anything but her daughter, and she grieves for her as any mother would."

Kiko and Tía Dippy have gone back to their respective homes, but they keep both the highways and the telephone wires humming between them, so who knows what the future will bring?

As for Mr. Álvarez, thanks to the mild sedative Bernice had given him, he slept through the showdown that took place practically under his nose. In an unrelated turn of events, he suffered a heart attack a couple of weeks later and died a peaceful death.

Up till then, out of concern for his health, Alicia had shielded him from the publicity surrounding Bernice. But perhaps he hadn't been hoodwinked after all. He had told "Rita" he'd changed his will, but hadn't told her how.

We learned that, in conjunction with his formal will, he had made a video confirming his surprising bequests. In it he stated in a clear and lucid voice:

"My dear Rita brought me much happiness in my golden years, but I suspect she'll have no trouble finding someone else after I'm gone. My daughter has a small pension. My granddaughter needs to get a job. None of them needs to rely on me for financial support, but I do not want them to think I forgot them. Therefore, I leave Rita, Alicia, and Vanessa the sum of $5000.00 each as a small token of my affection.

"I leave my house to the Village of Chama to be used as a museum. I leave the rest of my estate to the Chama Valley Humane Society in Max's name."

Of course, there was no Rita to collect, and Alicia was well-cared for through her inheritance from Mr. Álvarez's brother. I suspect Mr. Álvarez knew that, but kept it quiet so that greedy Vanessa wouldn't be tempted to think of ways to con it from her mother.

I expected Vanessa and Toro/Trog to break up now that their goal of extracting money from her grandfather vanished. From all accounts, Vanessa was still her surly self after hearing she'd been left with so little. But "Toro" surprised me by telephoning me at my law firm not long afterwards to ask if I thought he'd make a good detective.

"You say I observe good," he reminded me.

"That's true, and you do seem to enjoy surveillance."

I could picture his brow furrowing at this.

"But it's very hard work, uh, Toro. You'd have to go school—study for your license, study English...." *Study diplomacy, bathe.* "It might be a little overwhelming."

"I work hard."

I smiled. "I'm sure you do."

He hung up happy, and I figured it wasn't up to me to discourage him.

As for Ryan and me, we're back at our respective jobs. Yes, mine was still waiting, with a stack of new cases to look into.

Not long ago Ryan asked me if I had something in mind for Christmas vacation. I told him I thought it would be fun to get away for a romantic little holiday—just the two of us.

He thought that had a familiar ring, but agreed it was a great idea. Maybe we'll go cross-country skiing in Chama....

LaVergne, TN USA
25 March 2011
221617LV00003B/1/P